Fatal Godddess

Vasilisa Drake

CONTENTS

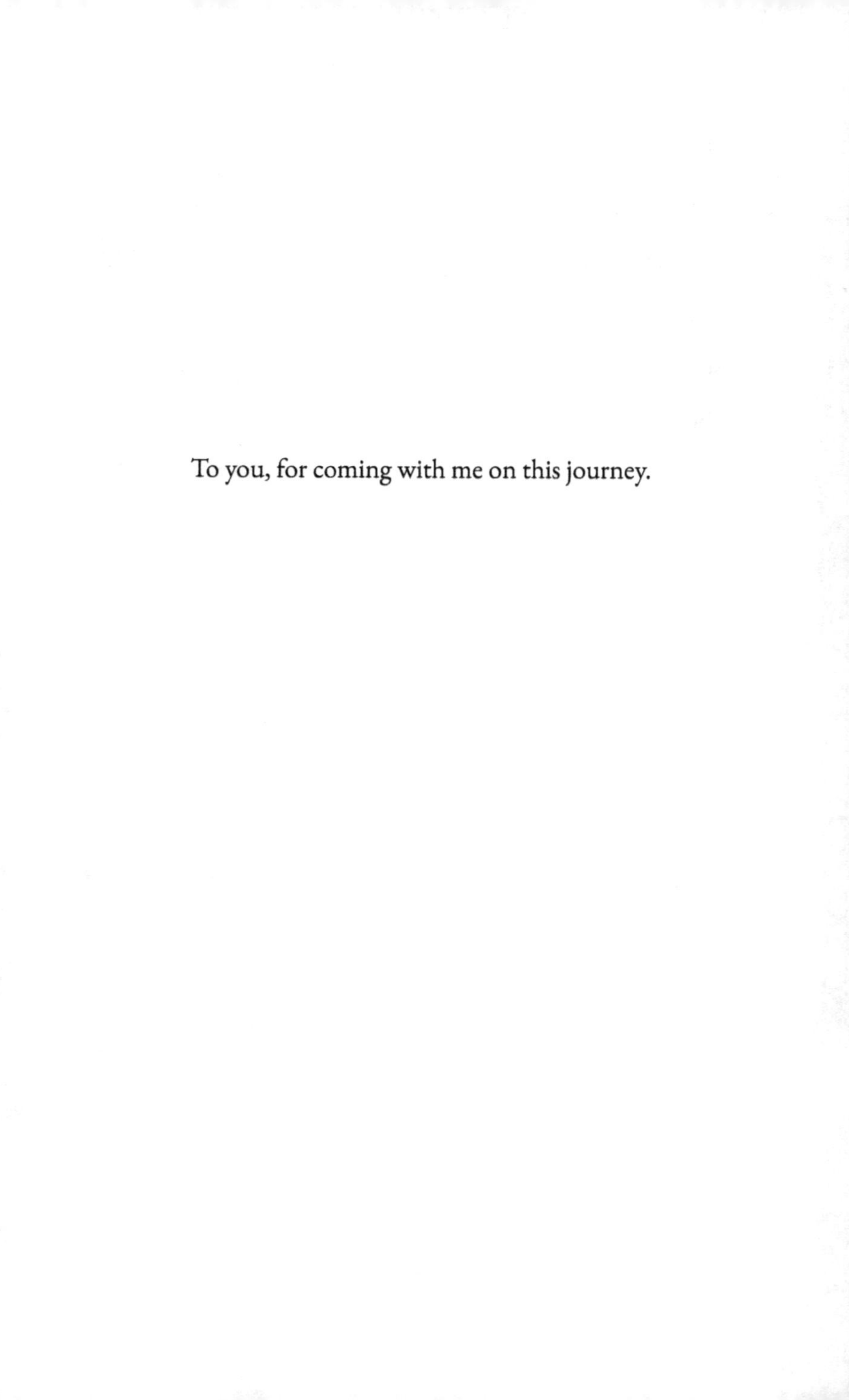

To you, for coming with me on this journey.

FANG PACK LAND
HUNTING GROUNDS
ALPHA MANSION
DINING HALL
PACK SCHOOL
TRAINING RING
MAIN STREET
PACK HOUSING
PACK SHOPS
WIND BLOOD PACK LAND
MOON GHOST PACK LANDS

PROLOGUE
SOME THOUSAND YEARS AGO...

THE KING NEVER WENT to the surface. He was not greedy; he did not covet. He was content with his lot in life—or death, as it was. He ruled the underworld, with enough violence and apathy that the natural chaos of the realm was restrained, if not utterly dominated.

It was an endless existence.

There was no reason for him to break the pattern and rise to the surface realm. Yet, something drew him upwards that night. He cast open a portal, uncaring where he landed, and cloaked himself in a web of darkness so as not to be seen.

The underworld had no seasons; day and night, yes, but it was the same, even temperatures. You were never cold, but never quite warm either.

Such was not the case in the realm of the living. Once he stepped through, the warmth of the night struck him, the heat of summer persisting even late into the night. The warmth hit his bones, potent and... pleasant. Not that it mattered.

The moon waned, only the slimmest portion of it lighting

the night. Not that the lack of light presented an issue for his enhanced eyesight. He cast a careless glance around. He was in an orchard of some sort. Perhaps he would walk among the trees for a few hours before returning to the mantle of the realm.

A shift in the breeze carried the scent of another to him.

He was not alone.

He inhaled deeply, tasting the notes of her on his tongue.

Delectable.

And there she was, not a hundred paces away from him.

The female wore a simple green shift, the basic cloth doing nothing to disguise her figure. Red locks tumbled down to her waist, swaying behind her as she moved through the orchard. The very ground bloomed beneath her feet, visible even from a distance as she took a step towards one of the trees and pulled a blossom to her nose.

"Do you find the scent pleasing?" she asked aloud.

He scanned the night, looking for others he had failed to detect, but there were no others. Still, a mortal should not be able to sense him...

"Come now, don't you owe me some conversation after I've allowed you to ogle me for several minutes?"

She still did not face him, but he could feel the smile in her words. Her voice was teasing, careless. As if she had nothing to fear by being alone in the orchard late at night.

And she would not, not as long as he was here.

He flinched at the thought. It made no sense to have such an inclination. But the thought came nonetheless.

"I have no use for pretty scents."

It was a lie. He had no use for flowers, true, but *her* scent?

He wanted to take her down to the lowest depths of the underworld and wrap her scent around him until, at last, he could breathe. Before this night, he would have said he had no such issues, no such passions. But just one inhalation of her natural perfume, one glimpse at her distant figure, and he was entranced.

"The trees do not bloom to be *useful*," she chastised, not releasing the flower as she drew in another inhale. "If anything, we exist to be useful to them. Are we not all stewards of the realm?"

Another question.

"You should not be out here so late." The words slipped from his tongue before he could stop them.

The female laughed, and he thought he might die all over again to hear the sound once more.

"And who might you be, oh dark stranger, to tell me what I should and should not do?"

He owed her no answers.

He was compelled to give them.

"I am Hades, King of the Underworld."

"King of the Underworld?" If he expected her to sound impressed, he would be disappointed. But he was not, because there was nothing the creature in front of him could do to disappoint him, save disappear from his sight. "Then you have no dominion here, isn't it so?"

A laugh escaped from his lips before he could stop it. The sound was startling to his own ears. When was the last time he had laughed, or even smiled? His mind traced through centuries of memories and came up empty.

"A king does not cease to be a king simply because he is not lazing on his throne."

"Is that so?" Once more, he could sense the smile playing on her lips.

How he wanted to see it! "Indeed."

A beat of silence, the night filling the space between them. He moved closer until he was standing behind her.

He wanted to turn her to face him, but he stayed his hand.

"Tell me, female, do you belong to another?"

A snort. "No one will ever *own* me. Not even a king."

A smile curved on his lips at her indignation. "Then, are there any *you* own? A male, perhaps?"

"Only all the living things in the world," the female said with a sigh. The words held a weariness he knew all too well.

This close, he could taste her scent like it was a physical thing, no longer contaminated by the other smells in the orchard. Pomegranate and budding flowers.

The scent was stamped in his mind from one breath to the next.

"Give me your name." His words were commanding, as was fitting of a ruler.

Yet if she knew him better, she would've detected that it was not the same distanced orders he gave those beneath him. This was an order he could not bear to be refused.

"I told you, Hades, King of the Underworld—you have no claim to make demands here."

"Then consider this me begging." The plea in his voice—never had he made that sound before.

Finally, she turned to him. Her pale skin seemed to glow in the moonlight, a smattering of freckles covering her face, moving like constellations over her skin as her lips tipped up into a smile. It was even more devastating than he'd imagined. Her green eyes lit with mischief, an innocence that was foreign to him after his centuries in the underworld.

"I am known as Persephone."

Chapter I

W HEN THE SOBS STARTED, they choked me.

It should have been me.

Blood caked my hands from where the skin had torn as I'd tried to pierce the ground.

It should have been me.

Time no longer mattered to me. It could have been seconds since he'd been taken from me. It could have been years. All of it was the same—time without him. The one male who had made me feel alive. Loved. Cherished.

The tears had dried on my cheeks, but I couldn't stop the sounds that left me. My wails were painful to my own ears, but still, they continued. I could do nothing as my voice shook, dried out, turning into a mournful rattle.

There was no catharsis in them.

The ground beneath me was perfect. Even, unbroken, for as far as I could see besides the pathetic dent I'd made in the ground.

As if it hadn't just swallowed the love of my life.

In the distance, someone called my name. I knew that

voice. It was a good voice, a voice that cared about me.

But it wasn't *his* voice. I couldn't make myself look away from the spot he had last been in.

Forgive me for leaving you alone.

He had said the words like it was so simple. As if because I'd been alone all my life, it would be possible to return to that state, now that I'd tasted heaven.

It should have been me.

When I failed to reply, someone pulled my face away. It hurt my neck, to move after bending for so long.

A stiff neck.

He was gone, and I was faced with the *tragedy* of a stiff neck.

It was enough to make me laugh, ending the hollowed-out sobs, and once I started, I couldn't stop. Not even as the women in front of me exchanged concerned looks. My best friend's concern was riddled with confusion. The other—her gaze was cursed with knowledge. Understanding, as if she could comprehend what I'd lost.

But no one could understand.

I laughed until I choked, the moment of airlessness returning a familiar sting to my eyes, and though I'd thought I'd emptied myself of tears, suddenly, I had found new reserves.

Daphne pulled me to her chest, wrapping her arms around me.

My own arms hung limp at my side. There was no strength

left to move them.

"Soteria, we must return to the castle."

"What's left of it," Daphne added grimly. "Avery, we need to regroup. It's chaos."

I heard the words, but all I did was return my gaze to the ground.

"He's gone."

The words were no more than a whisper.

I hadn't realized I'd hoped otherwise until Hecate murmured a sad confirmation. "He is." Finality rang through the words.

But if I'd learned just one thing, it was this: death was not the end.

My voice was stronger the next time I spoke. I ignored the look of shock in Hecate and Daphne's eyes because, to me, the path was suddenly clear.

"I'm going to get him back."

THE FORTIFIED WALLS THAT surrounded the city had crumbled. The city was in chaos. Soldiers called out orders, trying to organize the terrified populace.

The palace itself was a wreck. People looked expectantly at us as we returned. I couldn't bring myself to meet their gazes.

Hecate led us to the empty throne room. In a cruel irony, it was relatively untouched, with nothing more than a few loose stones.

"Tell me exactly what happened," Hecate demanded. "Why did you go into my rooms?"

I didn't ask how she knew. It didn't matter. I filled her in as best I could, telling her about the deal I'd made with a demon for the portal and answers. How he'd threatened Daphne's life if I didn't obey. How the magic of our bargain prevented me from seeking help in fighting off the deal, no matter how I tried. How I'd scried using Hecate's hidden Many Moon Mirror and seen my fated mate.

How he'd sensed me.

"This demon." Hecate was barely breathing as she spoke. "What was his name?"

"Phaidros." It was Daphne who spoke. "It was him, wasn't it?"

Hecate looked to me for confirmation, and I nodded.

The witch simply stared at me for a moment. Then— "Foolish girl."

Something snapped in me at that. "Foolish? You're damn right, I'm a fool. I'm the ignorant *idiot* you've all refused to give any answers to, so I had to make a deal with a freaking demon. This only happened because you and... he..." I choked for a moment, unable to say Cole's name. "Because the two of you refused to give me any answers. Time and time again. You kept me in the dark, and now we're all paying the price!"

All? a dark voice whispered in my ears. No. *Cole* had paid the price.

"He forbid me to tell you more."

"And where did that get him, Hecate? Where?"

She drew a breath. Perhaps my question had been rhetorical, but she didn't take it that way. "It took him to the pits, Soteria. Tartarus."

I'd suspected. An awful part of me had known, had sensed the malevolence from the ground, but the confirmation... Cole had once called the realm *unending torture*.

"How?" I demanded. "How did this happen?" When Hecate didn't immediately answer, I exploded. "You owe me!" I snarled, and the room shook around me. Here, my magic was plentiful and angry. Yet I'd been powerless—again—when the pits came calling. "You call me your savior? You're damn right. When that dragon came, I saved you all. This whole forsaken kingdom. You say he forbid you to give me answers? Well, look around, Hecate. Cole is gone!"

Slicing me in two would have hurt less than saying his name again. I shook, emotion rocking me. I didn't have to see myself to know my eyes were glowing with that furious magic; the worried glance Daphne gave me before approaching me, attempting to soothe me, was enough.

But I didn't want to be soothed. I wanted to be *angry*. Because anger... anger was better than pain.

"Tell me everything," I demanded.

I wanted to fight more. To snarl, to throw my weight around, even if Hecate could wipe the floor with me. Even if she wasn't really at fault—no, the blame lay squarely with me. Or worse... with Cole.

"Very well. I told you there would be consequences, Soteria. When you returned to the realm of the living, you were still a shade. You had no right to alter the lives on that plane, but you killed someone."

"Maddox was going to kill Daphne," I protested.

"The laws of the universe *do not care*, Avery!"

I flinched. It was the first time she'd ever raised her voice.

She drew a steadying breath. "Listen to me. There is a cycle of life. The living, in the realm you remember, the shades here in Hell, and then a final death that draws you to the pits. You moved one piece forward in the cycle, out of order. In turn, another must go forward—you, from the underworld to Tartarus. We hid you with magic, attempting to buy time to find some solution, even though there is no escaping fate. The *only* solution was for another to take your place. When you used the mirror to scry, you reversed the magic we'd crafted to hide you. It was never permanent—this outcome was inevitable—but Phaidros must have wanted to hasten the process."

"Is Maddox here, in Hell, then?" Daphne asked.

Hecate shook her head, the dark waves of her hair falling forward. "No. For shifters, the cycle is altered. The Moon

Goddess struck a bargain, and now, you're set among the stars for eternity, removed from the natural cycle. You will never go to the pits, but your soul will be enslaved by her forever."

When Hecate said it like that, it sounded really bad. Which made no sense, because the alternative was Hell and eternal torture.

Where Cole is.

I tamped down on the thought. "When I saw Jett, he mentioned the Moon Goddess. Our pack was never overly religious, but he seemed like a fanatic."

"The Moon Goddess is more than a figure in pack mythology, Soteria." She'd gone back to my title rather than using my name. "She is real, and she is the very opposite of *benevolent*." Venom dripped off the word. "No doubt, she has been the one pulling the strings, using your pack, demons, and even the laws of the universe to her advantage. Her goal is to see both you and Cole in Tartarus."

I could do little more than stare at Hecate. "And she got one of us."

She shook her head. "No. A hundred years ago, she succeeded in sending you to the pits."

I will not let her be taken again. That was what Cole had said to Hecate just hours ago.

It felt like a lifetime.

"But I'm not in Tartarus," I protested. "So it must be possible for me to get Cole back. A portal or something. A spell.

Just let me go and find him."

Hecate's gaze was pitying.

"There is nothing you can do for him, Soteria. He is lost. But the people need you, now more than ever before. You *must* become the Queen of Hell."

CHAPTER II

THIS AGAIN? OF ALL times?

"You can't just replace him with me!" I snapped. "He's gone and all you're thinking of is having someone else sit on that?"

I flung an angry arm toward the throne at the back of the room. As if in answer to my emotions, green vines sprouted, smothering the seat.

"The people need a leader, Soteria. This is not the end of the Moon Goddess's machinations. Of that, I have no doubt. You must step into your power. The shades will be lost without him after so many thousands of years, and he would not want you to abandon them."

Funny, because it was Cole who had told me he would never ask me to become queen. Never place that burden on me.

But Cole had left me. He had chosen eternal torment in my stead.

"We'll just have to ask him about it when I get him back." I wasn't accepting defeat.

Death is not the end.

Hecate sighed. "I understand this pains you—"

"Pains?" I almost laughed, but there was no humor left in me. "Pain is nothing compared to what I'm feeling right now. Knowing I brought this on him. I'm going to make this right, Hecate. *Help me.* You have to know something. A way to get into Tartarus."

"Getting in isn't the hard part. It's tricky; you have to find an entrance that has been hidden by time, and even I do not know their locations. The only other way would be to create your own entrance, and there is only one creature that can create portals to the pits. But getting out is impossible. You must convince the under-realm to let you out."

"If I made it out, then there must be a way," I argued.

"This is true." The words themselves were neutral, but they were laced with disapproval.

"What creature can make those portals? Phaidros?" I guessed.

Hecate nodded. "But listen to me, Avery. Do not seek him out. You are no match for the demon as you are now, and we have no way of finding him. Even if you did and he accepted a bargain, the cost would be far too high."

There was no price too high. Yet as I recalled the way he'd threatened Daphne—and the fact he was working with Jett—I decided to take that as a last resort. "Fine. I'm not looking to sell my soul, anyway. But you said there are entrances—even if you don't know where they are exactly, you must have *some* idea."

"All I know is they sit in the realm of the living. You need to use a portal to go to the realm of the living. Creating one is not possible for me, but when you take the mantle of Hell, your power will be unlocked, and you will be able to traverse between the two realms."

She wasn't going to drop it. But if I was going to rescue Cole, I was going to need to get stronger. Even now, my power seemed to increase every day.

Yet I'd been helpless when Phaidros had cornered me.

"Tell me how to become queen, then. I'll do whatever it takes if it means I can rescue Cole."

"Soteria? An audience?" a new voice called into the room, interrupting.

I turned. It was Stefan, Cole's captain of the guard. He looked like he'd aged a decade since I'd last seen him. Not in the ageless ways time just passed by in Hell, but a long, devastating several years. His gray hair was haggard, his normally impeccable posture stooped as he shifted on his feet while he waited to be granted permission to join us.

I looked to Hecate for guidance, but she offered none. I gestured for Stefan to come forward.

"What's wrong?" I asked, then nearly smacked myself. Everything was wrong. Starting with the fact Stefan was coming to me instead of Cole, who had thousands of years of experience in this mess apparently while I had barely been here a few months.

"The guards are doing the best they can to assess the damage, but the people are panicked. Several were hurt by falling debris. The castle held up better than the rest of the city, but the medical wing took some of the worst damage. Where should we take them?"

I frowned. I hadn't surveyed any of the damage, but I couldn't trust some key structures hadn't been hurt in the earthquake. Things seemed fine for now, and I knew Hecate's magic could keep us safe, but we shouldn't be keeping anyone in the castle who couldn't get out in a hurry. "We can use the market while the guards finish their assessment. Hecate, can you help with repairs?"

Hecate nodded.

"Okay. Then while she works on that, set the patients up and then send someone to take me to them."

Stefan nodded, the nervous energy around him dissipating now that he had clear instructions.

I should have told him about Cole. But that was the one thing I couldn't make myself do.

Coward. Instead, after Stefan left, I asked Hecate to update the palace guard on the leadership status.

"As you wish, Soteria," she replied.

The title hurt worse than ever. Because I was no savior. Not when I'd damned the man I loved to the pits. I stomped down on the guilt. Right now, I had a goal. Despite Hecate's insistence it was futile, she would help get me to Tartarus.

Hecate left, and Daphne stayed by my side. My best friend eyed me with concern but I refused to talk about Cole any further. Unless I could actually do something, there was no point. I went to Daphne's room, not wanting to go into my own and smell the scents that lingered there, to wash up and change out of my bloodstained clothing.

Hector tracked us down at Stefan's command an hour later.

The makeshift sick bay he led us to was emptier than I'd initially feared. There was a sea of bodies, but not an ocean, and only a few were seriously injured.

"Soteria. You honor us with your presence," one of the healers said as I approached.

I fought the urge to grimace. *I'm no one's savior.* "I'm here to help." My magic was well-suited for healing. *And more,* Hecate had hinted to me on more than one occasion.

"We've triaged the first two rows of patients," the healer explained, gesturing behind her. Each row had about thirty people in it, at a glance. "We'll work on triaging the remaining four. The ones with the worst injuries have been marked with a red scarf."

They had acted fast. I made my way to the first red marker.

The patient had a wound that made me wince. Most had escaped with minor injuries, but this woman had a wooden beam speared through her chest. Blood had pooled around, drenching her frock. I was stunned she wasn't howling in pain.

I was also stunned, momentarily, because I recognized the patient.

"Don't waste your energy on me," the barkeep who had tried to poison me a while ago snapped.

The poison, granted, hadn't been the fatal kind. It had been closer to a laxative than anything else.

"You may die if I don't."

"I don't need you to treat me," the woman insisted.

Perhaps I should've respected her stubborn desire to die. But part of me felt responsible for her, for having been injured in the destruction I'd unwittingly caused.

"Too bad." I knelt down to get a better look at the wound.

Besides myself, I had only healed Cole before. Well, Cole and an undead dragon. Then, I'd been frantic, wild with my magic. I tried to imagine Hecate guiding me. I placed my hands as gently as I could around the puncture wound. The barkeep winced but didn't protest at the pain.

"I'm not gonna recognize you as my queen just because of this," she huffed while I summoned my magic.

She probably wanted to talk to take her mind off of the excruciating pain. "I don't expect you to." It was more surprising to me that anyone *did*.

"Why not?" she grumbled. "Seems like you'd take it as your

due."

"Respect is earned, not demanded." Not the way the Alphas in my old pack had tried to demand it. "Though an apology for trying to poison me wouldn't be amiss."

The barkeep was silent for a moment. Either because she was in too much pain as I slowly pulled the wood out with my magic, knitting the punctured organs together, or just because she didn't have another barb ready.

"If the king hears you say that, all your healing is for naught," she said, glancing around as though the King of Hell might step from the shadows at any moment.

I wished she had been right. She didn't know he was gone yet. No doubt, there would be chaos when word spread.

"You didn't tell him," she said when I stayed quiet. "If you had, I'd have been dead already."

Did part of me want to protest that Cole wouldn't kill someone for something that was a borderline prank, albeit a malicious one?

Yes, but I was a shitty liar.

I tossed the shrapnel aside. "How do you feel?"

The barkeep turned her attention to her newly mended stomach. Her eyes widened in shock. I knew from Hecate magic was common in different forms, but the magic to heal? That was managed by only the strongest creatures, and mastered by none.

"I can stand!" She stood on shaky legs.

"Good as new," I agreed.

Hopefully, I hadn't missed any internal bleeding.

I moved to the next patient.

IT TOOK UNTIL NEARLY midnight for me to finish healing the patients. I'd meant to just assist, but then it snowballed. The other healers were woefully ill-equipped to take care of that many injuries. Plus, their combined magic wasn't anywhere near as strong as mine. In the end, I'd been assigned every single red flag patient.

None of them were people I recognized.

I wasn't sure if it was a blessing or just a cruel reminder of what my actions could cost people.

The castle was almost fully repaired by the time I trudged back. Stefan assured me all that was left was some aesthetic fixes. I nodded, and noticing he seemed to be waiting, dismissed him for the night.

Hecate was the one I needed to see. I knocked on the door of her quarters. The floral and herb scent that had colored the air around it was tinged by something more sinister. More damage I caused.

"At least this time you bothered to knock."

I spun. The enchantress continued to walk down the hallway towards me.

"Tell me how to get the power of the queen."

Hecate was silent, just finished crossing the hall to stand by me.

"I need to make a portal as soon as possible," I insisted. "There's no time to waste."

She took a step past me to push open the door to her quarters.

"Soteria, you have been awake for over a day now. What's more, you've expended significant quantities of magic; I can sense how close you are to your limit. You're standing here through sheer will alone, and I respect that, I do. But there comes a time when one must know to rest, and before taking the queen's trials is such a time." I wanted to argue more, but Hecate silenced me with a raised hand. "First thing tomorrow. You have my word."

Reluctantly, I agreed.

Still unable to brave the bed I'd shared with Cole, I went to Daphne's room. My friend welcomed me with open arms, but there was another scent tied to hers.

"Hector?" I guessed.

She flushed. "He wanted to make sure I was okay after everything. I was going to go down and check on you, but they said you were working nonstop with the medics."

The reminder seemed to sap the remaining strength from my bones. "Would've come in handy to have all this healing magic when I was getting beat every other week."

"What will come in handy is all that magic to get Cole back. And you will, Avery. I know it."

I appreciated her confidence in me, because Hecate had none. Well, that wasn't fair. She seemed completely confident I could rule an entire realm. She just didn't think I could save the male I loved.

"So, you sleep with him yet?" I asked, desperate to change the subject. Anything to keep my mind from the dark place it was going without something to keep me busy, be it arguing with Hecate, healing patients, or gossiping like there was nothing wrong.

My best friend flushed a deeper red. "Avery, no!"

"So I won't get cooties if I sleep in your bed with you?" I teased.

Her expression softened. She opened her mouth, no doubt to say something comforting, reassuring, but I pushed past her, stretching my arms over my head.

"I'm beat, Daph." I flopped onto her bed. "Tell me about him. We barely got to talk after the ball."

So Daphne did. I heckled her about her crush, and she indulged me by telling me about every single flirty exchange the two had since she's come to the realm. I kept teasing until my eyelids refused to stay open and my lips moved with no sound coming out. Daphne settled in next to me, pulling the covers over us.

I couldn't bring myself to admit the true reason I didn't

want to sleep.

What if I saw Cole in my dreams?

What if I didn't?

But when I slept, I couldn't find him, no matter how my soul searched. Instead, my dreams were filled with fire.

Chapter III

*F*OR MOST OF MY *life, my sleep either went two ways—either it was empty, and there was only darkness until I awoke, or Cole was there. He'd found me—or as he claimed, I'd found him—when I was just a kid, passed out after the Alpha Clique had stuffed me in a locker. From then on, he'd been the one constant I had, the one person I could confide in without fear of seeming weak. I hadn't realized he was an actual person, of course. He hadn't even shown himself, cloaking himself in every dream after the first time I'd surprised him, as a muffled voice that teased me when my spirits were low and comforted me when they were lower still.*

Dying had muddied the connection, first making my dreams blank again, but then, I was able to seek Cole out in them—and vice versa—with much greater ease.

That night, I slept with another purpose. I was afraid to find him, hadn't wanted to fall asleep, but as I did, I couldn't stop my soul from reaching out for his.

Instead, all I found was pain.

My body was alight with it. The world was dark, dark, dark, and then there would be a flash of red flame, so bright my eyes nearly burned, the heat searing me. Then darkness again.

"Cole?" *I tried to call out.* "Are you there? Can you hear me?"

A fresh wave of torment hit me. I sank to my knees and screamed.

"Cole?" *I called again.* "Cole!"

But no matter how many hours I spent calling out, pleading, there were only three things.

Pain.

Darkness.

Fire.

I'D BEEN ON THE move for hours, my paws devouring the ground in front of me as I moved away from the capital.

"Those who have the potential to rule the realm, and only those, can find the mantle's resting place and claim it as their own," she'd explained when she met me in the morning, as promised. *"You must find it by feeling the pull within and let it guide you. Just as you did so once before."*

My dreams had not been restful, and I'd set out only minutes after she'd given instructions. It was a journey I had to make on my own. At first, my movements had been uncertain. I didn't immediately feel the pull Hecate described, my thoughts still wrecked by the nightmares of last night.

Or what I hoped was a nightmare.

It had felt only right to take my second skin. Once, turning into a wolf had been an impossible task. I'd nearly collapsed from the effort anytime I tried in the pack. But ever since I'd died, it felt easy. Like a missing piece had slotted into place. It was the first time I'd shifted since Phaidros' deal had trapped me as a wolf. Then, the three days had frustrated me.

Now, it was as if for the first time since Cole had left I could breathe. My wolf had the clarity I lacked. Her senses were sharper, less muddled by the torment and grief that threatened to drown me. She had one mission: Find the mantle. And nothing would stop her.

"I cannot promise you an easy quest, only that it will not be too far," Hecate had said. *"It's never more than a day's journey, for the realm never knows when it will need a new leader."*

An easy journey? No. But when the Scorpio demon attacked me as I followed the path I could only sense, I hadn't minded venting my frustrations. My wolf couldn't wield the magic I could in my human shape, but she had no issues sinking her teeth through the thick exoskeleton.

The Aries demon that had attacked from above when I'd paused to rest for a moment had met a similar fate. Its curved horns tried to ram into me. Instead, I'd split its throat wide and nearly sipped its blood for spite.

My wolf was focused, but perhaps more than a *smidge* unbalanced with the absence of the one male she cared about.

On and on, miles disappeared beneath my run. What had started as a small thread I struggled to grasp and follow had turned into a chain, reeling me closer. I wasn't sure I could've stopped if I wanted to.

Mountains turned to forest which turned to rolling planes. The scene grew familiar.

For a moment, I expected to see a castle of black stone appear on the horizon, a moat around it threatening all visitors to stay away.

But Cole had destroyed that castle, and everything in the pocket realm, when he'd returned to his seat of power in order to find me.

The familiarity went deeper. A sense of déjà vu spilled over me. I was on the right track. The pull grew stronger and stronger until I reached my target at last.

The mantle of Hell.

The enchantress hadn't described it, hadn't told me to go by anything more than feeling, but I had no doubts. There was a pool of lava, maybe thirty feet in diameter, that seemed to have sprung out of nowhere. The surface boiled, glowing bubbles of flame popping along the surface, yet there was no heat emanating from the pool.

It was familiar. So familiar.

I had come here in a dream, with Cole. The night of the Choosing, the ceremony where I'd been doomed to find my moon-matched mate.

"What if you're fated to someone in your pack?" he had asked.

"Fate wouldn't be so cruel."

How little I had known. I thought I'd known cruelty before, but nothing had prepared me for the shock of finding out my bully was my predestined partner.

A stab of memory hit me, a vision of the lake as if looking through a different set of eyes. I'd been here, not just in my dreams, but... another time. A memory tugged and tugged, threatening to rise in my consciousness.

But nothing came. All I was left with was a migraine.

I shifted back to my human form.

And then, guided by an instinct I'd only begun to trust, I walked into the lake.

The lava didn't scald me, nor did it smother me. I stepped forward until I was fully submerged, yet I was able to breathe and open my eyes.

"You've come for the mantle," a voice said.

The voice was neither male nor female, neither weak with age nor strong with youth nor raised like that of a child. It echoed outside my ears and in my head at the same time.

"I have." Speaking was difficult under the lava. Not for a physical reason—it didn't drown me—but as if an oppressive magic was pushing down on every part of me, testing my mettle.

"Strength, courage, and selflessness. A ruler must

have all three," the voice intoned. **"Do you agree to face the trials?"**

"I do." I wasn't sure I possessed any of the qualities, honestly, but turning back now was *not* an option.

There was no warning before what happened next.

CHAPTER IV

ONE MOMENT, I'D BEEN standing, submerged in the calm lake of lava, able to speak and breathe.

The next, the lake was a violent mess. Waves pushed against me, assaulting me on all sides. The temperature heated. The very magic of the lake came alive. If I'd thought all it had to offer was a spooky voice, I was very, very wrong.

The magic of the mantle was ancient. Potent. It had been cloaking itself, allowing only the barest hint of itself to trickle to the surface, as a way to guide any who sought it out.

Now?

Now, that hold was unbarred.

It flooded me with the magic. More than the waves or heat of the lava, the magic itself was nearly unbearable. I gritted my teeth, tensing my muscles, but there was no way to strike back at an enemy that surrounded you on all sides. Not physically.

I summoned my magic, green sparks lighting around me. First at my fingertips, then slowly spreading over my body. I tried to build a protective layer around myself, but each time I tried, another wave, each stronger than the last, slammed into me at a different angle and sent me stumbling.

I will not give up.

I reinforced my layer over and over first, simple green sparks that glowed around me like a second skin, then spontaneously summoned vines that slipped around me like armor.

The mantle was unimpressed. I was better able to withstand its blows, but I was still doing my impression of a punching bag rather than a queen.

Flashes of fire danced around me. Magic slammed into me with each wave, like a rocket launched at me.

I tensed, but I refused to fully flinch.

I shut my eyes to concentrate. It went against my shifter instincts to keep eyes on the enemy, but, as I reminded myself, the lake was not my enemy, not truly.

You want to see if I have the strength to be worthy, I thought at it. *I'll show you strength.*

It wasn't like the other times when I'd used my magic, where I'd been terrified and grasping around wildly. Deep down, I understood that wasn't what the lake wanted. It wanted control. It wanted precision. And perhaps, even though it was Hell, a realm full of monsters and cruelty and death, it wanted something more.

My lessons with Hecate had stressed the technicalities of magic. If you were powerful, you could perform any number of arts, but there would always be a specific type of magic that you were drawn to above all others.

For Hecate, that had been enchantments.

For me?

It wasn't anything so simple. Or the opposite: maybe it was far simpler.

My magic was life.

The vines I'd wrapped protectively around my body melted away, exposing me to the lake. Yet the mantle paused its siege as if waiting to see what I would do. The vines spread wider, encircling me first in a large sphere, then growing, growing, growing wider. They didn't stay simple green stalks. Instead, I pushed them to the perimeter, sprouting offshoots over and over until my net covered the entire lake.

Then I gave it one final command.

Bloom.

Petals exploded through the lake. Several disintegrated as lava flashed hot against them, combating the sudden onslaught, but they bloomed again, over and over as my magic fed into the vines. They weren't simple flowers, but a representation of my magic, the green sparks filling the center of every blossom as if it was pollen, filling my lungs as I breathed in deeply.

Eventually, the magic of the mantle stopped fighting the flowers. I had won.

Yet it was more than that, wasn't it?

"It's a gift." I wasn't sure what spurred me to say that, but it felt right.

"A gift." The mantle paused as if considering. **"Very well. You have passed the first trial."**

The second trial began instantly.

At least, it was that, or the mantle was thoroughly pissed off at my gift.

The lava was no longer turbulent, yet instead of easing up, a new feeling of animosity rose.

Images flashed around me on all sides, as I was surrounded by their portraits.

Sabine.

Richard.

Maddox.

And then, in front of me, Jett.

"Weak little Omega," Sabine hissed.

"Dumb bitch." Richard.

"Should've killed you in the womb." Maddox.

"My worthless mate." Jett.

If I thought all the mantle had for me were taunts, I was wildly underestimating the trials. The figures peeled off the portraits.

We collided.

Sabine was the first to land a blow. Across my stomach.

Phantom pain leaked into me. *Just like that night.* The night of the Choosing, when she'd ripped my organs apart. I'd begged that night. Pleaded. It hadn't been enough. They hated me, even though I'd never given them a single reason to, and delighted in their own cruelty.

I tried to summon my magic to shove her away.

It was gone.

It wasn't as if I'd expended it all in the past trial. I'd used a lot, but I should still be able to fight back. Instead, it was as if it was sealed behind a glass wall, visible to my mind but out of my reach.

Panic slipped into me, freezing me in place. I'd gotten used to having my magic at my back, strengthening my deficits.

Richard bit into my side, holding me in place while Maddox landed a vicious kick. Pain ripped through me as he loomed over me. It was like when I was a pup, hiding from his scrutiny, yet now, in my worst nightmare, he'd found me. There was no escape.

My wolf was silent. I couldn't shift, couldn't access my stronger form and slash at them the way they had me.

Just like every time they'd ganged up on me.

A hundred memories danced across my vision. Every time they'd bullied me, tormented me. They'd hated me, and they'd enjoyed letting me know it with every single cruel act. Sabine slammed me again, sending me falling to the ground.

I tried to fight, tried to pick myself up, but my limbs were sluggish.

I'd lived this scene over and over. It had never gotten better. The fear seeped into every part of me. I shook.

Jett emerged. He was larger than life. His hand snapped

out around my neck, squeezing as he lifted me high in the air. Sabine and Richard flanked him, hurling taunts spiced with hateful laughter, but I couldn't look away from my fated mate.

"Let... go..." I gasped.

His sadistic grin widened, teeth sharp like a shark's. "Or what, mate? You belong to me. I can do anything I please."

"Don't... belong..." *to you*, I tried to say but couldn't get the last of the words out.

"You're too weak to do anything to stop me, *mate*. You always have been and you always will be."

There was nothing I could do. I had no magic, no wolf, no shifter strength to stop him as he squeezed my neck.

But he would never own me. I forced my eyes open, even as the pressure grew and grew. I looked at him, and even though I couldn't speak, I thought my words.

You will never own me. I am not yours. You cannot win respect or submission through bullying, and I'll be damned if I let you try. I died to get away from you, and one day, I'll murder you myself.

Jett's smile slipped off his face. For one moment, he appeared furious, an avatar of wrath itself.

Then he and all my other tormentors shattered as though they were no more than panes of glass and fell to the floor.

My wounds healed the moment they disappeared into the ether, but the oppressive magic didn't leave the air.

When I saw him, a new wave of fear flooded me.

"Cole!"

He collapsed on the ground in front of me. I rushed over to him, scrambling to reach him.

Think, Avery, he's not really here. He was in the pits. But wasn't this magic ancient? Wasn't it powerful? What if it *was* him?

Blood pooled out of his chest, his eyes, his nose, his ears. I leaned over him.

"Little wolf." It was his voice. The same rumble I had heard in a thousand dreams, the same name he'd called me for years. "I'm sorry."

His eyes shut. His chest stopped moving. I screamed and pulled him up into my arms.

Live, I thought. *Live, damn you!*

My magic was no longer behind a wall. It was a violent, demanding thing. And it demanded Cole live.

A swirl of green lights struck him like an arrow to the chest. He didn't flinch.

"No, no, no," I murmured, pulling him closer. "Not again."

"You wanted power. You have it. But power is not everything." The voice echoed through the lava.

Power? What did it matter if it couldn't give me this?

Tears raced down my cheeks, as fresh as they'd been the day he'd been stolen from me and fallen into the pits.

"Tell me, Avery. If he is lost for good, would you still want the mantle?"

Did I?

In an instant, I thought no. Because if Cole wasn't coming back, there was nothing left for me in the world. My heart would never heal. My soul would never be complete.

But there *was* something. Buried under sorrow, fighting to come out. No, if I couldn't save Cole, I wouldn't give up. The images of Jett, of Sabine, and every other wolf who'd ever tormented me flashed through my head. Of Phaidros, who had orchestrated Cole's demise through me.

Cold rage seeped into the void left by Cole's absence.

"Yes," I breathed. I wanted it. I wanted revenge.

"You've failed, Avery Ward. You are unworthy."

CHAPTER V

A WAVE OF DEFEAT crashed over me.

After all that, I failed?

The lava burned hotter and hotter, scalding my skin. I began to push back, desperate to escape the violent change in the lake.

I failed.

The pain felt like justice, to a dark buried part of me. I'd known I could never be worthy. I'd deluded myself into thinking I was worthy of more, more power, more responsibility, but who was I? Just the Omega from Moon-Ghost.

An abrupt change rocked through the lake.

The burning halted. It was more than the mantle's magic. Something had changed, a third force entering the lake. Protecting me. Halting the rejection.

A vision flickered in front of me. Not like the torments it had pulled from the ether in the earlier trial, but something entirely different.

There, where I'd stood only a moment before, was a woman. She faced away from me. Her hair was the color of flames, even brighter than the lava. She wore a simple dress that looked hundreds of years out of style. At first glance, it looked like normal, braided fabric. But with my shifter eyes, I saw it was more. The dress was woven from plants themselves, vines twisting over each other, so fine and simple that it looked like less than the marvel it was.

The lake flashed emerald.

If I had any doubts about who I was looking at, they disappeared when the lake was filled with projections of greenery.

The former Queen of Hell.

Cole's love.

And... my previous incarnation.

"You have passed the first trial," the lake intoned. But it wasn't talking to me. This was an echo of the past.

The figure didn't speak.

"The second begins," the lake warned.

Another flicker in the projection, and Cole appeared in front of her. This must've been years and years ago, yet he looked exactly the same.

He cupped her face with his palms.

For a moment, jealousy flared. I bit down on a growl, instinct warring with reason. Not only was this before Cole and I had ever met, but this was supposedly my previous life.

But he didn't lean in to kiss her. Instead, the vines that had lingered around her crumpled as his death magic took control. He'd done it once to me, when we'd sparred and I'd trapped him. That had been Cole playing.

Yet even as a tender expression washed over Cole's face, his magic turned aggressive. It spiraled over the woman's body, cocooning her from the neck down in a black haze. Beneath the smoke, her body withered. Supple skin turned gaunt, then decayed.

It reminded me of the dragon before I'd healed it.

Yet she made no move to fight him.

Her gaze slipped from Cole as if she directed the mantle of Hell itself. "He is who he is, and our fate must be balanced by as much death as it is life. I am not afraid."

Her voice… it was bizarre to hear it.

It sounded exactly like mine. Or at least, what mine sounded like on recordings because it was always a little eerie to hear recordings of your voice.

That feeling was made a thousand times worse when it came out of some woman you had never met.

"You have passed. Tell me, Persephone, why do you wish to be queen? Do you simply want to stay at the side of the king? Or do you lust for power?"

Okay, so she'd been given a multiple-choice question. Slightly unfair.

But Persephone—my past self—shook her head. "I have no need for power for the sake of power, and he will be mine forever whether I take the throne beside him or not. I want the mantle to ease your burden. I will care for the people of your realm as I do my own. I would sacrifice myself for them if needed, even if it cost me Hades. That is what he has agreed to offer his people, and I would not dishonor them by offering any less."

The scene froze as if someone had hit pause on the television. The woman was frozen, still as one of Medusa's victims, but then her body split. One version of her stayed exactly as she did. Then, a phantom version of her stepped out and turned to face me.

She could have been my twin. Every freckle of my face was mirrored on Persephone's skin. The way she carried herself, however, was different. Her posture was regal, serene. More like Hecate's than my own.

"Hello, Avery."

It was an effort not to stumble back when she addressed me. "What? How?"

She cast a smile my way, like she could imagine the hundreds of questions flashing through my mind. "I am not alive if that is what you're wondering. When I took the trials, some of my magic was left here. It allowed my essence to gather, to be here for you, to show you my own struggles."

"Struggles? You passed with flying colors!"

She shook her head. "I nearly failed the second one. Power, it's not hard for you or me. But I faced few trials in my life before I met Hades. Even if I had faced titans, none could have compared to the sheer terror loving the Lord of the Dead would bring. I feared, when I took these, that it would destroy me. I decided I didn't care." She narrowed her gaze. "And yet, that is not even a fear you have. You love him with your whole heart, and you trust him."

"How do you know all this? Are we the same person, like everyone says?" I wasn't sure that I could refute it, when faced with... well, her face.

Persephone shook her head. "We are the same soul, reincarnated. I did not know what would happen when I put that in motion, but I had faith our soul would find its way back to him. But you and I, we are not the same. My demons were different. Yet our enemy... she *remains*."

Up until then, Persephone had appeared the picture of serenity.

With one word, I understood why everyone had begun to back away when I got angry.

Her eyes flared neon green, replacing everything from the pupil to the sclera. Green lightning flashed along her skin like chain mail, while vines flared to life, covered in thorns.

"You must defeat her, Avery. But it's not for revenge."

"Why, then?" I asked, refusing to fear my own soul. Even if she looked like a demon at that moment.

But the magic ebbed away. Both the frozen ghost, and the phantom faded until they were barely visible.

"You know why. For the same reason you will take the mantle..."

Her voice grew softer and softer until it faded into silence. The previous Queen of Hell disappeared.

Immediately the lava began to heat again, threatening to dissolve my body.

Shit.

You know why.

"Wait!" I called out to the mantle. "Let me change my answer!"

I half-expected the mantle to dismiss me and continue with the destroying-the-unworthy-pretender shtick.

The lake paused. It didn't cool the lava, just left it a shade below the temperature of boiling water. My magic sheltered me, but barely.

A bead of sweat dripped down my back.

I thought back to my previous answer. I'd told myself I wanted to live for revenge. To have the power to hurt those who had hurt me.

Yet there was more to it than that.

Phaidros had threatened Daphne. All I'd ever wanted was to protect her. I loved her. I wanted the power to make sure no one could hurt her like that again.

I wanted the power to rescue Cole. And even if Cole was lost, I wouldn't abandon his people.

There was a bigger threat out there. I'd spent so long wishing I'd had someone to protect me.

I'd wanted the power to intervene when Sabine had found

a new victim and I'd had to walk away.

I wanted the power to be that person for the entire realm. For the imps who had to steal bread, for undead dragons that had been malformed through magic.

"What is your answer, then?" the mantle asked, impatient, like it really had somewhere to be.

"I've wanted power ever since my pack turned on me. Wished for it. Cursed the fact I didn't have it. But then, I wanted it to protect myself. I thought I wanted it to fix the fact I hadn't had it, to fix what I thought had caused all my problems." I drew a breath, hoping the lake wouldn't smother me with lava if it didn't like my new answer. "I don't want the mantle for the power, but the responsibility. Both realms have been too long without guidance. Where the strong pick on the weak. With the mantle, I'll change that."

"Both realms?"

"I'm only asking for power for this one. But I'm not going to abandon my old pack either. I'm going to take on Jett. And I'm going to set things right there, too. For all shifters."

Maybe it was hubris that made me think I could do that.

But when I thought of Daphne in the cell... when I thought of the little shifter Sabine tormented, the latest in a never-ending cycle of victims, I realized I couldn't turn my back on them.

I held my breath, waiting.

"Then the mantle is yours."

Chapter VI

A WAVE CRASHED INTO me. I slammed my eyes shut, bracing. The lava turned searing, but it didn't hurt me. Not in the typical way pain worked. No longer did the heat of the lava burn me. The raw power itself seared me. The lake imbued magic into every ounce of my being, soaking me in ancient power.

It was a fraction of a second. It was a year.

New clarity rolled into my mind. A fog lifted. My magic was *more*. More abundant. More controlled. More dangerous. More healing.

I opened my eyes. The lake looked different, yet I knew it wasn't. The resting place of the mantle was unchanged; it had been here for thousands of years and would lie unaltered for thousands more. But I was changed.

I walked out of the lake as if it were nothing more than an empty pit. I stayed in my human shape. On a whim, I tested the magic. Once, it had been hard to call forward. Now, it buzzed under the top layer of my skin as if eager to come out and play.

I conjured the vines that had become so familiar, yet instead of brandishing them like bulky weapons, I pulled one in front of me and split it, over and over, growing each new strand and splitting it again. With a flick of my wrist, the strands braided together, knitting themselves into a sheet. Another flick, and I had styled something resembling the clothing I'd seen Persephone in.

This is kind of handy.

It wasn't as skilled. Instead of a dress, I made a simple top and skirt. Pants were beyond me.

It was effortless to *poof* myself back to the palace. It was as simple and instinctive as turning into a wolf. One step, I was in front of the lake. The next, I stepped through to the throne room.

It had come a long way from the nearly crumbling room I'd stood in from the aftermath of the pits. Walls were repaired, banners lining the stone behind the thrones I'd materialized in front of.

The castle felt different. Like another layer on my skin. Not unpleasant, but present all the same. I twisted around, trying to pinpoint the change.

But it wasn't the castle that had changed, just as it hadn't been the lake. It was all me. The mantle seemed to have dialed me into the capital, not just the physical space but its very life force. And the souls of those in it.

There could be no other explanation for how I sensed the

guard a moment before he turned into the room.

Hector saw me, eyes flaring wide with surprise as he nearly stumbled.

Then he knelt.

And kept kneeling.

For a solid minute.

Finally, it dawned on me he was waiting for some sort of acknowledgment. How strange, to have someone waiting for my command.

"You can stand," I told him, and instantly the soldier lifted himself from the ground.

He'd regained his composure but there was shining reverence in his eyes that made me shift on my feet.

I hope I'm worthy of the mantle.

"Soteria. You've returned."

I waved him off. "I've been gone all of a day. What's the most that could've happened?"

Hector frowned.

Oh.

"How long?"

"Six months. Lady Hecate insisted you would return," he added quickly, to cover the weariness those months must have left in their wake.

Bile filled my throat. Cole had been in Tartarus for *six months.*

"Will you take me to her?"

He led me through the twists of the castle—there had been some changes necessitated by the quake. I could sense souls around me, almost like shimmering lights in my mind, but at the moment, they were indistinguishable from one another. Others reacted to my reappearance in a similar way as Hector had. At first, I thought it was just the time passing but maybe there was more to it.

"Why do they all look like they've seen a ghost?"

He didn't glance at me as he answered, keeping his posture firm. Aside from that initial stumble, Hector was a steady presence. I could see the appeal Daphne so obviously found in him. He was clean-cut, a solid, square jaw unobscured by so much as a scruff. His looks were that of a simple soldier, fair-skinned with blond hair cropped close and bulging muscles that were obvious even in armor. He smelled like steel. It wasn't exactly my taste—I preferred dark, threatening looks in a lithe yet powerful body—but I was glad she had him.

"You look like the old queen."

"Aren't they used to that by now?" I prodded.

He shook his head. "Not simply your visage. Your entire appearance; the way you carry yourself, the way you clothe yourself."

I frowned. I hadn't noticed myself moving differently at all, but there was some merit to what Hector said. I'd mimicked the style Persephone had worn in the lava lake. The magic had changed me.

I just wasn't sure how, exactly.

Hector led me into the courtyard where I'd trained with Hecate before. The ancient, petrified tree she'd set me against, time and time again stood proudly at the center. It had survived the damage, or as much as a dead tree could. Not unscathed entirely; branches had snapped off and the tree had no life to regrow it, but it stood there all the same.

"Avery!" Daphne broke off from her conversation and ran to hug me. My arms wrapped around her, tightly embracing her.

Hecate gave a regal nod. "You've returned."

I mirrored the movement. "I have."

Hector moved away, but I didn't miss the shared glance between him and my best friend.

"What happened?" she demanded, returning to face me.

"As I told you, child. The mantle takes as long as it needs to settle," Hecate answered for me. "I don't suppose you could be dissuaded from your foolhardy quest, now that you have earned the mantle? The people of this realm have been without a leader for too long."

I stepped away from Daphne, stiffening. "Tell me you didn't send me to claim the mantle in hopes I'd be convinced to abandon my plan to rescue him?"

The mantle wouldn't be given to me unless I was willing to give myself to the realm. I did plan to serve them. Had burned the promise on my soul.

"I did not," Hecate replied in an unhurried tone. "I serve you, Soteria. I have never done any less."

"And I *will* serve the realm. Starting by rescuing its king."

I stepped towards the petrified tree and laid my palm on it, as I had a hundred times before.

Then, there had been something buried, the seed of something my life magic couldn't quite grasp. I'd sweated in frustration at the impossible task.

Impossible—the word had a different meaning now. I shut my eyes and concentrated on the thread connecting me to the roots of the tree.

Dead. Petrified from age.

My life magic could do a lot, but it couldn't undo death itself. Surely not.

Yet this tree... it reflected my magic back at me. It wasn't only one kind of magic, but two. Sometime, probably hundreds of years ago, it had grown from my own magic. The tree was massive; growing something like this would've been well beyond my abilities before.

I focused. My magic was life, but taking the mantle had given me something else.

A greater understanding of death.

Death is not the end.

It was not just my own magic of green sparks I summoned when I pushed my energy into the tree. Black, death sparks drew around the trunk as well.

Death had shackled the tree. Chains around a coffin.

I unlocked them, a skeleton key into a lock. And as the coffin opened, I pushed my life magic into it.

The tree flared to life. Grey wood darkened to a vibrant brown, branches grew, and leaves sprouted until they grazed the ceiling. Even the roots grew, cracking the floor beneath them as they stretched wide, hungry for nutrients after decades of decay.

I turned back to the witch. "I'm going to rescue him," I repeated.

Hecate dipped her head in understanding. "Very well. Then there is no time to waste."

NOW THAT I HAD the mantle, I could conjure portals. The catch was, they didn't come anywhere near as easy as teleporting within the realm. Hecate explained that within Hell, barring pocket realms like the one I'd found Cole in to begin, my power was near limitless. Piercing the realms to move between them was only possible with the mantle, but it was far from effortless. Portals took a great deal of magic and focus.

Returning to the realm of the living was never meant to be easy. It took Hecate hours to guide me through, the task especially challenging since Hecate had never cast a portal herself. The ability was limited to just two creatures: Libra demons, and the rulers of the realms.

But first, we had to agree on a plan, and that had proved challenging. I wanted to go by myself. I could move faster, I was more powerful, and there was no sense endangering anyone else.

Hecate countered that, as the only ruler of the realm currently, I was the one that shouldn't be endangered, and if I insisted on going—which I did—then I needed reinforcements. Preferably a dozen soldiers.

Hector had immediately volunteered, even before I could shoot down the idea. Daphne had joined in. After all, since she was still technically "alive" as she'd only come to Hell through a portal, she could protect me from others without the pits demanding their due. Hector obviously wasn't happy about the idea, but at least he had enough sense to not argue.

In the end, we agreed to keep it to a small group. I didn't know if we would have any run-ins with Moon-Ghost, or any other hostile packs.

But there was one pack that could offer help. One that kept the old ways and just might be able to help me.

Aiming a portal wasn't easy, but it was at least possible to guide it to where I had been.

We were still in the courtyard, in the shade of the massive, revived tree, when I finally got the hang of it. Hecate had encouraged me to rest, but one look had told her exactly how likely that was.

Six months.

I summoned a portal that shimmered like an emerald, although the circle kept shrinking and enlarging in a way Phaidros's never had. It was too bright to even see the other side, but I prayed my aim was true. I didn't know what to pray to anymore. Never the Moon Goddess, not again. Maybe to the stars themselves. To the magic that had been entrusted to me. Hector and Daphne went through first, while I poured all my focus into keeping the magical door open. I didn't want to know what would happen if it shut while one of them was halfway through.

With a final look at Hecate, I began to step through.

"Be careful, Soteria. I fear your journey will not be easy. Be mindful of what it may cost you."

I gave a quick jerk of my head and then rushed through, the portal slamming shut behind me.

CHAPTER VII

"WHO ARE YOU AND what are you doing in my territory?" a familiar voice snapped as I stumbled out of the portal.

Hector and Daphne had taken defensive stances in front of me, but the Wing-Blood Alpha Heir's voice was easy to identify.

I pushed myself up from my knees. The portal had taken a tremendous amount of magic; truth be told, I wanted to curl back in the dirt and sleep. But we didn't have that time. I elbowed my way between them.

Xander's eyes flared in recognition. The past few months had aged him. When I'd seen him last, he'd been beautiful, playful. Now he had grown, taken on more muscle, and lost that boyish edge. Something had happened.

"Remember when you said a certain wolf might be able to find allies in your pack?"

The Alpha Heir nodded.

"Well, we need help." I wasn't even sure what to ask. "Can I speak with your pack elders?"

A new voice joined the fray. "Who do we have here, Xander?"

The newcomer looked like a bigger, badder version of Xander. If I'd met him a year ago, I would've cowered. Now, I held the male's gaze.

"Alpha," Xander inclined his head. "This was the... visitor we found a few seasons ago. The one Grandmother mentioned. And she brought friends."

His peridot eyes flicked over Hector and settled on Daphne for a beat before returning to me.

"My name is Avery Ward, and this is my friend Daphne. We used to be part of Moon-Ghost. And this is Hector..." I trailed off, not exactly sure how to explain his presence.

"The queen's guard," Hector helpfully filled in.

At the twin looks of disbelief on our Wind-Blood hosts, I smacked a palm over my face. We already had a lot to explain with the portal. Our sudden arrival had drawn attention—appearing in the heart of a pack's territory was rather conspicuous—and now we seemed insane. Or dangerous. Two things shifters responded super well to. Fantastic.

"So the red wolf returns." A figure pushed their way through the crowd, settling between the two alphas in front of me. The pack elder who had healed me after her grandson ripped out my guts. "Come. Speak with us."

She led us back to the cottage, her long silver braid swayed as she moved through. Onlookers parted for her. She still had the energy of an alpha, even if she'd resigned from the post. Even if she walked with the pack's alpha and alpha heir, it was her they moved for. Once in the cottage, she began to boil water and mixed a comforting set of herbs.

"Speak, red wolf. Tell us how we may aid you."

A glance at the other alphas revealed a hint of confusion at the elder's reaction. I summarized the journey as briefly as I could—how I'd been murdered by my fated mate, as the rumors said, and returned from the land of the dead to rescue Daphne, only to return anew. There was no easy way to explain I was now the queen of Hell, but Hector had already spilled the beans on that one.

"The black wolf you described. The one who rules over death." I held the elder's gaze. "He's trapped because of me, in a realm of eternal torture. I can open portals between this realm and Hell, but I can't go to where he is. There's supposed to be a passageway somewhere in this realm, and I was hoping you might have an idea where to look. We don't have much time."

Hecate had warned that appearing on the surface would make us vulnerable. I didn't dare risk spending any longer than necessary.

But I would not return to Hell without Cole.

"Avery, this is..." Xander started, but the elder cut him off with a flick of her wrist.

"I know of where you speak. Xander will take you."

He raised a brow in question.

"The center of the caves. Our pack has watched over them for many years, awaiting your return. Even as the tides shifted to favor the Moon Goddess, we knew the true one would return. And so we shall help you in any way we can, red wolf."

Xander nodded, accepting the order. He may not have understood what I was asking for or why, but he would obey his orders.

In silent agreement, he guided us deeper into the territory. I hadn't spent long here, but even the air smelled different than it had in Moon-Ghost. Less tainted.

"If we need to hurry, it would make more sense to shift so we can cover more ground quickly," Xander said once we were outside of the center.

I glanced at Hector. He wasn't a shifter.

"I can keep up," he assured me.

"Then let's do it," I decided.

We shed our clothes and changed behind some bushes. Hector collected Daphne's discarded fabric and placed it in his saddlebag; I let my vine clothing sink into the ground, since I could simply grow more of mine when I shifted back. Daphne brushed my shoulder, her dove-gray fur pressing into my side in comfort. I nudged her in return, grateful for her having my back on this. It was the first time our wolves had spent time together—after my failures shifting as a pup and the contempt my red fur earned me, I hadn't bothered to change very often once we'd gotten to know each other.

Meanwhile, the ash-furred shape of Xander appeared. He was large, even for a wolf. Maybe only twenty pounds less than Cole. His attention fixed on Daphne for a long moment, head cocking as he examined her, breathing in her scent.

A growl began to stir in my throat at the delay the same moment Hector said, "I'll remind you, my lady said time is of the essence."

Xander made a sound in his throat like he didn't care much for a guard keeping him on schedule, but he broke his stare. He turned east and began to run. His pace was too slow for me at first, and I nipped at his heels, urging him on. It earned a growl, but he sped up. A glance back at Hector confirmed that, true to his word, he was keeping pace with us. He might not have the supernatural speed of a wolf, but he had some preternatural gifts and had years of military training to hone them.

It took half an hour to reach the opening of the caves. I paused at the entrance, half-expecting to have reached the entrance to Tartarus itself. Xander huffed, chastising me in a wolf way for stopping.

We entered the caves.

It wasn't possible to run through the winding paths, so we shifted back. Daphne changed back, while I grew another dress for myself and attempted shorts for Xander.

"I think I'd show less if I was naked," he griped.

"I'm a magical wolf, not a seamstress," I retorted. But I did manage to loosen them with a twist of my wrist.

The caves were pitch-black. Our gifted vision could only do so much. I summoned a ball of light like Hecate had tried to teach me. When she had first shown me, I'd tried and failed to replicate it. Yet the magic didn't hesitate to unfurl in my desired shape. Since claiming the mantle, there was a whole world of magic that was now possible for me.

"How far do these caves go?" I asked.

I wanted to rush through, but the caves were a labyrinth of forking tunnels. Without Xander's guidance, we'd be lost.

"The elders have said they go everywhere. Under all Wind-Blood pack territory, to the moon rock and beyond. Even reaching to other dimensions." He slid his green-eyed glance my way. "I'd thought it was just a myth, but apparently it's true."

"Myths are truths diluted by time," Hector said.

Like the Moon Goddess. What had been the center of shifter religion was actually my enemy.

There was no way to go any faster, so the four of us spoke to pass the time.

"So how did you die?" Xander asked Daphne.

"I didn't."

He frowned. "Didn't Avery say you all came from the land of the dead?"

"Hell, not to put too fine a point on it," she replied.

"Hell." He snorted. "Does it live up to the name?"

"Absolutely."

I nearly stumbled. I expected Daphne to say no. After all, it was a place of relative safety over pack life, plentiful food, a city to explore.

"The people are violent, there's no end to the magical horrors and curses you encounter, including star-skinned, pompous demons. People try to poison you if they don't like you; it's not like in a pack where you can just challenge someone. And the air... there's like this miasma, some foul energy that clings to my skin and enters my lungs with every breath. I can't shift when I'm there. My wolf can't break out of my skin."

How bizarre. I'd never felt any evil in the air. But then again, I had died. Daphne existing there as a living creature who didn't belong was unlikely to be welcome.

"But," she continued, "it's a thousand times better than living among people who would let you be caged like an animal for protesting some psychotic wolves killing your best friend."

Xander looked at me for a long moment, then back at Daphne, putting the pieces together. "You're the wolf Avery was looking for two seasons ago."

I nodded in confirmation, even as my stomach clenched at the reminder. Cole had been in the pits for months.

"If you were in Hell, how did you know she was imprisoned?"

I explained how scrying worked. That led to questions on the rest of my magic, but I didn't have much in the way of answers to offer. The magic simply *was*, just like shifting *was*.

"They talked about the red wolf presiding over plants and life, but obviously there's a lot beyond that."

There was.

I hoped it would be enough to let me do what Hecate had deemed impossible.

"And the black wolf, is he as powerful as you?"

"More."

"And he rules over death."

It wasn't a question, so I kept walking.

"Are you sure we should be rescuing him then?"

My fingers twitched at my sides, green sparks flaring. I bit down on the urge to slam him against the cave wall for even implying leaving Cole to his fate could be an acceptable option. But we needed Xander, and he didn't mean any harm.

"When her eyes look like that, it's a hint to *back off*." Daphne pulled Xander farther ahead. "We'll rescue him, Avery. I promise."

I shook my head, trying to shove the magic down.

"Death isn't bad," I said once I felt capable of doing something other than exploding. "But prison is. What Daphne was put in was cruel. It's worse than what they did to me. And what the black wolf—what Cole—is going through? It's worse than any of us could imagine. There's nothing more despicable than trapping a wolf, and I will do anything to save him from that."

That was a bit of a downer, so I slid out of the conversation. Mainly, Xander and Daphne talked, occasionally volleying questions to Hector or me to keep us involved. I only half-listened, my own words ringing in my head.

"Almost there." Several hours had passed, but no one had complained.

Xander led us around a corner, and there was no doubt we had reached our destination.

The walls turned smoother than the rough stone of the others, as if they had been carved. It was a long, straight passage, without any of the winding or offshoots the others had.

But most of all, at the end was a final wall of crystal. The green light I'd cast refracted back. Energy pulsed in the air, dark and foreboding.

"This," Daphne whispered. "This is what it feels like to be in Hell, but way worse."

I grit my teeth, pushing forward.

"Be careful, your majesty," Hector said. He was trying to keep pace beside me, but the energy seemed to repel him. It wasn't exactly easy for me either, but I was doing better than any of my companions.

"You three stay back. I'll go by myself from here."

Daphne started to protest, but I shook my head. "If something goes wrong, I won't have you trapped there with me. Keep them safe, Hector."

When my guard readied his own argument, I cut him off with a stern look. "That's an order."

"Be careful," Daphne called after me, her warning bouncing off the walls.

It was like walking through snowdrifts. Ice slammed into my bones, the energy an assault, trying to keep me away.

Nothing will keep me from him.

Sweat trickled down my forehead. My hands balled into fists, my nails digging so deeply into my hands that they drew blood. When I reached the crystal wall, I forced my gaze up. It was nearly ten feet tall, with white fragments protruding like weapons.

I slammed my palms onto it, letting the stone taste blood as I summoned my strength.

But like Hecate warned, getting into Tartarus was the easy part.

The hard part would be making it back out.

Chapter VIII

TARTARUS.

Toxic air slammed through my lungs. Every cell in my body rebelled at my presence in this forsaken place. It was like it was twisting every atom and turning me inside out. I looked around, trying to ground myself, but my surroundings were mind-bending. What first seemed to be the ground I stood on was somehow the ceiling, and the moment I realized that, I fell down, down, down to the ground. Shifter instincts let me round off my fall into a roll that spared me the worst pain, but the pain was the least of my concerns. I shut my eyes, trying to slow down the ringing in my ears from the fall, but the air continued to suffocate me.

I bent over my knees and vomited.

That made me feel only marginally better. A thousand invisible centipedes crawled over my skin, worming their way under my clothes and warring with each other. I wanted to howl, to shift, to run, but my wolf wanted nothing to do with this hellscape. She recoiled, as though it was something that had already hurt her.

Control yourself, Avery.

I tried to imagine it was *his* voice in my head, coaxing me the way he had when I'd faced other challenges. I didn't have time to lose my shit.

I forced my eyes open.

The under-realm had only ever been referred to in vague terms. The pits. Eternal torture.

Both, I found, were apt. The term pits felt particularly accurate. I was in a cavernous room, but it was more than a simple cave, like the tunnels I'd walked through before. Stalagmites and stalactites lined the various peaks and protrusions like teeth. A ringed path wound around the chamber. But it quickly became clear this wasn't a simple place. Every time I tried to orient myself, the space shifted. The initial fall was the worst of it, when gravity reversed, but that was far from all. The under-realm continued to play tricks on me. If I carelessly rose on two feet, I'd suddenly find myself sliding back as if the ground was tilted and frictionless. If I turned clockwise to assess the space, I'd find myself turning into the same scene over and over until I shifted—and then, when I turned back, it was entirely different. The air continued to poison me. I half-wondered if I was hallucinating. A pounding headache had taken up residence, like someone was slamming into my forehead with a silver ice pick.

Any attempts to call my magic failed.

No wolf. No magic.

Fine. I'd dealt with that hand for twenty years. It wouldn't stop me now.

I kept my gaze moving at a snail's pace. When I moved quickly, the realm reacted like it was an invasion. But slowly, I was able to better understand my surroundings. Throughout the mind games and revisions of the cavern, the winding path remained. It took ages for me to reach the edge of the room. I put a palm to the wall to steady myself and immediately regretted it.

Scalding hot. Like sticking my hand on molten lava, even though there was no heat in the air to warn me. Blisters erupted over my palm. I didn't let myself look at them, too worried about the path disappearing. Instead, I forced the pain to anchor me while I began the climb. It dulled after a few minutes.

At least I had my shifter healing.

The path was not as simple as it had at first appeared. At some points, it thinned until it was barely a foots-breadth wide. Once, I fell, barely catching myself by my still-stinging palms before I tumbled to the ground. I didn't want to know how the realm would react to that.

I tried not to think about the fact this was likely to be the easiest part of my journey.

Finally, I reached the end of the winding path. My stand widened, bracing for what new torments would emerge.

Unlike the rest of the cavern that was hewn from natural

grays, the path ended with an entryway of utter darkness. There was an opening, lined in flat obsidian. Beyond the entrance was only blackness, the kind of void that seems to be carved from outer space, where not even a shred of light can touch it.

My gaze snagged on the top of the archway. Carved into the obsidian were words, big, bold, jagged marks of warning. The shape of the letters was unfamiliar. It wasn't a language I'd ever learned.

Yet somehow I understood the meaning instantly.

QUAKE BEFORE TARTARUS; THERE IS NO HOPE; THERE IS NO ESCAPE.

My vision turned double, the letters blurring into a mess. I choked. Water filled my lungs. It wasn't like the miasma that had assailed me since walking in without abating. This was new. I crumpled to the ground, clutching my throat. I refused to look away from the archway. I wouldn't give the under-realm another chance to move, to hide itself from me.

The drowning sensation abated a moment later, the taste of seawater coating my tongue. It was like what I'd experienced with the nixie, only worse. Because I hadn't felt like I was starting to drown; I felt like I had been drowning for hours. The difference mattered.

"This won't stop me." I forced the words out, a promise to the realm. "I *will* get him."

I forced myself through the obsidian archway.

TAUNTING A REALM MEANT to torment and break souls was, in the opinion of someone certainly smarter than me, unwise.

The darkness continued while I walked. It shouldn't have been possible for the sensations to get worse, but when you're being psychologically tortured, your only asset is your vision. Vision that lets you reassure yourself there aren't a million tiny bugs crawling over you, slithering, tasting your skin. Vision that proves you are not, in fact, being sliced open as you walk through, not when it feels like blood is rolling down your arms as they burn and burn with open wounds, but you don't taste any blood when you put a finger to test. Shards of glass were embedded in my feet, even through my shoes. I came to realize it didn't matter if none of these things were happening. They felt real. It might have been less painful if they *had* been real, because then my body could heal. But there was no healing, just more invisible cuts across my skin. Sometimes they slashed the same part several times in a row, a slow, methodical cut that repeated until my very muscles seemed to tear apart.

I cried.

There was no escape from the pain, except for some pathetic tears.

I wouldn't stop, however. Every step was a battle, but losing was not an option.

My skin began to burn like it was encased in silver as I continued. That sensation, on top of the other cruelties, nearly broke me. I wanted to beg for mercy.

I will not stop.

Those four words were the only ones that tethered me through the pain. Over and over again, I chanted them. Sometimes I opened my lips to mouth the words, but that just let worse sensations in.

I will not stop.

I didn't need to sleep. That was the only gift the realm gave me, and taking away the blissful escape of sleep was anything but a kindness. Still, gratitude pulsed through me, because if I needed to sleep, if I had a reason to stop, I might very well cave in. The darkness went on and on. There was no way to tell time with any meaning; there was no light, no movement, not so much as a change in elevation. But days passed. I was certain. Days that felt like centuries while every part of my body screamed at me to relent, to give up.

I will not stop.

The darkness ended abruptly.

When I lifted my foot, I was blind.

When I put it down, I was suddenly able to see.

I was no longer in a simple cavern.

The ground was still hard rock and dirt, though it had been

turned a copper-red. Lifeless; it was more than an absence, it was a sensation. No wonder my magic was repelled. The planes in front of me spread out for miles, ending in blackness on all sides. Above was the same blackness. Not quite a ceiling, but I couldn't call the vortex a sky. I turned back, and the same space stretched around me.

I turned back and there was a lake in front of me.

The drowning sensation returned in force.

It wasn't just a sensation in my throat, though. My entire body was encased in water; when I blinked, all I saw around me was water.

I choked, crying out a name I couldn't even recall. A thousand desperate thoughts flickered through my mind, competing for what little air I had. As if they'd always belonged there and rushed to the surface.

Endure. Endure for him. Endure. It will not be forever. It will not get worse. Endure.

My body was emaciated under the water, skin barely hanging on. A tangle of red hair long enough to strangle me encased my already drowning chest. My lungs burned and burned, desperate, my lips open, begging for air only to be slammed with more salt water.

And then, in another blink, it was gone. I gasped, my chest heaving. My body was dry. My hair was tied back. My arms had muscles.

But it felt so real... so familiar...

Of course, it does.

Because my soul had spent a hundred years here, in this very realm. And I knew—knew in a way I could never prove, but neither could I doubt it—that the lake the under-realm had put in front of me had been the site of my own torture.

Those were *memories*. Memories that filtered back in, echoes of pain that still scarred my soul.

There is no escape.

I had been an exception. I *had* escaped. Or had I, because I was right back here where I had been imprisoned. Maybe I had never left. Maybe it was pointless. Sorrow pierced me, hopelessness pushing me towards the water. I took a step, and the water drew closer of its own accord.

Wasn't it easier not to hope? Not to fight? To accept it?

I raked my nails down my arm, drawing real blood—not like the unseen invisible slices. The pain shocked me, breaking the temporary hold Tartarus had on me.

"I will not stop," I snarled.

The lake vanished.

And the land in front of me was utterly changed.

Chapter IX

T HE REALM HAD BEEN empty, or at least the part of the pits it revealed to me.

But when I resisted the siren call of my old torture, it dropped the facade. Now, the plains that stretched for miles and miles were no longer deserted.

A cacophony erupted, hurting my ears. Yells of agony, pleas for mercy. Thousands and thousands of voices, all belonging to those now presented in front of me.

Every manner of brutality was on display for me. Creatures of every description had only one thing in common: they were in pain. My eyes darted around, unable to process what I was seeing. They were impaled on spikes; they were encased in blocks of ice, eyes flickering desperately; they had bites taken out of them, entire stomachs missing only to regrow; they were flayed; they were whipped; they were hung upside down while blood streamed down their entire body.

The copper hue of the dirt took on another meaning.

The scent of burned flesh and rotted blood filled my senses, compounding with the poisoned air that had chased me throughout the realm. I ran to the first one I saw, a humanoid creature who was bound to a table. His body was male, though his head was covered in a shroud. Two cranks at either end of the table magically continued to move, pulling at the shackles on his hands and feet. His arms and legs were distended, the body never built to survive such manipulation.

"I'm... I'm going to help you." It was hard to get the words out. I was torn between sobbing and throwing up again, but I shoved both sensations aside.

The male didn't respond.

I pulled at the shackles, but that did nothing. "Just hold on." I tried for the crank, but still, nothing happened.

I growled in frustration. No. I wouldn't stand for this.

I reached for the chains. I'd avoided them because they glittered like silver, but they were my best bet. I wrapped my hands with parts of my vine clothing and yanked.

Nothing.

I tapped into my fury. The unfairness of this, the vulgarity.

The thought that Cole might be going through something even worse.

I pulled with all my might and the chain snapped.

"One down," I promised the male.

He said nothing. I reached for the other. Sweat poured down my brows from exertion as I finally snapped the chain, the silver burning an exposed edge of my palms.

Success. I pulled the hood from his head. That, at least, was effortless.

Unfocused eyes didn't meet my own as I peered down.

"Your... your hands are free."

Still, no answer.

"Here, sit up," I urged him, putting my hands on his shoulders.

The male began yelling. A wordless, pained cry.

I yanked my hands back.

The yelling stopped a moment later. I stared in confusion. "Please, you have to let me help you. Your hands are free. I'll undo your legs as well, and you can escape this."

Finally, the male sat up. He stared at me, but his eyes went right past me.

"There is no hope. There is no escape." The words were rough, like his vocal cords were mangled from too much yelling.

He laid back down, slapping the hood over his face, and extended his mangled arms over his shoulders once more. The ends of the shackles dangled inches from the rest of the chain. Links regrew between them. The crank wound, unbidden, tightening the grip.

The torture resumed.

The sight shook me. Another trick of the realm, surely. To try and convince me it was hopeless.

But then I turned to the next victim, one who was being sawed in half, over and over again.

Even when I fought my hardest to free the creature, it just brayed at me in fury and returned to the pose. The saw resumed.

So went the next.

And the next.

And the next.

True torture, I realized. Worse than being hurt. Not being able to help anyone. Fear crystallized into shards of ice within my chest as I, for a moment, just a second, imagined that Cole might have the same reaction.

The thought had me dry-heaving, bent over my knees.

I wouldn't accept that. Surely they all had been here so long they had given up. Cole would fight back. He would fight to survive. He would fight for us.

Even though he chose this, an insidious voice whispered.

As I journeyed deeper, I finally stopped trying to help people. It was taking too much time without any success, and my entire body was in pain. The momentary drowning spiked at random when I'd hear a cry that almost sounded familiar as I waded through the pits or caught sight of a particularly awful scene. But that wasn't the only memory coming back to me.

Thoughts teased at the edge of my consciousness as I continued. Maybe I was simply delirious. They were different from my own, older, out of context, but they fit in. Words, strings of phrases, then images.

I paused mid-step as one slammed into me.

I was in an orchard at night. Moonlight bathed the ground, and a figure emerged from a shadow behind the tree. He had long onyx hair and a black swath of cloth covering him.

"You've come again, Hades," my voice said.

"As if I were capable of staying away," Cole replied.

It wasn't as if I was fully there, not like the scene in the lava. Instead, it was like these memories had always belonged to me, a birthright that played in my mind as I reclaimed them.

That was not the last of them.

They came without context, flitting into place as I stumbled through miles of savagery. They were a balm for the wounds I now carried. But they were a poison too. I'd had so little of Cole. This other me had more of him.

And even as I learned her reasons, I couldn't help but wonder how she had managed to curse Hades... curse *Cole* to such a miserable existence.

A hiss of snakes took me from my thoughts.

Suddenly I found myself face-to-face with the creature that had nearly killed me.

Medusa.

I did not turn to stone.

In fact, it may have been impossible for her to turn anyone to stone. Where her petrifying eyes had once been were now two empty sockets, the hollows oozing blood. Her body was naked, a mess of green scale and gray skin. Her hair of snakes was a mess, a few, weak skinny ones moving about while thicker strands ended in stumps.

"A living soul."

I started. She was the first to acknowledge me. The *s* was drawn out into a hiss. Her voice was far more serpentine than it had been before, as if torture had stripped her of the civilized veneer.

"I know this soul—"

Her words bit off with a howl of pain. One of the snakes had tentatively wormed its way up and immediately sparked into flames.

"We... we met. You turned me to stone."

"That hardly narrows it down for—" A snake spontaneously exploded. "—For me."

"It was right before Cole killed you." My words were nearly a snarl, for the pain the memory ignited, the way Cole had frantically carried me to Hecate, but I immediately felt bad. He had killed her to avenge me, and she had been here ever since. Even she didn't deserve this.

"Ah, yes. The second coming of the soul." This time, she ground her teeth to avoid crying out when the next snake was destroyed. Even as the third one wilted, a new one grew half as thick as my pinky finger. "In my defense, I could hardly have harmed the old you."

"You knew me before?"

Even as I said it, new memories flickered through, as if I was looking at them in a stream. I had met the gorgon before—ages and ages before. In fact, I had been the one to insist we keep her in the dungeon instead of ending her existence entirely.

"Every living soul d–did." Another snake gone, mid-word.

"Let me help you," I said. "Then you can give me answers."

Medusa roared with laughter, even as it was punctuated by cries as her snakes suffered and hissed in pain. "The only help you could give me would be ending my existence, and you alone cannot take on the very fabric of our universe."

"I've tried to help the others," I said, helplessly, "but even when I free them, they refuse to escape."

"That is what this—" The word bit off as a snake head swelled up to the size of my fist and burst. "This place does. There is no hope, life-giver. Not for those of us trapped here."

"That's not true. That *can't* be true." I refused to let it. "I got out—or at least my soul did. Cole is here, and I'm not leaving until I get him out."

"Oh yes, the old king," she rasped. "He was nearly as much of a prize as you were." She paused, perhaps bracing for the next snake to be destroyed, but nothing happened. Maybe that was part of the torture—forever bracing for the strike that would eventually come. How odd, to see such a con-fident monster struggle to hide her fear. "The under-realm whispers to me, you know. It likes having us old creatures. It tells me it's still displeased to have lost you all those years ago."

The last words came out in a cry, another snake disfigured.

"You agree people can escape then," I reminded her.

"And in what state did you return? A simpering wolf, scared of her own shadow. Not any kind of goddess."

I said nothing.

"Fine," she spat. "I'll tell you how to find the king. The under-realm plays tricks after all, but as it whispers to me, I grow wise." The realm, disliking this, took three snakes at once. Her roar of pain shook the cavern. "It's simple, really. You find what you fear here. So drop the brave front, and imagine the worst, worst things that could happen. Imagine him torn in two at his own hand, imagine him on his knees, then cut off at them, imagine him in pain, begging for it to end, and knowing it never will. Then you will find him."

Even though her words made my stomach feel like it was turning to stone all over again, I thanked her.

She laughed and laughed again, the hollow rattle fading to a cough. "Oh, you shouldn't thank me for this."

CHAPTER X

IT WAS THE OPPOSITE sensation of summoning my magic. Instead of focusing on life and survival and hope, I let all the insidious thoughts I'd sheltered myself from filter in. Every pain, every torment I'd seen, with the male I loved taking center stage. My attempts to find him in my dreams, when there had only been smoke and pain, the fear that those were more than simple nightmares.

My newly returned memories of my own torture hit me in visceral waves. When I imagined Cole going through that, it nearly broke me.

I walked on aimlessly, barely able to see through my tears. The fear and horror grew. What would I find? Would he be broken by the time I reached him? I wanted to believe otherwise, but every creature I'd encountered so far had gone insane from the torment. My own existence had fractured to escape.

I didn't pause to try and help anyone else.

The red plains emptied of bodies the farther I went. The ground was splintered with streams of lava, and the farther

I went, the wider they grew, until I was perilously balanced on sinking bits of ground to move forward. My mind only half-processed what was happening around me, still sinking into the depths of my terror.

It grew hot, my hair plastered to my forehead and back as I dodged bubbles of lava.

The ground was no longer flat. An incline grew, the sharp angle making my legs burn from exertion, my shifter stamina worn thin after fighting mental battle after mental battle.

And then I saw him.

I didn't want to believe the figure ahead of me could be Cole. For a brief moment, I wished I would never find him, rather than see him in that state.

His skin was a sea of blisters, dark red cracked skin mottled over the sensitive, exposed flesh. His body was spread wide, shoulders wrenched back at an unnatural angle, while glittering spears impaled his hands and feet into stone. My body recoiled even at this distance at the volume of silver. His head was hung low. His normally night-black hair was cropped short, uneven in patches, with gray powder coloring it nearly white. Large boulders towered over either side, leaning in, and the tops of the stone melted, sprinkling down bits of rock onto him, which cooled on his body, turning to cinders.

I rushed forward, scrambling up the lava-riddled path. A sulfurous smell made me gag, even as it mixed with the sickeningly sweet scent of burning flesh.

"Cole? Cole, it's me!"

I lifted his head to meet my gaze, gripping him between my fingers.

He looked at me. But there was no recognition, not so much as a flicker.

"I'm going to get you out of here," I vowed. I released him as gently as I could, wishing desperately for my healing powers. *Soon*. Soon I would get him out of here. I would never stop, not until we were both back where we belonged.

The spears in his feet would be the first to go. I had seen them from a distance. The sight up close was utterly grotesque. His body had tried to heal around the puncture, even as the metal burned him. I tried to grip them with my makeshift shirt, but the metal was too hot to touch without the vines burning.

There was no way I was leaving him here like this. Not a chance.

I bit down on my tongue, bracing for pain, and wrapped my hands around the steel pole.

Even while pain exploded behind my eyes, I yanked up, not letting my mind process the awful sensation.

But the pole gave way.

"I'm going to get you," I repeated. A glance down confirmed my palms were covered in blisters, though they didn't begin to compare to Cole's tortured body. I made myself wait for them to heal, which took agonizing minutes. If I was too rash, I could very well burn my hands beyond use. All the while I whispered reassurances, promises, even taunts, anything I could do to try and rouse him. Cole, who had never been anything less than powerful, now brought this low.

And it was all my fault.

All of it. I knew that now that my memories had returned.

The next pole was no less painful to remove. His legs slumped forward, lower half free. I set to work on his hands, his body falling on mine for support. I held him as best I could. The final spear was the most difficult to remove. I cried out when I removed it, then grabbed Cole and moved him from under the melting boulders. I drew him to a relatively safe part, where he rested on the ground.

I wanted to sigh in relief, but we were so far from okay. So, so far.

"Cole? Do you... do you know who I am?"

His eyes twitched, as if trying to rise to meet mine. I gently lifted his head in my palms.

"Red... you're not real."

"I'm real," I promised. "I'm real, Cole. I came."

He didn't need to speak to convey his disbelief.

No matter. Once I got him out of here, he'd snap out of it. I'd allow nothing less.

Getting out wouldn't be easy. My memories were still filtering in.

The only way to get out of the under-realm was to convince

the realm to let you. To make a deal.

I had said no. A million times I had said no to the deal that was offered. The price was too grave to pay, even to save my own damned soul.

But there was no price I wouldn't pay for his.

"I want to make a deal." The words were little more than a whisper as I cradled Cole against me.

Silence.

"I want to make a deal!" I shouted. "Answer me!"

"So quick to make demands."

The voice filtered in my mind. Like the mantle, but not. I wasn't able to stop from flinching. The voice was malevolence personified. Worse, it was familiar, a starring sound in my worst memories, though they hadn't done it justice.

"Didn't I say you would be back?"

"I want to make a deal. Release Cole's soul and let me bring it back to the underworld."

"You know the price of this, life-giver. If you set him free from below, you will unshackle the one above as well."

The poisoned offer. The one I had sworn never to accept for myself.

"I—"

"No."

I glanced down. Cole's eyes were still shut, his body starting to heal, painstakingly slow for a shifter.

"Not this," he murmured, voice growing weak from just a few words. "Get out. Leave me."

"Not without you," I said, pressing my lips to his. "We'll figure it out." Or so I hoped.

We'd failed to figure it out for the past thousand years.

"Do you agree to the bargain or not, life-giver?"

"I do."

"Then begone. Though I'm sure I will see you both again before time is done."

COLE AND I WERE released to the land of the living in a heap.

"Avery! You—you got him!"

Daphne rushed to my side, and the violent air coming from the crystal momentarily ceased. I clutched Cole closer to me, even as she fell over my body in relief.

"You saved me," he rasped, looking up at me. He tried to lift his hand to cup my face. I bent my cheek, feeling the rough skin on my own. His own scent was muddied with blood, but I drank it in all the same.

"My liege." Hector knelt before Cole.

"It's all true," Xander murmured. The Wind-Blood Heir drew close, taking us in. His eyes were wide with shock. Though he'd obeyed the words of his elders, he had doubted like any living creature would.

Scratch that, every single creature had doubted us. Doubted that I could get him back.

But he was here. I hadn't failed. Cole was here, in my arms. So drained he was barely able to keep his eyes open, but he fought to do so, just to keep that amber gaze on me. I drank their depths in, memorizing every part of him, still whispering assurances in soft words.

I was so focused on him I didn't even notice the sudden presence of cloves in the air.

"Isn't this a pretty picture?"

My head snapped up as Phaidros stepped from the shadows, a portal shutting behind him.

I moved in front of Cole on instinct, even as he tried to shield me. My magic was back, but I was utterly drained. I barely had enough juice to do a show of sparks.

"I should kill you," I snarled. "You set me up."

"You made that deal of your own accord, darling." A careless shrug of his shoulders. "Not my fault you're so easy to manipulate."

A growl rose. Not from me, but from the shifter behind me. Daphne.

His attention flickered to her and then stayed, a slow, sensual perusal. "Hello again, love. As much as I love to see my mortal enemies brought low, I didn't come here to chat."

"Then why are you here?" I was stalling, trying to rouse my

magic, but what precious little I had, I needed to conserve to heal Cole and get us back to Hell.

"A warning, darling." He swayed forward, as if to take a step, then smirked as we all readied ourselves without so much as moving. "So jumpy."

"Spit it out," I demanded.

His attention shifted to Xander, lifting his empty wrist as if checking an invisible watch. "Your pack is being attacked, in, oh... three, two... five minutes ago."

Xander jolted.

"Why warn us?" I snapped. "You're not on our side."

He snorted. "Maybe I'm not on that moronic Moon-Blood Alpha's side either."

"Thanks," I grumbled.

"I still didn't say I was on your side, either," he purred.

And in a blink, faster than a body should be able to move, he lunged and drew his sword in a single gesture and stabbed Hector straight through the heart.

CHAPTER XI

PHAIDROS WAS GONE, DEVOURED by darkness, before we could so much as react.

Hector fell forward onto the ground, a pool of blood pouring from his chest. Daphne surged for him, rolling him on his back. His lifeless eyes looked back up.

"Save him, Avery," she sobbed. "Do something, please!"

I was already moving, trying to gather my wisps of power and shove them into his body. I gripped his shoulders, shuddering as my magic tried to knit him together. It couldn't find a purchase within him. His soul was already gone.

"I'm sorry." The words tasted like failure. Yet again, someone I cared about had been hurt. Because he was here, with me, and Phaidros had wanted to hurt me for spite.

Her hand flew to her mouth as she muffled a sob, shoving me out of the way as she clutched his body in goodbye. But even that was denied—in a matter of seconds, he crumbled to dust. It was a twisted kind of sense. His real body had died centuries ago when he'd come to my kingdom.

And now he was doomed to the pits. Bile rose in my throat.

"He was a good man," she growled. "He didn't deserve this."

"We'll avenge him," I vowed.

Her eyes flashed, her wolf flickering behind them. "I'll rip his goddess-damned throat out."

"He was a good male," Xander said, tension rolling off of him. The alpha in him was obviously furious at having his territory invaded and threatened. "Unfortunately, there's no time to mourn. I need to get back to help my pack, and unless you want to be lost down here, you'll want to follow me."

I shook my head. "I can do one better. I'll teleport us back there, and then immediately take a portal back to Hell."

I was loathe to risk entering the fray with Cole barely breathing and my own magic resources depleted, but it was my fault Xander's territory was attacked. My own moon-cursed mate was leading the charge.

Hecate had warned me they'd sense my arrival and charge after us.

Xander nodded.

I helped Cole to his feet, supporting him as he wrapped one blistered arm over my shoulders for stability. I gathered my magic and imagined the center of Wind-Blood territory, where we'd first emerged.

A blink later, we were there.

The sky was burned with a red sunset, as if drenched in blood. For the briefest moment, I thought we were back in

Hell.

Then the din of war pierced the air, battles raging around us. All around, shifters fought. Some with fists, some with claws.

Xander didn't hesitate to shift, leaping on a nearby foe.

I summoned my magic, forming the green sparks of a portal with practiced ease even as I struggled with my fatigue. I'd be no help here. If I took another living life, then I'd put us back in the same place. Lingering was dangerous. Already, our sudden arrival had been noticed, and gazes shifted from current fights to decide if we were enemies to be prioritized. I didn't care where we wound up in the underworld as long as we got there fast.

"Let's go, Daphne," I said, urging her as I took the first step through, clutching Cole's body protectively.

Bloodlust lit her eyes. "I'm staying."

There was no time to argue. And... my friend belonged in the world of the living, even if I no longer did. Even if it meant leaving her among this.

"I'll find you again," I promised.

She nodded, already shedding her human skin.

I pulled Cole the rest of the way through the portal, watching the battle desperately, helplessly.

Daphne bounded after Xander, who faced three wolves on his own. The elders were nowhere in sight.

And there was the Alpha, facing off in human form against

Jett. Jett, who spotted me as the portal began to shut. His gaze was more than furious. It was ravenous. Power-hungry. Obsessed.

He jerked his clawed hand forward.

The portal shut in time for me to see him rip the Wind-Blood Alpha's still-beating heart out of his chest.

WE'D LANDED IN OUR bedroom, atop the same bed I'd refused to sleep in since he'd left me.

I rolled over to tell him something, to say anything, only to find his eyes shut.

Passed out. Not dead, I reassured myself, pressing fingers to his pulse and resting my ear against his chest. But recovering. My magic returned quickly, but Cole was already healing. His body seemed to heal before my eyes, new skin growing where patches of exposed muscle had been minutes before. More than shifter magic; the mantle of Hell had settled back into him.

But Tartarus was not an easy place to recover from.

I summoned Hecate with my magic, letting her know of our arrival. Her shock at Cole's return was palpable. And then her eyes flickered to mine.

"Soteria," she whispered.

How odd, how unchanged she was in my eyes. She recognized the knowledge in my gaze, the memories. They weren't complete—more flashes of moments, conversations in the garden I built with her, jokes over dinner. Not just my teacher, but my friend. My confidant.

"It's coming back to me," I murmured. "Pieces. I think the pits returned a piece of me they'd held onto. I'm still me, but... I *remember* things. How to use my magic. How we met." My gaze went back to the male who was still asleep.

She nodded. "It makes sense. The others?"

I shook my head. "Daphne will stay in the realm of the living. Hector... he didn't make it."

"He gave his life to protect you," she assured me.

But that wasn't true at all. "He lost his life because he was by my side and a cruel bastard wanted to punish him for that." Another person I'd been too weak to protect.

I told her of Phaidros, and how the Moon-Ghosts attacked the Wind-Bloods. In my entire life, I'd never heard of a pack invading another's territory like that. Border disputes, squabbles, sparring during the full moon meets, yes. But never *war*.

"She's making her move," Hecate warned. "We will be ready."

Would we?

I rested a hand in Cole's hair, feeling the soft strands.

"I'll stay with him until he wakes up," I told her. "Please see to the rest of the castle. Let them know their king and queen have returned."

I wouldn't shy from the crown. The Moon Goddess would pay for what she had taken from me.

My body intertwined with Cole's, I shut my eyes at last, breathing in the scent that, in my darkest hours, I'd thought was gone forever.

Sleep was a dark, deep embrace. In my dreams, I tried to find him. But there was only fire and pain and screams.

I woke with two hands locked around my throat.

CHAPTER XII

S OMEONE WAS SQUEEZING MY neck like they wanted to murder me.

My eyes snapped open in an instant, magic already swirling in my palms to take down the intruder.

But the figure above me wasn't an assassin.

It was Cole.

I fought to get out of his grip, but even in a weakened state, Cole's brute strength outmatched mine. My magic sputtered, not wanting to hurt him. Survival won, and I tried to slam him with a ball of green energy, but it didn't so much as shake him. His eyes... I'd never seen them like that. Pure rage tormented them, the amber shade darkened with shadows and fury.

"It's... me..." I sputtered in desperation. "Wake... up..."

Cole's eyes flared wide at my voice. He leaned back, shocked.

"Avery?" He shook himself. "This is a new torture."

"This is real," I assured him. "You're safe now. I got you out of Tartarus."

"I thought it was a dream." His voice was rough. "Then a nightmare. Where someone attacked you." His gaze slammed to my throat. "I hurt you."

He looked disgusted.

My neck was going to be ringed in bruises, and not the fun kind. But none of that mattered. I circled his wrists with my hands and pulled him towards me. "None of that matters. It was a nightmare, Cole. Understandable after... after everything." I bit back a sob. The little bit I'd seen him go through had been my own torture. And he'd gone through that for much, much longer.

"You're here. This is real," I repeated, pulling him to me.

I wrapped my arms around his neck, tasting his lips.

"I'd given up."

"I never did," I said, tasting him again.

"You feel too good to be real," he said, catching my lower lip between his teeth.

My claws sharpened, digging into his freshly healed shoulders. "Does this feel like a dream?"

"Little wolf, you have no idea."

I shivered at the nickname. Emotions swirled inside me, a million disparate feelings, but they all crystallized into a single intense need. Magic or not, I was a wolf at heart. I needed to feel skin on skin, to wrap his scent around me.

I pulled Cole's body against mine, refusing to let him get away. His body responded, hardening against me. His hand gripped my hair, unmistakably possessive. His other made quick work of my makeshift outfit, the vines turning to dust with nothing more than a touch. I leaned back, dragging him with me until we both lay on the bed. Unwilling to simply be led, he took control. His hips rocked against mine, taunting, threatening.

Need was a raging fire in me. I urged him on, bucking against him.

If he'd been feeling weak before, any sign of it was hidden. There was nothing but dark, demanding intensity in every single one of Cole's movements. Still, he controlled the pace. He wanted to drive me to madness before succumbing himself. Wanted to see me lose control. Wanted to force me to.

I was on board with his plan, for the most part. Except I intended to take him down with me.

"Give me more," I insisted. "Don't taunt me, Hades." The name slipped out before I could stop it.

He froze above me.

"Cole," I corrected. "I need you."

"You remember."

"Pieces." I didn't want to talk about it now. Soon, we would talk. About my memories and a dozen other things that seemed to strangle us. But tonight, all I wanted was him. "For example, how much you like *this*."

I arched up and nipped at his jaw, then exposed my throat for him.

He took the invitation, capturing the flesh between his teeth and sucking. Every part of my skin felt ultra sensitive, as if keyed in to his touch alone. I ran my fingers over his arms as if assuring myself they still held me.

He moved lower, teasing my breasts. My nipples had turned to stiff peaks, aching. When I tried to massage them, he snatched my hands away, pinning them above my head.

"*Mine*." The word came out as a low growl. "In any shape, by any name, little wolf, you are mine."

"Yours," I promised. It felt odd to be owned, but right, too. Like I belonged in a way I never had before. As if a missing piece had snapped into place. "Take what's yours."

"I should savor this," he rasped against my skin. "Should stretch this out to eternity. A perfect dream I won't let end."

"Savor next round," I growled. "Now, take what belongs to you."

"I can't be gentle," he warned. "Not tonight."

"I don't want gentle. I want *you*."

My words snapped the male's careful control. He didn't so much as loosen his grip while he shifted over me, lining his length against my entrance.

He slid his cock into me in one single thrust. I gasped at the sudden invasion, writhing against the cage of his body. "That's it. Good girl, take your male."

Words left me. All I could do was moan, shifting my hips to try and accommodate his girth.

He moved out before I could adjust, then slammed in again. My hiss of pain didn't stop him. He trusted my words. I didn't want gentle, and I wondered if it was for the same reason Cole didn't either. I needed to feel him, needed the pain that told me this was real. Not some sweet dream that would devastate me when I woke up. I wanted to ache in the morning, to carry the proof with me that he was back with me again.

In and out, he moved. Discomfort gave way to pleasure. Soon, I moved my hips in time, eagerly meeting each savage thrust.

"Gods, you feel good," Cole groaned. "You like this. You need this as much as I do."

"Yes. *Yes.*"

"You're going to hurt after this," he warned, not slowing his movements. "Going to feel me for days."

"I need to," I whimpered against him, clutching him closer. "I want to feel you with every step until I can get you inside me again."

"Little wolf," he grunted. "You don't know what your words do to me."

I hissed as he slammed into me with greater force. "I think"—*gasp*—"I'm getting the picture."

"Going to make me spend." He kissed me, a brutal, searing kiss. "I want to feel your pleasure when I do. Be a good girl and come with me."

"I'm close." Pleasure had built at a steady pace in my center, need spiking with every filthy word. "So, so close, Cole."

"I love my name on your tongue." He was relentless. "I love having you tight around my cock. Love having your perfect body beneath me, exactly where you belong."

"I belong on top, too," I quipped between breaths.

"Then show me."

In a swift, smooth movement he moved, so I was atop him without ever breaking contact. "Pump yourself up and down on my shaft. Want to see you come."

The sudden change in angle made me moan, his length pressing against me in a new way that was utterly delicious. I moved up and down at his command, taking him over and over, leaning forward for friction. His fingers dug into my hips, a bruising, possessive grip. I may have been on top, but I was no more in control now.

"I'm about to come, Avery." The words were sharp, bit off as he held back. "Come for me. Now."

The raw dominance in his voice sent me over. Euphoria erupted inside me, my head rolling back. Tension eased from every part of my body, an overwhelming sense of rightness taking its place. It was nearly an out-of-body experience. I was weightless. Everything was as it should be. Cole came with a final feral thrust, then tightened his grip as if I could even think of moving while his seed coated my insides. I squeezed my core around him, milking every drop of his pleasure. He was looking up at me with male satisfaction when my body finally became my own again.

I sank down against him, curling my fingers over his chest.

He traced a hand through my mass of hair and met my gaze. "Perfection."

CHAPTER XIII

I F I'D THOUGHT SEX with Cole was going to settle the rampant emotions unfurling inside me, I was sorely mistaken.

Uncertainty leaked into my spine. I spread a hand out on the other side of the bed.

Cold.

Empty.

No. No, it couldn't have just been a dream. He was real. I'd tasted him. I imagined I still could on my tongue. The soreness in my body should have been proof that it was nothing more than a silly fear, but when I sat up...

The room was empty.

My chest tightened with panic. I summoned a robe of vines with half a thought, wrapping it around myself as I ran from the bed to the bathroom. Empty, too. Cole's scent lingered in the air. I honed in on it, feeding it to my panicked wolf.

I chased his scent through the halls, moving in short leaps as my magic moved me entire hall lengths in seconds. Awareness tugged at my chest the further I went, the twinkling sensation almost familiar. It grew stronger as I went higher and higher through the castle.

I found Cole on the roof.

His back was to me, though he couldn't have missed my arrival. His hair had been ruined in Tartarus. The rest of his body had healed in a single day in Hell, but if he wanted his old hair back, it would take magic. He'd slipped on a familiar ensemble of black pants and a black silk shirt. On the roof, in the dawning hours of the day, I could almost imagine we were back at the other castle. The one that had been just for us, where he'd trained me and we'd sparred, verbally as often as physically. That castle had been home. The first I'd ever had.

Anguish surged in my throat. We didn't have that castle anymore. Didn't have the safety he'd indulged me with. When life had been as simple as learning how to reach my wolf and grow stronger physically.

But none of that had been real. We were trapped in a game that started thousands of years ago. The ignorance Cole had left me with had been a gift, a way to shelter me from this burden, but it had been an illusion.

An illusion that shattered when I'd seen him swallowed by the pits. A fate I'd fought against a hundred years ago, though even now the details remained unclear.

"You left me." The words were a whisper.

He didn't turn. I surged toward him, inches from his back.

"You weren't there when I woke up." My hands curled

into fists against his back in anger. Still, he didn't turn, and I slammed against him, desperate to make him turn and face me. "You left me, you left me, you left me!" I knocked my fists against him with every word. "How could you leave me?"

My voice cracked, and I was asking about more than just this morning.

Forgive me for leaving you all alone. A paltry apology for ripping my heart out.

At last, he turned.

The look on his face devastated me.

Self-loathing was carved into every pane of his face.

"What changed?" I fought to keep the tears that welled in my eyes from falling. I wanted to be angry, not to see my own emotions reflected back. "Why did you leave this morning?"

"I left you there."

Not in the bedroom. The hollow sound of his voice could only mean the pits.

"A hundred years ago, I left you there," he repeated. "My wife went to the vilest place in our universe, and was brutally tortured for what would've felt like millennia, and I did *noth-ing.*"

"You left me *here,*" I accused. "Not a lifetime ago. You abandoned me."

"There was no choice."

"There's always a choice." I slammed my palms into his chest, his back hitting the battlement. "You could've told me!

We could've found a solution."

"Oh, like we did last time?" A hundred years of bitterness coated the words.

"Maybe!" I snapped. "You didn't even give me a chance. You just... You gave up and left me."

"And what's the alternative, Avery? Do you think I would ever let you go back to that place? Never again. *Never,*" he snarled.

"The alternative is that you stop being so angry over the past for a moment and just *talk* to me. Don't disappear on me, Cole. Not after this."

"Angry?" He scoffed. "You want to talk about me being angry? Yes. I'm furious. Because you saved me, Avery. I failed you, a thousand times I failed you, failed to even try, and then you saved me."

"I've had enough of the masochistic bullshit." An animalistic growl burned in my throat. "You respected my wishes. We *survived*, Cole. We both survived an under-realm that's meant to be the end of souls. Nothing else matters."

"And for how long?" he demanded. "I should never have drawn you into this world. It was a mistake."

Of everything he could have said, that hurt the most. That he could actually regret having met. Having loved. Yes, there had been pain, and no doubt we would face more, but the idea that any pain could outweigh what we had together enraged me.

My magic flared to life.

Cole moved out of the way instantaneously, appearing halfway across the roof. I was in front of him in a blink, hooking my fist around.

He caught my palm and twisted, deflecting the blow. I didn't care. I hit him again. Over and over, we danced across the roof. Cole refused to engage me, and that just set my wolf off more. A fight was one thing, but to be denied the respect of it?

"Fight back," I snapped. "Don't just throw us away. *Fight!*"

"You want me to fight, little wolf?"

He slammed me back with an open palm, knocking me on my back. He moved to tower over me. I wasn't going down that easily. I hooked my legs around his ankle and jerked, knocking him off balance.

We flipped back onto our feet at the same time. His amber eyes blazed back, a familiar sight from all the days we'd spent on the sparring mat. We circled for a moment, sizing each other up.

Cole struck first. I dodged, then summoned a mass of vines to wrench his arm away. He turned the vines to dust and charged, his own magic surging. I liked the taste of it, even in the middle of battle. It was dark, unforgiving, and best of all, familiar. The magic of the Lord of Death. I hesitated a beat too long, and his fist connected. As if surprised the blow had landed, he paused.

His mistake. I took advantage and landed a solid kick to his kidneys, teleporting away before he could catch my leg. He was on me a heartbeat later, startling me as he drew behind, wrapping my neck in a choke hold. I couldn't concentrate enough to teleport away, but I could summon a fistful of green sparks and throw them in his eyes.

Back and forth we went. He'd land a blow, then I would. A kick, a punch. Twin fists colliding.

"I don't want to hurt you, little wolf," he said when he managed to pin me on my back for a moment.

"Can't you see abandoning me hurts the most?" I snarled, and in a fit of animalistic fury, I bit him.

He jerked back, startled. I was on my feet in another second and surging at him.

"I don't deserve you," he said, weaving around my assault.

"It's not up to you to figure out what I deserve!"

He shook his head, moving behind me again, and shoved me off balance.

I spun. "It's too late for that."

I launched a high kick, and this time he caught me, pinning me down, my leg wide under his knee while he pinned my hands above my head.

"Didn't last night mean anything to you?" I demanded.

Yours, I had promised him. And yet he was trying to throw me away again. We were covered in blood and bruises, a parody of last night.

"Last night meant *everything*." His battle-roughened voice raked over me.

"Then fight for us, Cole. I don't want a life you're not in. I want to be your strength, and I want you to be mine. Don't regret us." The violence left my words, leaving only desperation.

"I need you to be sure, little wolf." He pressed his forehead to mine. "I can't lose you again."

"Then stay with me. Don't leave me, Cole. I'll bear any torture but that."

A growl rumbled in his chest. "I don't want you getting tortured at all."

"We both know our lives are too dangerous for that. But we'll protect each other. It worked for thousands of years."

"Until it didn't."

Everything in Cole was built to hate himself for that, I realized. He was an Alpha, the King of Hell. He was born to put himself in the path of destruction in order to save those he cared about, and I was the one he cared about most of all. Failing that had been brutal. It had been why, when he finally found me again, he tried to resist, even as fate drew us together. He'd been able to tolerate it when I was ignorant, but now he knew what I'd gone through—and with my memories, I did too.

But I didn't see it as him failing me. We'd been in an impossible situation, and there'd been only one way out. The details were still hidden in the cobwebs of my mind, but I knew that down to my bones.

"Don't leave me again," I repeated. "Vow you'll never leave me like that, Cole. Or if you do, I'll kill myself and find you in that miserable pit and make you sorry."

He looked stricken. "Don't say that."

I narrowed my gaze. "Don't test me."

"Then I'll vow it, my fierce little wolf. But only if you make me one vow in return."

"What's that?" I asked.

"Marry me."

CHAPTER XIV

I BLINKED UP AT him. Of all the different responses I might have expected, that was the last one.

"What?" I said stupidly. As if I had somehow misheard him.

"Marry me," he repeated. "Become my wife and rule with me."

"Hecate said I didn't have to marry you to rule as Queen of Hell."

"That's true." Then he leaned down, his breath teasing at my earlobe. "There are more benefits to marrying me than just that, though."

A teasing thrust of his hips punctuated the remark. My body jerked, still tender from last night, but eager for more.

"Talk about hot and cold," I said, fighting for my composure while his words rattled in my brain. "One minute you're trying to end us now... now, this?"

"What can I say, little wolf? You're very persuasive, and I'm willing to be persuaded."

I was pretty damn sure I wasn't angling for marriage when

I'd tracked Cole down.

"You're supposed to ask bent on one knee, not while you have me pinned underneath you."

"Really?" He made a theatrical show of considering my words. "I'd consider it an improvement."

It certainly felt more true to form, I'd give him that. "How's that?"

"Stops you from running away." His grip loosened on my wrists, and he propped himself up on his arms atop me.

"Wasn't our whole issue you wanting to be the one to run away?"

"No." He nipped at my lower lip. "My little queen likes to disappear on me."

I huffed. "That was *one* time."

"One too many." His fingers trailed around my throat. "I should put a bell on you."

My pulse pounded under his fingertips, the words sending a thrill in me. "You'll find I'm not the domestic kind of wolf."

He chuckled, low and sensuous. "I wouldn't have you any other way."

I wanted him to have me *now*. No matter how many rounds we'd gone last night, I'd never get enough of this male. "We need to talk about everything that's happened in the past few months."

Cole sighed as if put out, but I could read him well enough to know he was covering his own concerns. "No doubt

Hecate has spent them strategizing for how we may survive the apocalypse."

"She definitely had contingencies in place." I swallowed back my anger at the enchantress. How quickly she'd wanted to move on when Cole was gone. But it wasn't her fault—the feat I'd pulled off would have been considered impossible by anyone sane. Thankfully, with Cole gone, I'd been unencumbered by inconvenient things like rational thought.

"It's her way," he said gently.

"It is," I conceded. "Let's go talk to her."

I tried to rise, but he didn't let me. Instead, he leaned down again to kiss me. He tasted like sweat and blood, gifts from our fight. "First, we need to shower."

A heartbeat later, we were in the shower. We stayed there for well over an hour. By the time we found Hecate, the day had well and truly begun. Palace staff moved about, doing double-takes at Cole's reappearance. Even though I'd instructed Hecate to tell them their king had returned, it was another thing to find the ruler they'd believed gone walking the hallway.

The conversation we had wasn't easy. Stefan, the captain of the guard, joined us so he could prepare our armies as required. We gathered around a table in a quiet room, away from prying eyes. There, we discussed my memories coming back in frustrating fragments. Hecate urged me not to rush them and let them return to me in time. She agreed it was entirely possible that having returned to the last place my soul had been complete, Tartarus, put something right. Cole was unsurprised to hear I'd taken the mantle. I told her about the bargain I'd made, and though she had to hide her shock, the witch took it in stride.

"We knew war would come," Cole said. "Our enemy is who she is. This just levels the playing field."

"She's using the Moon-Ghost pack to do her bidding." I recapped the battle we'd fled. I wanted to check on Daphne and make sure she was alright.

Cole nodded. "It makes sense. The dead may only attack the dead; the living only the living. Worse, a living creature can defeat a dead one without consequence. The reverse... you know what happens."

Yes. Because I'd killed Maddox to protect Daphne and myself, I'd forfeited my soul to the pits. Cole had wiped that debt clear, but it could happen again just as easily.

"She's had a century to gather her own army of dead shifters in the stars," Hecate warned. "Now she has a living army as well. And that demon of hers moves with impunity."

"Phaidros?"

She nodded. "He appeared some years ago, but the rules don't apply to him the way they do to other demons who should be bound to Hell. It's clear he'd allied himself with her as well."

"It would help if we knew why," Stefan added. He stood

stiffly, taking everything in.

All I could see was Phaidros, driving a sword through Hector's abdomen. "It doesn't matter. I'll kill him for what he did."

"My vengeful queen." Cole's voice was approving. He certainly had no love of the demon.

"That's fine," Hecate said. "Demons are fair game to kill without damning your soul in the meantime. Your old pack, however, may prove problematic."

I ran a hand over my temple, fighting the growing headache. "We'll need to talk to Xander. His pack's elders seemed to know more about this. They went to the moon ceremonies, but they didn't seem to worship the Moon Goddess the way Moon-Ghost or the Fangs did. Is it safe to scry now?"

Hecate nodded. "It should be, since we aren't cloaking you any longer."

"Then that should be our next step," Stefan said. "Determine who our allies are, and ready our people for war. Whether the battlefield will be in this realm or that of the living."

"And inform them, for the first time in many years, they have two rulers on the throne," Hecate added, her eyes brimming with unusual emotion as she looked at us.

Stefan agreed and dismissed himself to spread the word to his advisers.

"In addition to Avery's coronation, we need to arrange for

one other event," Cole said as our conversation wound down. "Our wedding."

Hecate's face broke into a grin, while I gaped at him.

"I never agreed," I protested.

He snorted. "As if that's stopped me before." I glared, and his smirk fell, a serious expression reigned over his face. "Do you really intend to say no after you went to Tartarus for me?"

I winced. That was a fair point. "It's not me saying no, it's just that I haven't had time to really think about it."

He pulled me in for a deep, dark kiss, not caring who saw, that left me breathless. I'd never expected Cole to be the type to flaunt his affections, but even if he was the King of Hell, he was a shifter. We liked to show off what was ours.

"I'll persuade you later," he purred, a tender promise.

I was looking forward to it.

SCRYING OPENED UP A one-way mirror. If I wanted to talk to my best friend after, I'd have to risk making a portal and either going to the realm of the living and painting a target on my back or dragging my best friend to Hell for a second time. My gut twisted, remembering the way she'd described how she'd felt here, where her wolf was locked away. Maybe I'd be able to hold a portal open long enough for us to communicate. But the first thing was to see that she was okay after the battle.

I was in the courtyard under the shade of the once-petrified tree. I sat cross-legged, nestled in its roots. A bucket of water was in front of me. It wasn't glamorous, but it was easy to transport.

My magic reached out into the universe, searching for Daphne. I willed the pool to show me she was safe. I told myself I'd know if something happened to her. She was strong. The water shifted under my power, rippling as it turned from water into a window.

My stomach dropped as the scene unfolded in front of me.

Daphne was sprawled over a couch, her palm bloody against her stomach. I wanted to lunge through the water and get to her, to make a portal and heal her, but that would only risk alerting the Moon Bitch of where to strike.

I was prepared to do it, though. The only thing that stopped me was the way the water shifted, zooming out so I could see those by her side. The pack elder who had healed me, the Alpha's mother, was by her side, grinding a combination of healing herbs in a mortar.

The second figure was more surprising. Xander stood over his grandmother's shoulder, his back stiff. Curious, I waved a hand over the bucket, shifting the angle of the image so I could see his face. His green eyes were narrowed with concern. A fresh scar covered his face, running from his upper left brow across his nose to his cheek.

The male who had given him that was almost certainly dead.

"How long until she wakes up?" Xander demanded. Though they couldn't hear me, I could hear them as easily as if they were in the room with me.

"She'll be fine once she rests," the elder replied. "Which she'd probably do more easily if you stopped hovering. She's young and strong."

My heart unclenched as I forced myself to exhale in relief. Shifters were extremely durable—present company excluded, at least when I'd been alive. If the elder said she'd be okay, I trusted her.

"Now, go tend to our pack. Our people need you, Xander."

A haunted look crossed his eyes. Alpha Heir no more, I realized sadly. Shifters could recover from a lot, but not having their hearts ripped out.

I broke the mystical connection, not wanting to pry on Wind-Blood affairs. I'd check in again soon, once Daphne had time to recover and we had more of a concrete plan. At least the Wind-Bloods had survived the attack. It was foolish to attack wolves in the heart of their territory. Yes, you could take them by surprise. But they would fight harder, to the last breath, to defend what was theirs.

What a stupid loss of life.

I wished I could have believed that would be the last of it. But we were on the brink of war, and a lot more blood would be shed before we could have any semblance of peace.

CHAPTER XV

T HE WEEK PASSED WITH a flurry of activity. Daphne
recovered in a matter of days, which I knew because
I scried on her every few hours, if only to reassure myself
there wasn't another attack. Once she was up and about, I
reached out to her and Xander. I caught them up on what had
happened, and they filled me in on the battle. It was as devastating as I'd feared. Worse, there had been no clear reason.
Moon-Ghost had simply wreaked havoc and then retreated.

Jett had led them. He was still alive.

Stefan continued to ready the forces of Hell. I'd come to
learn Hell was more than just an empty plain and a single
city. In the main realm, there were hundreds of towns and
settlements, the largest of which had troops stationed. Stefan
had a point; there was no sense spreading ourselves thin. Any
attack would target me and Cole, so they should be close
to us. Makeshift barracks were established outside the gates.
I helped raise base structures with my magic, while soldiers
refined them so they were habitable.

There was so much to do, I barely realized the day had

finally come.

Cole had convinced me to marry him.

It hadn't been hard, really. All I'd ever wanted was a person of my own. One who I could count on. One I would die for. And in Cole, I had found that and so much more.

That said, I had definitely enjoyed making him work for it. He hadn't minded the task, bringing me to the edge over and over until finally, I agreed to be his wife.

The coronation and wedding would be one joint ceremony. There were two reasons for this—one, it was easier to secure. Two, it minimized the amount of time it took up. Cole had offered to put all that aside and have two if I wanted, but I didn't care about appearances. I just wanted him.

The male I would fight armies for. Go to Tartarus for.

Button a thousand impossibly small buttons for.

The latter one was proving a challenge. I'd gotten into the habit of wearing my own green creations and quite enjoyed the freedom that offered me. I'd tossed the idea out of doing something like that for the wedding. Hecate had firmly discarded the idea. She gave me a speech about how the ceremony was a show of power, and our looks should reflect our station, and when I'd pointed out that being able to make my own clothes with magic was a statement of power, she finally admitted they did nothing for my figure and she refused to let me ascend to the throne that way.

The enchantress just liked a good fashion statement. She

never looked anything less than perfect, and she wanted no less for me for the coronation.

When I saw the dress she had created for me, I was inclined to see things her way.

Until I got to the buttons that ran up and down the back. It was an intricate piece, sleeveless and cut tight to the body until it flared beneath the hips out into countless layers of tulle. The bodice was covered in intricate webs of gemstones that glittered in the firelight. I wasn't sure how it had been made so perfectly to fit my body, since no one had taken a single measurement. Magic, most likely. Unless Cole had been feeling me up last night for more practical purposes.

I managed the first two-thirds with ease, but for all my shifter strength, I couldn't get the last few latched. I twisted around, trying to see what I was doing in the mirror, but it made no difference. A growl of frustration rose in my throat.

"Now, what could have my future wife making a sound like that?"

I spun, fabric flailing everywhere while I hastily pressed a hand to the front of the dress to stop it from falling off. Not that my *future husband* would likely have complained.

"This dress is a torture device. I think it's Hecate's revenge for making her run the kingdom the past few months."

The right side of his lip quirked up. "I have to say, I'm rather fond of this kind of torture."

I narrowed my eyes at him. "You wouldn't be saying that if

you were the one who had nearly pulled a muscle trying to button all of these." I gestured to my back and spun around so he could see.

When I turned back to face him, the look on his face was one of pure hunger.

"We can't have that, now can we?" He strode across our bedroom.

"You're not supposed to see me before the ceremony, you know." Shifters didn't have weddings exactly. Your moon-matched bond was supposed to transcend that. Usually, the night true mates met, though sometimes after, they'd mark each other with a claiming bite to cement the bond. The mark was as good as wedding rings, though some indulged in those as well. Sometimes, if they gave up on their moon-matched mate, shifters would pair up in common matings, but those didn't end in claiming bites.

That happened when, you know, your mate didn't forsake you and then kill you. But I'd read plenty of books in the castle's massive library, and they were extremely clear on the human customs.

"You'll break the laws of the universe, but this is too much?" he teased, sweeping my hair to one side. His fingers trailed across my exposed back, barely more than a graze. The brief contact set every nerve alight.

I scoffed. "I have to have some standards."

"But then who would rescue you from all those

hard-to-reach buttons?"

Fair point. "Fine, you can stay if you get the top ones latched."

"Hmm. I don't know, at this point, I'm more inclined to undo the rest." His hand drifted lower, squeezing my backside.

My eyes flared wide in the mirror. "That comes *after* the wedding, remember?"

"Such a traditionalist." He *tsked*. "Besides, after you're my wife in truth, I won't have the patience. I'll just rip it off your body."

The words could have been a joke, but there was not a shard of doubt in my mind that Cole planned to do exactly that.

"If you're not here to help me with the buttons from, well, Hell, what are you doing here? Checking to make sure I didn't get cold feet and decide I didn't want to marry a possessive, demanding, grumpy male?"

"You forgot 'bossy.' I know you're fond of that one."

Okay, I did usually call him that too. "Did I mention know-it-all?"

"I'll add it to the list."

He didn't deny the accusation, though. Maybe there was a grain of truth to my accusation.

"Too bad," I said. "I've decided this possessive, demanding, grumpy, bossy, know-it-all male is *mine*."

In the mirror, I watched his face light into a grin. "Of all the things you've called me, that's my favorite."

"Mine?"

"Yours," he agreed. "In heart, in body, in spirit."

I melted at the affection in his words. I wanted to turn and kiss him, but he had dutifully shifted his attention to the buttons. I watched his movements in the mirror, then shifted my attention to us. What a pair we made. His dark features were accentuated by a matching dark suit he wore. It was a thousand times more formal than what he'd worn to the ball. This seemed molded from darkness, curved around his body. A crown adorned his head. It wasn't particularly large or flashy; a circlet of black metal with spires of varying heights. In contrast, my hair was bright and bold. My dress practically glowed. Opposites. Death and life. An unlikely, yet perfect, match.

"Tell me a memory. Something from our other life."

His fingers stilled. "What do you want to hear about?"

I knew exactly what I wanted to hear about. "Our wedding."

He considered for a moment. "You know I see you as your own person, right? The memories of your past life don't change that for me. I'd never hold you to promises made in another lifetime."

"I know." I'd been firm that we were different people, but when flashes of memory returned, there was no Avery and Persephone—there was only me. "I'm just curious."

For a moment, Cole looked uncomfortable. He actually ran a finger to straighten out his already immaculate collar.

I perked up, curious. "Tell me."

"I want to preface this by saying it was a different time."

I arched a brow.

"And I was not the patient saint of a male you know today," he amended.

"You? Patient?" I rolled my eyes.

He grabbed my ear between his teeth and bit in warning. "Do you want to hear about it or not?"

"Oh, now I *absolutely* have to hear it all."

He sighed and summoned a drink of whiskey from thin air. "We'd been meeting for some time. Stolen moments at midnight, that kind of thing. I always came to the realm of the living to see her. Persephone was... a novelty. I'd existed for a long time, but meeting her was perhaps the first time I felt alive."

My heart ached for him. The wonder he added to her name, the nonchalance as he skimmed past what must have been a heartbreaking existence.

"You could say I became a little bit addicted. Of course, she had her own duties. She was exceptionally focused on those responsibilities, and she refused to leave the living plane to see my world. I was fixed on the idea that we were meant to be the answer to each other's loneliness and began to take offense that she would not visit."

Cole trailed off. I looked up at him. "And?"

He took a long-suffering sip. "So I decided to kidnap her."

I burst out laughing. "That was your solution?"

"At the time," he ground out, "it seemed like the most expedient solution."

If Persephone had been anything like me, that would've been the furthest thing from a solution. "And she accepted that?"

Cole chuckled. "Not exactly. She immediately shifted into a wolf and tried to bite my head off. When that didn't work, she fled."

"Why not just make a portal back to the realm of the living?"

A flush worked up Cole's neck. "She... couldn't. In order for her to stay comfortably in the underworld for any length of time, she couldn't be among the living anymore."

My brows shot up. "You *killed* her?"

"Not precisely," he hedged. "My death magic shrouded her, marking her as one of the dead. She was balanced on a knife's edge, her own lively magic countering it until she gave in and joined me."

"You totally killed her to keep her in the realm with you."

"As I've admitted, I was more reckless in my youth. Since she couldn't return to the realm of the living, I decided to take my time, stalking her and wearing her down within my realm."

"Oh good, kidnapping, homicide, *and* stalking."

"As I said, I was impatient in my youth." He sighed, but there was a light in his eyes as he told the story. "I chased her through every corner of Hell as my own wolf. It was the first time I'd ever changed to the shape she often favored."

I frowned. "Wait, you weren't a shifter before then?"

"I was the King of Hell. My magic was so vast and different from anything that there were no terms to define what I was—what I am. I simply existed. I had no need to take on a wolf's shape until I saw her do so. After that, it became part of me. Shifters didn't exist back then as they did now; the world was different. Magic wasn't constrained to the rigid rules and roles of today. The contracts of the universe were still being written."

Sometimes I thought I was beginning to understand the world I'd entered; then Cole said things like that and I realized he had lived through a lot more than I could ever have conceived of.

"For six months, I followed her. First, she did everything in her power to escape me. Then, in time, she either respected my tenacity or took pity on my obsession. She didn't let me catch her, but she did permit me to begin to show her the realm. It seemed to change as we went through; the sky turned from the red you know today to the same blue of the sky in your realm. The violence that simmered beneath the service cooled, as if pleased to have two creatures such as us instead of one. It was no longer Hell as I'd known it for countless years. After half a year, she finally relented, and I captured her. She became my wife that night."

I arched a brow. "Did you ask her as nicely as you did me?"

He chuckled. "As you may recall, I'm not one for asking. But she became my wife of her own free will. Our wedding took place on the night of the new moon, in an orchard she had tended to for hundreds of years. It was important to me that we married in the realm where she was strongest, where she could walk away. The six months had taught me much of her nature, even if we'd never said a word, and my feelings had grown from obsession into love. There were no others present, but our vows were sacred all the same. She wore a shroud of white, and I, black." He looked us up and down in the mirror as if imagining that now.

"And then she just moved to Hell with you?"

He sighed. "Were it only so simple. Her time gone from the realm of the living had left a vacuum. When she finally gave up her life above to remain with me, other ambitious powers attempted to claim the realm. Our years were not peaceful, but we survived."

His voice trailed off. They'd survived, until they hadn't.

"Now, enough stories, little wolf. I'd like to marry the woman who captured my heart in two lifetimes."

CHAPTER XVI

THE CEREMONY WAS SPLIT into two parts. As eager as Cole was to make me his wife, it was more important to him to first see me crowned queen. The realm was ruled by a king and queen, as Hecate had explained, and though they didn't need to be wed, many still expected it, especially given the past precedent. He wanted it to be clear to the entire realm that I was worthy of the crown, not because I was his wife, but because I was a crazy powerful woman in my own right. And though he repeated on the way down that I didn't have to become queen if I didn't want to—it became clear the cold feet he expected were about becoming his queen, not his wife—I reminded him I'd already claimed the mantle. This was just a formality.

He eventually relented. For a male who so clearly wanted me tied to him in every way, he constantly tried to give me reasons not to.

Too bad I was already all in.

The ballroom was packed. I'd thought I'd seen it full before, but every inch of the place was crammed full. Beings with animal heads, beings with horns, beings no bigger than my pinky, and several feet taller than me.

I wanted to teleport us straight to the dais that had been brought into the very center of the room. Instead, we moved slowly through the crowd. They parted immediately upon seeing us, calling out in approval.

Cole didn't offer me a hand up the steps. I understood why. I was a queen; I would walk on my own two feet.

The ceremony was brief. Cole led it, making it clear he was only a vessel for the realm. It wasn't like the lake of lava was going to make a guest appearance and crown me. I dipped my head, and he placed the crown of the Queen of Hell on me. Twin to his, it was made of white gold with spires topped in opal that reflected a dozen different colors. I lifted my head and turned to the crowd.

As one, they knelt, fists crossed over their chests in respect. Thousands of eyes stared at me, waiting for my guidance. Unlike when I'd taken on the mantle, I didn't feel any different magically. Instead, I looked into the eyes of everyone before me and recalled my promise to the realm. I would guide these people. I would lead them into war, and I would eliminate the threat. I would eliminate any threat to them.

The wedding ceremony took place on the same platform. Hecate joined us, wielding twin rings the size of our crowns tied together with a string.

Everyone around us disappeared. All I could see was Cole.

Not the King of Hell, not the warrior who made everyone quake in terror. I just saw him. The male who had coaxed me out of my shell, who had made me believe I could be strong. The one who made me laugh and held me when I cried. The one I would go to the pits to be with a thousand times over.

"The bonds of marriage are not a simple thing," she intoned. "One may go their entire life without pledging themselves to another. It is a choice made but once, and it cannot be broken like you would a simple shackle. These ties go back to our furthest tradition. Do you, my queen, wish to wed this man?"

"I do," I said. Tears pricked at my eyes. "I want to be your wife. I want to be the person you look at in the morning and confide in at night. I want to protect this kingdom with you and all the people we love. You're my pack, Cole. You're a better person than I could have ever hoped to call my own, and I am proud to have you as my husband."

Cole's gaze lit with emotion. He held my hands in his, his body turned to face mine as if nothing else mattered.

"And do you, my king, wish to wed this woman?"

"More than anything." His voice grew thick with emotion. "When I was in the depths of the pits, in a realm of unending, eternal torture, when I could no longer remember my own name or who I was, you were the only thing that kept me sane. I held on to every piece of you I could and now that I have you in my arms again, I will never let you go. Avery Ward, you are my soul, my sanity, my queen. We are eternal. There is no title I have ever craved more than that of your husband. I vow I will honor you. I vow I will protect you. And I vow I will love you as no other has or ever will."

Hecate lifted the rings above our heads and passed them back and forth. "Then let it be so. I pronounce you two wed."

A cheer erupted through the crowd. Cole clasped my face with both hands and pulled me towards him, and I welcomed him with a smile. He dipped me low, and the cheers grew louder. *Husband.* He was my husband.

When we broke apart, he smiled at me. The easiest, happiest smile I'd ever seen on his face.

Unable to resist, I kissed him again, then turned to face our people.

"Let the celebration begin," Cole declared.

On his cue, music began playing, a jaunty, cheerful tune.

"No slow first dance?" I teased. It wasn't like Cole was anything less than an exceptional dancer.

"If I don't have you alone in the next five minutes, I'm going to take you in front of the entire kingdom."

A bolt of arousal went straight to my core. I glanced around, blushing in case someone had heard.

"Unless you like that idea," he said, considering. "Though I hate the thought of sharing you with our guests."

My face was in flames. "Just get me out of here."

Cole could've made us disappear in a blink, but he seemed

to relish shepherding me through the crowd with a possessive arm draped low on my waist. I'd never thought I could have this, not even with my moon-matched mate when I'd been just a girl dreaming of a way out of that awful pack. Then, I would've settled for someone I could tolerate for a few hours as long as they were part of another pack. Someone who I could trust, someone who was proud to be with me?

I'd never let myself imagine it.

Cole extricated us from the ballroom with practiced ease despite dozens of attempts at conversation by our attendees.

"We're awful hosts," I mused. "Sneaking out just minutes after getting married without so much as a toast."

"We can toast in a few hours."

"A few hours? Isn't that bad manners?"

"Do I look like I care?"

No. He looked like a man with only one thing on his mind.

He wound me down an empty hallway. Though there was nothing particularly secluded about it, I felt Cole's magic around me. It was like having his fingers graze the back of my neck, familiar and sensual. No one would disturb us here. "We're the monarchs of Hell. We can bend a few rules here and there."

"Well—"

My next teasing protest was cut off with a gasp as he spun me against the wall so my back pressed all along him. Damn, even through this thick dress I could feel him.

"Besides," he rasped, the sound low and wanting. I arched into it. "There's not a creature in that room that could blame me for wanting the bride alone after seeing you in that dress." His hands ran the length of it from my hips until they curved around my chest with a squeeze.

"This old thing?" I tried to be coy, but there was no point. Not when his touch turned my voice into a husky plea.

"Do you want to tease me, little queen? Or do you want me to give you what you need?"

"You mean what *you* need?" He had me pinned under him, but that meant I was in the perfect position to jerk my hips back and press against his length.

He hissed.

"Better get started on those buttons." I tilted my head back and to the side to move my hair out of the way. If I twisted just enough, I could see Cole's expression. The hunger in it called to me, moving from my eyes to my lips to my neck, a dangerous, wild hunger. Something spurred me on to tease him rather than give in. Just because we were married didn't mean I'd start letting him steamroll me. "I'm not having you shred my wedding dress while I still need to go back to our guests."

"Maybe we won't go back at all."

"Then we'd be *terrible* hosts."

"That's a conundrum." He held my gaze, a daring glint in it. "Then maybe we should go back right now. Since you don't want to ruin your dress."

I growled at him. "Put those talented fingers to work and get started on the buttons, Cole."

"Talented fingers, hmm?" he mused.

Those cursed fingers didn't move to the buttons. Instead, they were everywhere else, squeezing, playing, taunting. Sensual need stirred low in me. I squeezed my thighs together, trying to calm the ache.

The smirk on his face said he could scent my arousal and approved.

Two could play that game. I twisted in his grip so I was facing him, chest to chest. I reached out to his tented pants and squeezed, feeling up and down his length.

It was his turn to growl. "Feeling what's yours, little queen?"

Damn, I loved when he called me that. Even now, when it could be a taunt, there was reverence in it. Love and desire that burned through every word. Of course, if I'd meant to tease him with my touch, I was still tormenting myself as well. Feeling how much he wanted me was a massive turn-on.

I lifted on my toes so I could press my lips to his ear. "Do you want your queen on her knees? Taking you, here in the hall?"

His cock jerked in my hand as he groaned. "*Yes.*"

I pulled back so I could sink down to the ground, eager to watch him come undone, but he stopped me.

"There's one thing I want first. If you're amenable."

I angled my head in question.

"I want to claim you."

I frowned, lifting my left hand, which held a simple golden band on it. "Been there, done that, got the wedding ring."

He didn't laugh. "I want to claim you as the wolves do."

I blinked.

A claiming bite.

Something I'd given up on when my moon-matched mate had forsaken and killed me. No, something I'd given up on the moment I'd found out I'd been paired with him. Because I would have never let him do that to me.

Not every wolf got a bite. It was only for predestined pairs.

"Are you sure?"

"I want this more than nearly anything. I want to see my mark on your neck and know you chose it. I want other males to see it and know you're off-limits."

I was going to jest about him being awfully possessive, but then he added, "And I want to wear your bite, to feel it in my skin with every step, and know that you claim me as fiercely as I do you."

My heart beat faster, pounding so loudly I could barely think.

The wedding... marriage... it had made me happier than I'd ever been. It hadn't been something I'd expected, being raised as a shifter. Even though I knew the importance, it didn't hit me in the chest the way the thought of wearing Cole's bite did. Of getting to wake up every morning and see my mark on him.

If I'd thought I'd wanted him before, now the thought drove me wild.

"Yes. I want that. Badly."

"Are you sure?" he pressed. "If you don't want it, we don't have to. I meant every word of my vows. A bite doesn't change that."

"I want it for all the reasons you said. And I want it because you already own my soul, Cole. The ring, the dress, they're nice, but they can go. There's nothing more permanent than what we have. It transcends lifetimes and the barriers of life and death. Nothing would make me prouder than to wear that bond on my skin."

Something lit in Cole's expression at my words. Then he kissed me with a passion that could've burned the entire world down. He devoured my lips in a bruising kiss. I yielded, letting him take and take, showing him I meant every word. His fingers threaded through my hair, pulling it back. And when I was breathless and glassy-eyed, he broke the kiss and bit my neck.

I gasped at the contact.

I'd expected pain. I hadn't feared it, but being bit hurt.

But that wasn't what I felt. Heat exploded in me, spiraling straight down to my sex. When he broke away, I was even more breathless than I'd been before, and more eager than ever to feel him inside. Rules of hospitality be damned to the pits.

The look on his face was pure masculine satisfaction. He wiped the blood from his lips with the back of his hand, his amber eyes never leaving me. I pressed a hand to my neck, feeling the skin knit and begin to heal under my palm. The scar would remain, though. Claiming bites stayed, for whatever magical reason, despite shifter's healing abilities.

"Now your turn."

My fingers flew to his collar, tugging at the fabric to expose his neck. I wanted him to wear my mark even more now that I'd felt his claiming bite. Felt how connected it made us. How complete.

"Well, isn't this cozy?" a smooth voice cut in.

CHAPTER XVII

"**S**ORRY, GOT TWISTED AROUND on my way to the party." Phaidros had suddenly appeared, leaning against the wall opposite us as if he didn't have a care in the world. The scent of cloves pierced the air with his arrival. He was dressed as finely as any of our guests, a finely stitched, white silk shirt stretched over his star-covered skin. "Seems my invitation was lost in the mail."

I lunged forward, even as Cole moved an arm out to block me. "I'll kill you for what you did to Hector."

The demon's eyes narrowed. "We're at war, darling, in case you only just noticed. He was a soldier and he died. That's how this works."

"He had done *nothing* to you!"

He shoved himself off the wall. "He was *your soldier*. That was enough. Now, I've come to discuss something you'll want to hear. Are you going to keep whining about some soldier you barely knew or listen to reason?"

"Take another step towards my wife and I'll rip your spine out through your mouth." Cole didn't growl when he made the threat, didn't so much as raise his voice. The violent promise was enough to carry the message.

Phaidros lifted his hands up in surrender, ever dramatic. "So insecure, and just moments into the honeymoon too. If I was freshly married, I wouldn't feel so worried about some other fellow stealing her, but then again, I do look like this." He gestured to himself.

"You get one chance to say why you're here. Otherwise, we'll both rip you to shreds," I said, while summoning my magic through the walls. I kept it moving slowly, undetected.

"Very well. The Moon Goddess wants to meet."

I startled. I hadn't expected that. Even across all the memories that had scattered through my mind, I had no recollection of ever meeting the creature that had wreaked such havoc on our lives.

"Have you ever met her?" I asked Cole softly.

"No." His body was tense. He didn't take his attention off Phaidros. "The heavens are impenetrable to our magic, much like Tartarus. The only way to go there would be through the goddess herself."

"Where does she want to meet?"

Phaidros flashed his white teeth into a grin. "Why, in her domain, of course."

"And how exactly will we get there?" I asked.

"I'll be your escort. You're familiar with my portals, re-member?"

"It's a trick," Cole snapped. "No simple demon can go to the heavens."

Phaidros's cocky smile never faltered. "Oh, but I'm not just some demon." He paused, enjoying keeping us in suspense. "I'm her son."

I stared at the demon, trying to piece together this new bit of information. He didn't just serve the Moon Goddess; he was her kin. Which begged the question: how had the Moon Goddess's son wound up in Hell?

"Impossible," Cole said with finality.

"Like how bringing a soul back from Tartarus is impossible?" Phaidros quirked a brow. "Oh, and there's no 'we.' This offer goes to the freshly crowned queen alone."

"Absolutely not."

I moved aside, finally getting out from behind Cole. "You don't make decisions for me, Cole."

"It's not safe."

"I'm more powerful than I've ever been," I argued. "I'll be careful." We needed to know more about her. Why she was doing this. How to stop her. In all the time we'd been in conflict, we had precious little information. If I was going to be queen of this realm, I couldn't ignore an opportunity to avoid needless conflict.

"And I'll add," Phaidros interjected, obviously delighting in our argument, "this is a one-time offer."

I tugged on Cole's arm, forcing him to look at me. "Trust

me."

His expression softened. "It's not you that I don't trust." His gaze slid back to the demon. "What guarantee do we have that once he brings you there, they don't simply imprison you? Each ruler is strongest within their own realm, in the seat of their power. You aren't meeting on neutral ground; you're on her territory."

"Oh, she'll be perfectly fine, you worrywart," Phaidros said, ignoring the vengeful look Cole sent his way. "When you wish to leave, I'll take you right back here."

"And you'll vow it to the Styx," I growled.

Phaidros rolled his eyes, as if the idea of us not implicitly trusting him was somehow ridiculous. "I vow to the Styx that once you say to me you want to leave the moon realm, I'll portal you back here."

"Without delay," Cole added.

"Without delay," Phaidros parroted, mimicking Cole's low rumble.

I eased my magic from the wall. Today, I'd let him live because we needed him. But I would ensure Phaidros paid for what he'd done. "It's settled then. We leave in the morning."

Phaidros snorted. "What do I look like, your on-call portal-maker? This is a time-sensitive offer. We leave now, or you can kiss the chance to meet your mortal enemy goodbye."

I wanted time to talk things through with Cole. To discuss what I should do.

"In an hour," I bargained.

"Now. Or never. Your call, darling."

I glanced at Cole.

"I still think it's a terrible idea," he said, resigned. "But we may not get this opportunity again. If you want to do it, I trust you. But if your instincts tell you not to, then don't."

I swallowed. My instincts were at war; part of me believed this was a terrible idea, because everything related to Phaidros was terrible. But there was a chance I could learn more about the Moon Goddess and how to save all of us. It would be cowardly to ignore that. If everything was reversed and it was Cole getting the offer, I'd want him to say no, but at the same time, I'd understand why he had to say yes.

We owed it to our people. It was as sacred as the vows we'd just made to each other.

"Fine." I straightened and took a step toward the demon. "Let's go."

Phaidros summoned a portal behind him and held out a hand. I ignored it, brushing past him as I walked through.

"Sorry to ruin your wedding night," he said with a chuckle, falling in step right behind me.

My snarling response halted in my throat as the magic passed over me. The portal hadn't been anywhere near as painful and discombobulating as the last one he'd led me through. Prick. Unlike the rough-and-tumble approach, this was as easy as stepping through a doorway.

I blinked, unable to believe what I was seeing.

The sky stretched above, a midnight shade dotted with stars that were bigger and brighter than I'd ever seen. The ground beneath my feet was made of clouds, the same shade as my dress, though my feet felt solid atop them. Stretched out in front of me was a throne room. The room itself was demarcated by winding towers of ivory marble that practically glowed under the starlight. Unlike the simple twin thrones in the castle, this room had one single massive throne that stretched up at least twenty feet, a large staircase leading up to it, keeping it apart from the rest of the room.

The figure atop the throne was the most ethereal woman I'd ever seen. Her hair was so white it almost appeared violet in the light, a straight wave that disappeared behind her shoulders. Her skin was pale as the moon itself. The fabric that stretched over her was nearly sheer, a shimmering gossamer that managed to be regal rather than sultry. Her features were petite, her face unmarred by so much as a freckle or wrinkle. There was an unnatural coldness to it, as if she didn't consider herself part of the world at all. Like the moon itself, apart, influencing, not truly alive. Her presence filled the room, a power that made my body want to yield like the tides itself.

For a moment, I was simply speechless.

"Have fun with her, love," Phaidros said.

I startled at his words and turned to face the demon.

He was gone.

And with him, my way out of this realm.

CHAPTER XVIII

"WHERE DID PHAIDROS GO?" I demanded.

The deity rose from her throne. The very way she stood was unnatural; an elegant unbending of the legs until she rose to her full petite height without so much as adjusting her shoulders. She floated down the staircase without moving; the only indication she was alive was the slightest rise and fall of her chest on thirty-second cycles. If not for my shifter vision, I'd have missed them.

She wore the shape of a person, but there was no mistaking her for anything less than an avatar of the moon.

"You ask about my son?" Her head cocked at an unnatural angle, like she was imitating the gesture. "Who could say with children? Never there when you require them, and forever underfoot when you despise them. Besides, life-giver, it is hardly polite to give attention to a lesser creature when you're in the presence of the moon itself."

I raised my brows to gesture to the white orb in the sky, not taking my eyes off her. "Last I checked, the moon was still in the sky."

The Moon Goddess rolled her eyes—as with everything to her, it was unnerving to see. Rather than a sardonic gliding, her eyes jostled from one edge, upward, and then to the other side before they fixed on me. Her irises were nearly as leeched of color as the rest of it, black pinpoints embedded in a silver circle that now fixed on me. "I am the Moon Goddess, the one who controls the lunar world; the one whose power is limitless in this domain; the warden of all shifter souls and fates. Armies have risen to fight in my name and they will do so again. My soldiers are as numerous as the stars themselves. I am the daughter of the sky and the planet itself. I may not be a hunk of rock in the sky, but that is only because I am more. I am a goddess without equal, an eternal force that cannot be stopped by any magic. Those who try to lock me away shall always fail."

Okay, clearly Her Pastiness didn't get to make conversation very much. I wondered if I should have brought a crate so I could stand on a soapbox of my own.

"That's a bit of a mouthful. How about I just call you the bitch who has been ruining my life for the past few centuries?"

"Your *life*." She scoffed, as if the word itself was a joke. "If in this incarnation you're meant to be so vulgar, Persephone, you're succeeding. Since your feeble mind struggles to understand greatness, you may simply call me by the first name I was given." She paused to let the overwhelming generosity—and suspense—bring me to my knees.

I kept standing.

Finally, she gave the name. "Phoebe."

"Phoebe." I just stared at her as I repeated the name. All of that, and she was named *Phoebe*.

She inclined her head, the movement smoother than any other, as if the magnanimous, regal tilt was one she had practiced more than any other. "I will also accept 'Your Luminescence.'"

"Oh, I can think of a lot of names that would be more appropriate," I snarled.

The Moon Goddess—Phoebe—shook her head in disapproval. "Vulgar, Persephone. But then, you and your beasts always were. It's only under my guardianship that I've offered up a civilizing influence."

Memories flashed through my head—memories of another life. One where the wolves had roamed free and in abundance, had moved easily between packs, without the constant trappings of today's civilizations. "You call what you've done civilizing?" I recalled every cruelty my old pack had bestowed upon me. "They're more savage than ever, and in your name. And *my* name isn't Persephone—it's *Avery*."

Her lips thinned. "Whatever you call yourself, I care not. Understand this, life-giver. The wolves are mine. Their packs, their powers, their very souls, all belong to me. You abandoned them when you ran off with the Death God. Who could blame me for picking up such... interesting toys?"

There was glee in her eyes, even more disturbing than the apathy. She was worse than the foulest Alphas I'd ever met. She didn't just see herself as superior to them. She saw herself as a creature so far beyond comprehension that they were nothing more than toys to play with. "I'll kill you for what you've done to them. Trapping their souls in the stars, rewriting their history."

The Moon Goddess laughed. It was beautiful on the surface, but there was a disturbing chord that ran through the sound. "If you could kill me, you would have done so long ago. The best you managed was to trap me and damn yourself in the process. And when you grew weak and reincarnated, you fell perfectly into place."

My brows furrowed. "What do you mean?"

She grinned, flashing teeth full of fangs. Not canine, like a wolf's, but jagged like shark teeth. "Do you not remember this part?"

I ground my teeth in frustration. My memories had trickled back, but I still was unsure what had happened.

My obvious ignorance pleased Phoebe. "It's amazing what a few decades of torture will do. See, while I was trapped on my throne, with limited abilities, you suffered every pleasure Tartarus had to offer. Then, one day, the realm reached out to me. You wanted to make a deal, after all this time. Guess the status quo wasn't quite what you'd hoped. You wanted to set your soul free, back to the realm of the living. I agreed, in exchange for a boon of my own. I was less selfish; rather than starting from scratch, I carved off a sliver of my own soul twenty-one years ago."

A chill went down my spine. "Phaidros."

She shrugged. "Children are so hard for people like us. Yes, I got my son. And you got to escape the pits." A flash of shark teeth. "A shame you hadn't bargained to keep your soul in one piece as it reincarnated. I understand it's quite painful to have it spread across three realms."

My eyes widened in shock. That's exactly what had happened. I'd been born again, weak, a fraction of a shifter. Somehow, she'd rigged the deal so part of my soul was left in the underworld. And the final piece had been in Tartarus, where I, by rights, would never have returned.

The memory was hazy, as if it was split in three itself, a hazy collage of images floating through my head. "It was you. You kept my soul from forming again." Kept me from being able to reach Cole, forced me into the body of a weak newborn, and... a thought occurred to me, but no. I refused to consider it. Everything else was enough to stir my fury.

I reached for my magic to attack her, but there was no magic to be had. It wasn't like Tartarus, where I'd been painfully stifled. No, I was certain my magic had been there this entire time until I'd wanted to use it.

I growled in accusation.

Her beatific smile was confirmation. And I knew it wasn't

just my magic she had manipulated.

"You should know better than to try and attack a goddess in her own domain, life-giver. I should smite you for your insolence, but I find I'm a gracious host. Perhaps in a strange way, I am grateful, because your hubris then and now will lead me to my final victory." She took a step back and spread her arms wide. "That gratitude is why I handpicked your mate after all."

I nearly stumbled. *No.*

"Even you can't control fated mates," I hissed. Even if she had taken control of the wolves for centuries…

Warden of all shifter souls and fates. One of the many titles she'd touted. I wanted to believe it was just ego, but the pit that had formed in my stomach cautioned otherwise.

"Of course, I can control your *moon-matched* mate. I didn't expect him to reject you, I'll confess, though having seen your pathetic form, I hardly blame him."

I flexed my fingers, feeling my claws dig into my skin. My wolf wanted to burst from my skin, to rip out her throat before she could make another sound.

But as dainty as the woman before me looked, she emanated power. It echoed off every moon-white column, beamed back from every star in the sky.

Her expression was one of triumph.

"Never let it be said I'm not charitable, *Avery*. That's why I decided to reunite you two."

A jerk of her wrist and there stood my moon-matched mate, his hateful eyes promising every cruel act I'd ever imagined him capable of.

CHAPTER XIX

J ETT STOOD JUST FIVE feet away. His eyes glowed with hatred. He'd gotten bigger since I'd last seen him. His body was one built for violence and honed by cruelty. He wore simple pants and a shirt that seemed more like something Phaidros would wear rather than the Moon-Ghost Alpha. His right hand, covered in blisters, flexed around a brilliantly shining blade.

He was wielding silver.

I wanted to take a step back. I wanted to put as much distance between myself and the creator of my living nightmare as possible.

I'm the Queen of Hell. I will not back down from this male.

"You're no match for me, Jett. Not anymore," I said, staring down at him the way he had stared at me. More than a few fights were won on bravado.

But Jett had been too comfortable seeing me as weak to consider that. "Oh, you don't make the rules here, *mate.*"

He charged at me, his silver blade waving. I was probably better with a sword than him, but I was barehanded and, oh right, still in my wedding dress. I barely dodged in time, bending backward to avoid getting slashed across the face.

"What are you even doing here?" I snapped. "Don't you have a pack to order around?"

Jett's eyes flashed the same moonstone white as the Moon Goddess's. "They'll be fine. When the goddess calls you to her holy war, you answer." He lunged again. I danced away, the blade slicing the fabric of my dress.

"I'm not going down that easily." I ripped off the bottom of the dress to free up my legs.

His face contorted into a sardonic grin. "I'm going to enjoy this. Just think, with this I can send you back to those pits you so enjoyed." At my shock, his smile grew wider. "Oh yes, I know all about what happens to you after I kill you. And where you get sent back if you lay a hand on me."

"This isn't your fight," I snarled. "Walk away and deal with your little pack, Jett. You don't know what you're messing with."

"Oh, but I do." Jett's growl was guttural. "I'm dealing with my slut of a mate who let someone else mark her."

Cole's mark. I locked down the wave of want that went through me. Hours ago, I'd been happier than ever before. Now I was fighting for my life—again. "He's ten times the male you are. I will *never* accept you as my mate. You're a bully and an asshole."

He swung his blade again, careless in his fury. This one

was easy to dodge. "You belong to me. You were given to me by the goddess herself. Don't think this betrayal will go unpunished."

I wanted to laugh. "Betrayal? I don't owe you a shred of loyalty."

Jett was ready to volley back another insult, but the Moon Goddess's voice cut through the air.

"Get her out of my sight, Alpha." She had returned to her throne and watched us with casual detachment. "Resist the urge to kill her a second time. I would find it inconvenient."

Stars forbid the bitch who had manipulated my fate to be inconvenienced.

A silver sheen washed over his eyes again. Jett attacked me with renewed vigor, his swipes coming impossibly fast. My magic was still good. My wolf wanted to burst forward, but I didn't dare risk the half-second it took to change. Not when he had that blade. My wolf was an even bigger target.

He continued to attack with his deadly blade. My attention constantly flickered between his sword hand and the rest of his body, watching for any hint of where he would strike next. He wasn't skilled. It was unbelievable he was able to still hold that blade. Cole had once said when the wolf was perfectly balanced with the human, a shifter could wield silver as if it were any other metal. Not only was that incredibly rare, but Jett was in even *less* control than normal. No, the blade clearly hurt him, but he was ignoring it.

From my own experiences with silver, it was hard to believe. It was like something was blocking him from feeling the pain.

"You can't win. You can't hurt me without damning yourself, *mate*," Jett taunted. "Just surrender, Omega. Roll onto your back like a good submissive, and I'll be gentle."

Fury lit inside me. My wrist snapped out, grabbing his sword arm when he finished a slash far too wide. I snarled at him and crushed his forearm with my grip. It wasn't a clean break. I put all my force behind it, feeling the bones crumble under the force. He hadn't expected it, and the sudden pain cut through whatever mind-numbing magic the Moon Goddess had worked on him. His sword fell with a clatter, useless beside him. The Moon-Ghost Alpha fell to his knees with a cry.

"You crazy bitch!"

My foot snapped out in a front kick, hitting him squarely in the jaw. He crumpled to the ground.

"Just because I can't kill you doesn't mean I can't fight, asshole."

I reached for the blade, but the metal burned. I settled for kicking it away.

"So, this incarnation has some brawn to her," the Moon Goddess said from above, displeased. "Rise, Alpha. You are stronger than her. Bind her."

Jett rose, slowly, until he stood in front of me. His right arm hung limp at his side. His normally dark eyes were once again the same shade as the Moon Goddess's. He swayed towards me. I moved aside easily and slammed a kick to his ribs in retaliation.

An exasperated sigh came from above. "This is beneath me," she muttered.

I wanted to snap that she should come down from her throne and see how she fared, but all at once, I couldn't breathe. My hands flew to my neck, frantically grabbing and failing to find purchase. A collar of light choked me. I gasped for air. Enough came in that I stayed standing, but I could barely manage more than that.

"Has anyone ever told you that you're a rather unruly guest?" The goddess's words were accompanied by a beleaguered sigh that went on and on, like she had no idea when to end it. "Secure her."

Jett came forward. Gone was his cocky attitude; his eyes glowed brighter than ever. He grabbed my wrists and shackled them in front of me. The burning sensation that immediately followed left no doubt they were silver. Next, he lifted something to my face. Horror rolled over me. I jerked backward, trying to escape, but he swept my feet. With the collar, I was still gasping for breath. I ground my mouth shut, trying to avoid the inevitable. But all Jett had to do was wait, and when my need for oxygen won out, he slid the silver gag between my lips.

Agony. It was agony. My mouth felt like it was being carved

open, my lips constantly flaring, trying to escape the metal, trying to breathe around it, but all that did was make the sensation that much worse. Panic rose, pure animalistic panic. I flailed, but my hands couldn't even get close to the closing mechanism. I helplessly pulled at the gag itself. All I managed to do was burn my fingers. My vision blurred, first from the tears I couldn't stop, then because the combination of crippling pain and asphyxiation made me pass out.

Chapter XX

I AWOKE TO A world of pain.

There were different kinds of pain. There was the sharp pain of a fresh wound, and the eventual dull ache when your mind resolved that nothing could be done immediately, but at least it wasn't getting worse, so suck it up and move on.

Silver never turned to that second kind of pain.

I nearly passed out again. My mouth ached from the violation. It would've hurt less if they'd cut my tongue out entirely. I could breathe now, the collar of light gone, but I wished it was still there. Instead, my neck was now circled by a ring of silver. I kept my eyes almost entirely shut for the moment, trying to understand my circumstances through the barest sliver of vision in hopes I didn't tip off anyone who was guarding me. I was in some kind of cell, bars rising higher than I could see. They looked more like Greek ionic columns than prison bars, but I knew them for what they were. The floor was that same cloud-like material as the throne room. In fact... I suspected I was still in the throne room. If I was there, there was no point in playing at being asleep. I adjusted my head slightly and confirmed what I'd guessed.

"I see you're awake, *mate*."

The word was intended to be a blow, but I was glad of it. I'd existed afraid of Jett, ashamed of our fated connection. But now I knew it meant less than nothing. With every repetition, it cut less. I'd been raised for two decades to believe that word was everything. Now, it was like any other insult he had tossed my way.

I sat up and let loathing fill my expression as Jett towered over me.

"What? No bitchy remarks to make?" He laughed, like he was a one-man comedy troupe.

I lifted my cuffed hands, middle fingers first, not caring if the movement agitated the silver burns on my wrists.

It was worth it to see the anger on his face. He really was too easy to rile up. Unfortunately, riling up Jett wasn't a good thing, however satisfying it felt. He reached through the bars and backhanded me, sending me flying. My back slammed into a column barely a foot behind. My cell was small.

"Take my new pet for a walk, Alpha. To her new home."

The Moon Goddess remained on her throne, far above. The walls of my prison sunk into the clouds, clearly having served their purpose.

Jett reached out, fast as an asp, and locked a chain onto my silver collar. I couldn't move in time, sluggish from all the silver poisoning my body. Outrage flared. If I'd had my magic,

I would've ripped him apart with a thought.

They had collared me. Now they dared leash me, like some pet?

The twisted grin on Jett's face said he enjoyed the sight. "Exactly where you belong."

He tugged on the chain. His mangled arm had been healed while I'd passed out. I frowned. No, not healed exactly. Not like my magic did. Instead, it was like... like the pieces of his arm had been frozen together, into a functional shape. It wasn't healed, not truly. He might never have use of his arm again if it didn't heal right. Shifters recovered from a lot, but forcing the bone to fuse the wrong way could permanently handicap him. Did the Moon Goddess lack the power to properly heal him, or did she just not care? All lives were disposable to her, after all.

He did, however, wear black gloves now. I wondered if it took a lot of her magic to constantly overwrite Jett's desires, which is why he was left with as much free will as he was.

Of course, his desires aligned with hers, so maybe not. He led me out of the throne room. I had the choice to remain seated and get dragged or stand and try to salvage my dignity. I opted to walk behind him, plotting his death.

He would pay for this.

The moon realm had appeared to be one wide open space, but that wasn't exactly right. The sky itself parted as Jett led me out of the throne room. A narrow strip of clouds remained, forming a corridor. I half-wondered if I should jump to escape—could I cross the realms like that? But deep down I knew it wasn't so simple, no more than you could dig in the dirt far enough to reach the underworld.

I stared. The night sky glittered, millions of stars scattered through it.

My magic was locked away, inaccessible, but there was something more innate that the Moon Goddess couldn't control. Something that reached out psychically and recognized those stars for what they were.

Souls. Souls of dead shifters, denied rest, trapped in the sky at the whims of the mad goddess. Their pain, concentrated over years and years of slow suffocation, ricocheted into me. It was like they were crying out, pleading for help, and I was the only one who could hear them. I stumbled and fell to my knees. I tried to cry out around the gag, but that only earned more burning. Jett didn't so much as pause, yanking the silver lead. I snarled on reflex, my teeth grinding against the metal. For a moment, the pain flared so brightly I couldn't even see, my vision a flash of white.

It was at that moment that Phaidros entered the hallway.

The Libra demon spotted me and for the briefest moment he stumbled, something close to guilt splattering across his face before he recovered, a cruel grin twisting on his lips.

"So, this is what it takes for your mate to spend time with you." His voice was light, teasing, as if he was inclined to banter with the Alpha. Yet there was no happiness in his eyes.

Jett's lip curved up. "It's where she belongs."

Hardly. I tried muttering the phrase we'd agreed upon to tell Phaidros to take me home, but I couldn't form words with the gag in my mouth. My tongue burned from the effort, blood coating my mouth. I swallowed it, nearly choking on the coppery taste.

Jett tugged at the collar again. "Quit your moaning."

I forced myself to focus on the demon rather than the agony of millions of shifter souls that were still crying out, begging for release. Jett, I couldn't kill... not directly. But the demon? Oh, the demon would suffer for his betrayal. The pits would look kind compared to what I would do to him.

Jett strode by Phaidros without another word.

Phaidros's arm snapped out, gripping Jett by the shoulder. "What are you doing with her?"

Jett shoved off the touch. "I don't see how it's any of your business. If Mommy Dearest wanted you to know her plans, she'd tell you."

"Everything with her is my business." Phaidros kept his tone casual, but there was a clear order in his words.

Jett scoffed. "I may serve the Moon Goddess, but I'm still an Alpha."

Phaidros's expression hardened, the carefree expression gone in a blink. "Watch yourself, *pup*. You're nothing more than a pawn here, and if you stop being useful, I'll take you off the board."

The shifter straightened, rising to his full height. "Any day, any time. You let me know when you want me to put you in your place."

Phaidros rolled his eyes. The movement was quick, flawless, unlike his "mother's" stilted movements. She'd probably learned all her expressions by imitating the demon she'd carved from her soul. There was no doubt in my mind in a fight, Phaidros would win. Jett had no idea how badly he was outclassed. As much as I wanted to coat my claws with Jett's blood, I'd settle for Phaidros saving me the trouble. Especially if it got him condemned to the pits in the process.

Jett continued down the hall. Phaidros turned on his heel and followed, clearly pissing off the other male.

"Why are you still here?"

I didn't need to see the demon to know he'd just rolled his eyes again. "If you think I answer to you, you're even dumber than I thought. And that would be impressive."

The sound of teeth grinding was audible to my shifter hearing. If it was possible to smile around the gag, I would have. We continued down the hallway of clouds. Each step was a fresh kind of torture, as more and more souls detected me and reached out. I had thought I had come here to find a way to save my kingdom. I'd vowed to protect the living and the dead. But these creatures were even worse off, trapped in an undeath, like the dragon I'd faced against. Not quite in one existence, nor the other.

I had to find a way to save them too. There was nothing I could do while I was bound, though.

If I could get the gag off, I could command Phaidros to take me home. There were just two small issues with that plan. One, I had no way to remove it. And two, even if I did, I'd be in the exact same place as before. No, I needed to do something while I was here. But if I was being taken away from the Moon Goddess, then I couldn't even engage with her or figure out what she wanted. Well, aside from absolute control of all the shifters and killing me and everyone I loved.

The undead wolves continued to reach out, their cries turning to whines. *My soldiers are as numerous as the stars themselves.* As much as I wanted to believe it was an exaggeration, I suspected she was being quite literal. If she could raise the undead wolves from the stars and form an army, then we would be in big trouble. She had control of Moon-Ghost as well. Soldiers who could hurt our armies without consequence. She had a demon who could jump through portals with little more than a thought. And if we met on her home turf, she could lock away our magic. She wanted me and Cole back in the pits, and if I had to guess, the only reason I wasn't there now was because she had something even worse in store for me.

This did not look good.

It looked even worse when I saw where Jett had led me.

CHAPTER XXI

F OR A MOMENT, I was brought back to those months ago during my training with Cole. The day he showed me the silver box. What was in front of me was a smaller version of that, a silver cube with a door swung wide in ominous invitation. It wasn't big by any stretch of the imagination. Small, infrequent air holes dotted the bottom. It would be completely dark, so dark. And unlike when Cole had trained me, there would be no crying for mercy.

The Moon Goddess might not intend to kill me yet. But if I stepped foot in that box, I would wish she had. There would be no escape. Memories of drowning, over and over again, swelled in my mind. It was hard to breathe—on my gasps, I inhaled silver.

No. I wasn't going in that box. My mind spun as Jett shoved me forward, a maniacal grin on his face. I planted my feet to try and resist, but he was having none of that, a yank of the chain dragging me closer.

"Like your new home, mate? You'll be staying here for a while."

My gaze flickered from Phaidros to the box. A half-formed plan came to me, borne of desperation. It was stupid. It would take a dangerous amount of luck to work. But the alternative was the box. A box so small I'd have to be on my hands and knees to fit in it. The metal would burn every inch of my exposed skin. A cage that would prevent me from protecting my people. There was no time to hesitate.

My wolf was suppressed by the silver and the Moon Goddess's magic, but I was a queen and Alpha in my own right. No one would take my wolf from me. In a split second, I focused and managed to shift my hands. Not even my full hands, just a few fingers, my nails lengthening to sharp, deadly claws. Jett paid no notice. He was having too much fun carrying out his mistress's bidding.

My hands were shackled. My skin rebelled at any movement, but there was no choice. If I wanted to escape, I had to strike now.

I lifted my clawed hand and slashed.

Right through my own throat.

Blood choked me. With the silver gag, it had nowhere to go. Flashes of my previous torture slammed me as the air cut off. The coppery taste was the only way to tell the difference.

My eyes rolled back. I'd had a plan, but all I could do was panic and flail like an animal.

"What are you doing?" Jett growled.

Hands wrapped around my neck. "Getting this gag off, you

fucking idiot. Can't you see she's choking?"

Someone tugged me away. "Let her die." I half agreed with the voice, but *no*. I had to fight. Had to stay alive.

"The Moon Goddess doesn't want her dead, not yet." I was snatched back, and then the metal gag fell away with a loud snap. "If she dies, you'll be following her."

Blood flew from my mouth, spilling all over me. I tried to breathe, but I couldn't. My throat was punctured.

"The Moon Goddess will fix this," Jett said, yanking at the chain that still collared me.

No. Not back to her, not in this state.

It took everything in me, but I forced the three words out of my broken windpipe between mouthfuls of blood. "Take... me... home."

Phaidros's starry eyes snapped to me.

"Don't listen to her!" Jett yanked on the chain again, and I nearly blacked out as the silver rubbed against the exposed wound.

But the bargain compelled Phaidros to act as soon as the words were spoken. And though he might have indulged Jett enough to think they were equal in power plays, portal-making demon trumps brainwashed-alpha-asshole.

His star-skinned hands wrapped around my wrist, and he pushed us through a portal.

I didn't care where we landed. All I needed to feel was the barest flicker of my magic come back as we returned to Hell and I began to heal my throat. The skin mended under my magic, but if it had taken even a minute more... I'd have been back in the pits.

Cole would have been alone again.

Phaidros was gone by the time I recovered enough to breathe. A glance around said he'd used a rather liberal definition of home. The forest in front of me was devoid of any life. Even the trees were barren. But I had reclaimed the mantle. *Any* spot in the realm was home to me. I felt the glimmer of Cole's soul under my skin, and I knew he would sense my presence in the realm as well. The silver burned still. I might have been freed of the gag, but my mouth was still covered in blisters; my wrists and feet shackled; my barely healed throat was encircled by the burning metal. Teleporting back to the castle took the last of my reserves.

At least my aim had been true. I landed in a heap at Cole's feet.

He'd been in the library. If I'd felt any better, I would've teased him, wondering if he was reading anything particularly erotic—or looking for tips.

But he wasn't in a teasing mood. And I could barely speak. He flew to me.

"I will kill them," he snarled.

His fury was a caress. Cole tore my shackles apart, ripping the cuffs off with his bare hands. The wolf lit his eyes as his gaze hit me. I tasted copper, swallowing the blood that had pooled in my mouth.

My body shook. His arms were around me, as healing as the magic that worked over my skin to heal the silver burns. He was steady, an anchor. But I was a tempest, shaking, rocking back and forth. I buried my head in his chest, my eyes clenched shut, as if I could escape the memories of the past day.

"You're safe," he promised, fingers threading through my hair. A gentle massage meant to steady me, to ease the frantic energy.

"I'm not scared." I lifted my head to meet his gaze. "I'm *furious.*"

The library shook with my displeasure, but Cole didn't glance at the books that fell from the shelves.

"She has them trapped, Cole. All the souls, ever since that fucking deal. And now that I freed her, she can force them to fight for her. If you could have heard them… they're in agony. Just being near them, I could hear their screams. They're crying out at me, angry I've abandoned them, desperate for mercy. It's Tartarus all over again. She's made slaves of their souls and left them to suffer. And I will *kill her for it*," I snarled.

"We will," Cole promised. "And we will free the shifters she's trapped."

I didn't know how. Worse, I knew Cole had no idea how to do so either. They were in her domain. I'd let her have them in her domain, left their souls unguarded, and now she was their goddess.

Just as I had once been.

I *HAD RULED THE realm of the living for centuries. It was the source of my magic; it was my responsibility. I was the goddess of all living things, but most precious to me were those I had been born among—the wolf packs. Those who walked in two worlds, as I did: one on four legs, the other two.*

And then I met him.

The King of the Underworld. My opposite in every way. But more than my opposite, he was my equal. Something I could not find among all of the living creatures in the realm.

It was no wonder I fell for him.

But straddling two worlds... it was not as simple as wolf and human. Life and death can coexist in moments, not in centuries.

When I became Queen of the Underworld, the realms demanded a trade. No longer would I be allowed to rule over the living. It was too much for one individual. It would unbalance the universe.

At the time, it seemed fair. I would have given up everything to be with him, just as I knew he would have for me. And while I had borne my burden with relative ease, my king was crumbling under his. Oh, he was powerful. He was without equal in his realm. But loneliness is a kind of poison. And besides, unlike the realm that had been Hell, the realm of the living had been peaceful before me. Not perfect; I influenced it for the better. But in my naiveté, I decided the realm could do without me.

Nature abhors a vacuum. I grew into my role as Queen of the Underworld. While I tended to the souls that made their home in that realm and as I grew to love them, and them, me, the Moon Goddess made her move.

She was subtle, to her credit. My ties to the land were almost entirely gone. It took ages to detect her scheming. While she ruled the heavens, she had no one to rule over. When she thought the living realm was abandoned, she decided to annex it into hers. She chose to start with the shifters.

I should have known her greed would not stop there.

From there, there were decades of back and forth while we played a game of chess with all the souls of the universe. Many pieces were taken off the board. But while the Moon Goddess had nothing to lose—she had no family, no citizens, no love in her—I had a tremendous amount to lose.

The deal we struck had Cole raging. It was the only way. It was what I willed.

It was devastating.

A soul for a soul. Neither of us would claim the land of the living. Instead, we would be locked away in opposite dungeons.

Within her realm, her powers bound to little more than a trickle. And me, to the pits.

But while we had both ceded the world of the living, she used a loophole to steal the souls of the shifters. Once they died, they should have belonged to Hades. Instead, she siphoned them away, and in his grief, he was unable to stop her. Tartarus itself had whispered taunts of the world above, told me what had happened to those I had cared about so fiercely. It was a worse torture than the drowning.

Tartarus was more than just the realm of eternal torture. The realm was the one that brokered deals when we gods and goddesses wished to shift the scales.

To get out of that prison, we'd struck a new deal. My soul had reincarnated; for her, rather than risking herself in such a process, she sliced off a sliver and created Phaidros.

Our game began again.

Chapter XXII

Having gone to all the realms, my memories finally slotted into place, understanding rolling through me. At the time the Moon Goddess had been locked away, she'd held onto the barest essence of her power. The tendril was enough to reshape the mythos of the shifters. To raise fanatics like Jett. She was a master manipulator, and extremely patient.

If she was ice, I was flame. I wasn't patient. Not in the face of cruelty and injustice.

"This will not go unpunished," I vowed to Cole.

Cole agreed.

"You will have your vengeance, wife," he promised. "And for what she did to you, so will I."

For what she had done to us. The years and years of pain.

I ran my hands over his shoulders. Already, my wrists had begun to heal where they had been burned. His shoulders were firm, unyielding even as he knelt on the floor with me. I slid my palms down, feeling his chest, feeling his heartbeat pulse. Strong, racing. From relief... and from my touch.

"Were you worried about me?" I whispered.

"I could think of nothing else. What they might do to you. The fact I was not there to protect you. When you are not by my side, little queen, you are my every thought." His hands shifted, running down to the dip between my hips.

I arched against him. "You know, I don't know exactly how long it's been, but I'd still count this as our wedding night."

Cole leaned back, even as desire heated his eyes. "We don't have to. You've been through a lot this past day." He eyed the blood dried around my throat.

I cleaned the skin with a thought of my magic. "I *want* to."

His lip curved up. "Then I'll deny my queen nothing."

His magic whisked us away. When I blinked my eyes open, we weren't in our bedroom as expected. Instead, we were in the middle of a forest. There wasn't a soul around, at least not that I could feel. The red sky above us was a dark, burnt color. I must've been gone a full day for it to be this late.

It was perfect.

He captured my lips, tasting me. The kiss started slow, as if he was still assuring himself I was in one piece.

But I wasn't so easily breakable. I fisted his shirt between my hands, pressing further, demanding. I was so, so alive. Cole met my challenge. His wolf was not one to roll over and submit, even to his queen. He took control, and I yielded. There was nothing more glorious than cleaving to my husband.

There was nothing left of a tender embrace. No, instead we

pulled at clothing, moving through the forest until he caged me against a tree. The bark dug into my bare back, but I hardly felt it. I was strong, and I was more inclined to nip at his lips and draw his blood than worry about my own.

"This reminds me of when you kissed me the first time," I rasped when we broke to catch our breath.

A single dark brow arched. "Actually, you were the one who kissed me."

I huffed. "That's not how I remember it."

A smirk played on his lips, almost boyish. A sharp contrast to Cole's normally severe features. I adored it. "That's how it happened."

"You had just set a demon on me. I definitely wouldn't have kissed you for it."

"And yet, you did."

"Only you would think setting a demon on someone counts as flirting."

"It worked." He leaned in, nipping at my shoulder. "Apparently, demon killing is an aphrodisiac for my queen."

I rolled my eyes, trying to keep my composure even as he sucked at that sensitive spot in my shoulder that made me want to moan. "I can certainly think of one demon I'd like to kill."

He sucked harder, a hand sliding between my thighs where he cupped my sex. "I *know* you aren't talking about another man on our wedding night, wife."

I gasped, unable to stop the sound. "Fantasizing about murder shouldn't trigger any jealousy."

"And yet it does," he growled, fingers teasing at my entrance. "I didn't tell the whole truth before when I said I think of you when you're away."

I frowned. "Really?"

The emotion in his eyes made my knees buckle. Only his grip kept me upright. "The truth is, I think of you constantly. You consume my thoughts. If I'm not worried about you, I'm thinking of how I can be between your legs. Worshiping you with my tongue and bathing you in my seed."

His words sent a warm flare through my stomach. "I'd take some fingers."

"You'll take what I give you, wife." The dominance in his voice was *delicious*. "After what you've put me through the past few days, you're going to be a very good girl for me this evening and do exactly what I say."

I opened my mouth to argue but was cut off by a gasp as he adjusted his grip, his fingers grazing my entrance. Slowly, tortuously, he eased one finger between my folders. He found me wet and needful. He dipped the finger in and out in short strokes, his thumb brushing over my clit. I thought I might come from just that, but his finger was gone just as suddenly.

I snarled, and he chuckled.

Then he lifted that finger, slick with my desire, and placed it between my lips. His amber eyes flared as I sucked his finger between my lips, obedient, savoring the erotic mix of *us* on his hand.

He groaned, pulling his finger back. "You don't know what you do to me."

I looked at him from beneath my lashes. "If it's making you want to fuck me, then I'm succeeding."

He pushed his hips against me, the bulge obvious beneath the fabric of his pants. "*Want*, isn't an issue."

"Then fuck me, Cole." My brazen demand was borne of need. Raw, desperate need.

"I will." His fingers trailed over my jaw, down to my neck, where he placed just enough pressure to make my eyes go wide. "But as I said, I'm not taking orders tonight, Avery. Now, are you going to submit, or do you want to fight? I'll *fuck* you either way, wife. But I think you'll enjoy submitting to me. Letting go of that strong facade you have to wear with everyone else. Giving in, trusting me to take care of you, tending to you the way a queen like yourself deserves."

I tried to clench my legs on reflex, but he was still wedged between me. Fuck, his words...

"Which will it be?" His words were rich with dark promises. "Submit to my will or fight against me?"

"I'll submit," I gasped, and the pressure disappeared even as his hand remained in place. "For tonight." I might like Cole in charge—a lot—but that was strictly for the bedroom.

His lips curved up into a full smile. "I'd expect nothing

less." He kissed me, a gentle reward. "And I'll honor this gift."

And then Cole sank to his knees.

If I'd thought one finger might send me over, I was entirely unprepared for Cole's tongue. He licked me from end to end, tasting my need. He loosed a groan.

"Perfection," he praised.

His hands slid to my knees and forced me wider. I followed his silent command, and he rewarded me with another stroke. Then another. Slow, methodical. I bucked against him, trying to force him deeper on instinct. He stopped.

I glared down. Really, he expected me not to move when he did *that*?

"It seems you need a reminder of what it means to submit."

His death magic curled around me, dark wisps materializing from nowhere. They wrapped around my wrists and my stomach, pinning me against the tree. They didn't hurt, and if I fought, I could break them. Still, they helped me remember the role I'd agreed to enjoy for the evening. I forced myself to relax into them even as my pulse thrummed at a frantic pace.

"Better," Cole said with approval as I forced myself to still. "I love your reactions, wife. But the sadist in me enjoys seeing you fight them all too much."

Then he licked again.

It should've taken away from the pleasure, to fight my innate reactions. Instead, it made them all the more intense. As if because I couldn't move, the energy couldn't escape and instead sent my need rocketing higher and higher. He needed to feel me entirely under his control, and I needed to feel him all around me, his hands, his mouth, his magic.

His licking grew more exploratory. He dipped into my sex, and it took everything in me not to cry out.

Time meant nothing. There was only sensation. I tried my best to hold back, to obey, but obedience had never been my strong suit. When my wriggling grew frantic, he finally pulled away and looked up with raw male satisfaction.

"I think my wife is ready for her husband."

I whimpered.

Now that I'd been thoroughly teased and tormented, Cole wasted no time. He rose from his knees, his pants disappearing into the ether. He was magnificent. As tormented as I had been, he was definitely aching with the need to match mine. The tip of his cock glistened with precum. I inhaled his desire, the most potent aphrodisiac of all.

He ran his hand up and down the shaft, prolonging my desire for one final moment.

Then, with a single thrust, he slammed into me.

I gasped, an echo to his groan of release. His palms slammed into the trunk on either side of my head, his face inches away.

"More," I moaned. I was full, so full, but my body needed movement.

"I should make you wait just for that." The words slid out

through gritted teeth. "But I don't have any patience left in me."

"Lucky me," I teased, though I could barely get the thought out in anything resembling coherent sounds.

"We'll see if you're saying that when you're begging for a break in a few hours."

Hours?

And then he began to move. He gave a few shallow pumps, despite his words, trying to keep me comfortable. Then his ever-present restraint slipped away as he began to thrust in earnest. Each slam elicited a new gasp. I'd never felt so much, never been so full. We were both frantic with need. There was no pretending either of us was going to last long.

My orgasm ripped through me with a ferocity that almost overtook the pleasure itself. Cole followed immediately, his seed coating my insides. The raw, male possessiveness pleased a feral part of me. I wanted to feel him in every part of my body, and he obliged. His hand curled around the side of my neck, a featherlight touch.

"I love my mark on you. Love seeing it while I fuck you, the way your throat moves while you swallow down your cries." He bent to kiss it and murmured in my ears, "I hope you'll give me one to match."

If I'd thought I might be sated with that single orgasm, I was in for a lot of trouble. His words set my system alight with need. Normally, only the male marked the female... but he would take my mark. Of course. Cole was greedy for any part of me I would give him, and I would give him everything.

"I intend to," I purred. "But remember, turnabout's fair play."

Cole's smirk said he had no idea how much teasing I was going to do before I finally gave him the release he would need, based on his already-hardening erection.

He was going to find out, though. And I would enjoy every second of my wedding night.

CHAPTER XXIII

"**P**ROUD OF YOUR HANDIWORK?"

We were back at the castle—unfortunately, one night was all we could spare for each other while we prepared for war. Between countless meetings with advisers of every kind, political, military, and mystical, I'd stolen glances at Cole's exposed neck. The latest batch had left, and we were set for another meeting any minute to go over how our forces would work with those in the realm of the living. It was a serious time, but I couldn't stop looking.

Apparently, those glances weren't as covert as I'd hoped.

But who could blame me? Some would have thought the male weak to be marked by a female. Those people had never met Cole. Thinking about weak in the same sentence as Cole, except for "Everyone looks weak compared to Cole," was laughable. Instead, my husband had his mark on full display. His normally buttoned-up silk shirt was half undone, the collar almost pulled back so my claiming bite was on display.

Just seeing it made me want him again.

"I am," I admitted, a small smile on my lips despite everything we were facing.

His amber eyes darkened. "As am I."

And that was all he said before he whisked us away, meeting abandoned.

"We need to meet with the others," I complained. Or tried to complain, because once Cole's hands were on me, I was lost, already ripping his clothes away as fast as I could.

"They can wait." He nipped at my own claiming mark. "They've had centuries of my service. They can fucking wait."

"We'll be fast." I tried to sound reasonable while I pressed my hips forward, feeling the bulge of his erection against me.

Cole laughed a throaty chuckle. "As if I'd rush a single moment with you."

Any further protests were cut off with a kiss. Cole was inside me a second later, his hands supporting my hips as he lifted me against a wall. The bed that sat a few feet away was too far.

"It was that smile," he hissed. "Seeing you happy turns me on like nothing else."

"So what you're saying is if we're going to get through today's meetings, I need to stop smiling?" I laughed.

"Fuck no," Cole snarled. "I'm saying we're going to take a lot of breaks."

He moved in and out at a steady pace. His hands slipped away from my backside, replaced by those shadows, and instead found my nipples, tweaking them. "Understood?"

I gasped. "Yes, *sir.*"

There was no mistaking the sudden thrust coming a little harder, off-kilter. I grinned, liking that I had found another way to tease Cole. I wanted to learn all the little ways, to have a thousand years to play with him like this.

"Technically, it's *Your Majesty,*" he corrected, as if stern words could hide his reaction.

"Whatever you say, *sir.*"

His eyes narrowed. "Oh, you'll pay for that, little wolf."

He did make me pay, and I enjoyed every moment.

But unfortunately, everything had an end. As soon as I magicked on fresh clothing—an off-shoulder outfit that showed my own bite—we were back in the council room, where no one seemed to want to look us in the eyes except Hecate, who winked at me.

Despite the bit of levity, we were no closer to having an effective plan. Xander had rallied the Wind-Blood pack, and Daphne had been with him every step, educating the pack and then leaving to gain support with the Fangs. Whatever she'd said, she'd gotten the Fangs to agree to side against Jett's Moon-Ghosts. Then again, my old pack had made plenty of enemies, so even if they didn't believe us on the evil-Moon-Goddess thing, Jett-is-a-dick was easy enough to cash in on.

Even if our living allies, who could kill without getting a one-way ticket to the pits, did defeat the Moon-Ghosts, it would be bloody. And every soul lost would join the Moon Goddess's astral army.

The days grew long. It wasn't just meetings. It was scouring the library for any clue of how to fix this mess and hours of working out my frustrations with Cole. And not in a fun way—we were back in the ring every evening. He may have been happy to hear how I'd crushed the asshole's arm, but he hated the thought of me being vulnerable. Even if I faced the Moon Goddess in her realm and she took away my magic, she couldn't take away my innate shifter strength. We practiced fisticuffs, blades, in fur and with magic. Now that the memories of my previous incarnation had come back, I could actually face off against Cole as an equal. Without those memories, it would have taken decades, centuries, to match Cole's experience.

The Moon Goddess was older than both of us. In her realm, she was supreme, and she never left her realm.

I wasn't just angry anymore. I was frustrated.

I wanted a target to unleash myself on.

Twelve days after my abrupt return from the Moon Goddess's realm, a certain demon provided just that opportunity.

It was late, late enough that I should have been completely fatigued from the day I'd had, but instead, an expectant energy hummed beneath my skin as I wandered the castle halls. Although I—or rather, Persephone, whose memories I had—had lived in the castle for countless years, there were still new corridors to explore. Magic things hated being stagnant, after all. The deserted hallways were lined with massive paintings. The ceiling towered. My attention, however, was fixed on the one at the end. It was a massive portrait of a stunning woman with red hair. At first, I figured it was obviously Persephone. Then, as I drew closer, I realized it was *me*. Unlike my perfect "Goddess of Life" counterpart, I had some scars and a crooked nose even shifter healing couldn't salvage. Not me as I was currently dressed—all the crowns in the world couldn't deprive me of my sweatpants and tank tops. Instead, I wore the same gown I'd had at the ball, bright red hair tumbling down my back with a crown atop, twin to the necklace he'd gifted me which was also depicted.

I'd never sat for such a picture, but it was me. Something in my chest warmed. The kingdom may have longed for its once-forgotten queen, but Cole treasured *me*. I stared for a long moment, quietly contemplating the challenges we had ahead. And then, as Phaidros approached, I pretended to remain focused on it while I prepared the perfect gift for unwelcome visitors.

I didn't need the scent of cloves to warn me of his presence. Seconds before his portal opened, I felt his soul cross into Hell and gathered my magic at the spot he'd chosen.

"If you attack me, I can portal away before you even—"

His latest attempt to startle me with some patronizing warning was cut off with a flare of my power. Green sparks filled the hallway, and the demon was pulled from the portal and pinned to the floor. I threw myself on him, gripping his chest with both hands. My magic alerted Cole there was an intruder. I didn't bother to turn around and confirm he'd appeared behind me. Instead, I sharpened my human fingers into claws and stuck them into the demon's star-skinned chest. His fanciful clothes were shredded, and while that was the least important part of the situation, I enjoyed seeing the unflappable demon ruined.

"Before I can what?" I snarled. "I'm the Queen of Hell, Phaidros. You come into my territory with such impunity, after how you set me up. You really think you'll walk away from this conversation alive?"

I twisted my nails in his chest. He choked out a gasp.

If I wanted, I could've used my magic to rot him from the inside out. It was partly my gift, partly Cole's. The darkest part of my magic, taking away life, unlocked from him.

"It's in your best interest to hear me out," Phaidros snapped, sounding far too composed for someone who had a punctured lung.

I twisted deeper.

"Careful, demon. My wife rather dislikes people telling her what's in her best interest," Cole said mildly.

"It's true," I agreed cheerfully, the coppery scent coating my senses.

Phaidros writhed under my grip, his body instinctively trying to get away even though his brilliant mind surely realized he didn't stand a chance. He couldn't portal away, not while I held him like this, restricted his magic. I couldn't stop him from portaling forever, since that ability belonged to the between-realm magic, but I could make it difficult enough to trap him for a bit.

It felt good. Gods, it felt good to make someone hurt. I was so tired of feeling powerless. Of not being allowed to kill, either for my own morals or the laws of the universe. Here was someone I could make suffer, for the way he'd made me suffer. Someone I could blame.

"I helped you in the past," he argued.

The demon had balls on him. He was half-impaled by my claws, and he was acting like I owed him a favor still.

"You helped no one but yourself." I twisted deeper, hitting bone.

I could've killed him. Instead, I used my magic to heal him, just enough to know his suffering wouldn't end too soon. I waited for Cole to chastise me, to tell me to ease up or simply end him.

But my husband was an indulgent man. And he could be even crueler than I could.

"I'm an excellent multitasker, what can I say?" His bravado was cut off as he coughed up blood.

"You could say you're sorry," I hissed. "Sorry for Hector. Sorry for leading my 'moon-matched mate' straight to me."

Cole growled at the mention of Jett.

"Ah, love, but I'm not a liar."

"I don't think you're capable of a single truth," I countered. "Which means letting you speak is a waste of air."

I readied my claws to take the killing blow, but Phaidros's next words made me still.

"I want my mother dead, rotting in the pits of Tartarus."

Chapter XXIV

P HAIDROS SPAT THE WORDS in a rush, aware they were his last chance at staying his execution.

Unfortunately, they worked.

"Speak," I demanded.

"In open combat—even if you could draw my mother into such a thing—you don't stand a chance. It's true," he snapped, when I twisted a little more.

It *was* true. But that didn't mean I liked hearing it.

"Your only chance is to change the game. I will convince her to commit to a series of trials, one for each realm—the underworld, the living, and the heavens. That will give you a chance to end this conflict once and for all."

I stilled my grip.

"Why?" I hated that I was considering it, but we'd been at this for over a week—no, we'd been at this for centuries and had only heartbreak to show for it. I needed to keep the people I cared about safe.

"If my mother is the Moon Goddess, my father is the pits. I have his penchant for deals, as you may have noticed. I have the authority to bind her in vows to the Styx, and she won't be able to resist when I tell her the prize."

There was the catch.

"And what would that be?" Cole rasped from behind me. His death magic worked through the room, encircling both the demon and me. Only, it wouldn't hurt *me*. Phaidros would be less likely to survive if his answer was unsatisfactory.

"Both your souls bound to the pits for eternity," he said blithely.

Wrong answer. Our magic collided, sparks of black and green forming a bubble around Phaidros's head. Miraculously, the demon kept talking.

"It's the only way she'll accept. She could have either of you, but by the time she gets the second in, the first will have found a way out. If you both agree to go, no take-backsies to wriggle out from eternal damnation. And she will play for the same stakes."

"Why would she agree?" I repeated. "You know as well as I do that her army is nearly as big as ours. Our living allies are evenly matched. We can't even get to her realm without you taking us there."

"It is difficult for unwelcome visitors to get there," Phaidros agreed. "But she will agree. Because as powerful as my mother is, she is ten times as conceited. She will see this as an easy way to prove her superiority over your feeble powers and enjoy a game of strategy rather than inelegant warfare.

Most of all, she will agree because she is bored, and I will make the offer sound very attractive. Which I can only do if you get your prickly claws *out of my starsdamned chest* and let me speak to her."

I eased slightly, not fully removing them, while Cole drew closer. He towered over us, staring down at the demon. "Who gets to decide the challenges?"

"The realm's ruler. For the realm of the living, it will be up to me, as the judge."

So he'd already picked his role in this. "So you're saying you'll rig this in our favor if we agree to get rid of your mother for you?" Or rig it in hers and use this as a ploy to take us down to Tartarus with barely a fight.

The demon shook his head. "No. They will need to be fair contests, and the four of us will swear to that. But if you're clever, you'll still find a way to tilt the scale towards yourself in your own realm, which I'll ensure happens first, and then if you succeed in the realm of the living, you never need know what my mother will concoct."

I opened my mouth to argue but Phaidros cut me off with a beleaguered sigh.

"I can't do it all for you. I can bring her to the chessboard, but you still have to know how to play."

Only Phaidros could manage to be so condescending while I was still bathing my fingers in his blood.

"First, you will vow to do no harm to my wife or me."

"I vow to the Styx I will not harm either of you, *tonight*," Phaidros grumbled.

That began a long series of back-and-forth between the two, where Cole demanded increasingly specific vows to ensure our safety while Phaidros mostly agreed... though he did throw in a few adjustments, usually time limits. Neither of us pressed the issue.

"Then we're agreed," I said when Cole had covered every conceivable scenario.

The three of us stood in the hallway, staring. Cole was at my shoulder; Phaidros leaned against a nearby column like he didn't have a care in the world, least of all his blood-drenched shirt. Of course, he may have been leaning because he couldn't properly stand on his own. I was such a good sport I even stopped half of the internal bleeding I'd caused in Phaidros when I finally let him go.

"We will have a trial for each realm against the Moon Goddess to settle who has claim to what realms. *If* the Moon Goddess agrees, neither will attack the other for the duration of the trials. Losing rulers go to the pits."

Phaidros nodded. We made our vows and Phaidros left. I was left wondering if we may have found a way out—or a surefire way to damn ourselves and save our enemies the trouble.

WORD CAME BARELY A day later. The Moon Goddess had agreed, and the first challenge would be set for just four days later.

The challenge had to be fair, as we designed it, and Phaidros had explained for us that meant we couldn't both design it and participate. After a long discussion between myself, Cole, and Hecate, we agreed that the two of them should design our realm's test. I would compete on our behalf.

Cole could tell me nothing, lest he skew the odds in our favor and the challenge be declared null and void. Phaidros was the judge, and though he claimed to be working towards the same goal as us, I had no reason to trust him. In fact, I had a lot of reasons not to.

Starting with the fact I still planned to kill the demon.

Cole, ever pragmatic, assured me we could and would kill the demon once the Moon Goddess was dealt with. We spent those next days separated, Cole devising the test with Hecate, while I trained in the arena. I didn't know what the test would be—it could be anything from a fight to the death or a coin flip. But exercising took my mind off of it. My wolf needed the release as well. She had truly become part of me since I'd gained my memories. We weren't two people, but two sides of the same coin. Even so, my animalistic side was restless. There was a threat to her mate—and the bite did declare him as her mate—and she would not rest until it was destroyed.

Cole did his best to soothe that rage in the evenings. The

fact he was my husband... it shouldn't have changed things. He had forfeited his life for me; I had gone to the pits to get him back. Something as innocuous as marriage shouldn't have held a candle to that.

Yet it did. Saving each other was one thing. We did it on instinct. There was no choice when it came to putting our lives on the line for each other. But marriage was a choice. One we chose for *us*.

I really loved sleeping with my husband.

That said, "marital bliss" and "trying to end decades of torture to souls while you yourself risked eternal torture" were about as far from synonymous as you could get.

The morning of the challenge, Cole teleported me far away from the castle, all the way to the other side of the realm. Hecate remained in the capital.

"You'll be great." Cole's fingers caressed my spine, tracing over bare skin. "Relax, little wolf."

I was in a vine-knit crop top and hip-hugging sweats. I arched against his touch, liking the way his scent was now blended with mine when I breathed it in.

"That or I set us up to spend our honeymoon and the rest of eternity in Tartarus."

Cole chuckled. "That's not how we'll spend our honeymoon."

"Oh?"

"After all of this is done," he promised, "I will take you

somewhere far away. Where no one has heard of us or the moon itself. I will spend every morning and night with you, and I won't let you think about anything except what I'm going to do to you."

His words were warm with sensual promise, but that wasn't the image he painted that made me relax. It was his utter confidence that there was an *after* at all.

"I'll hold you to it," I said.

"I keep my word, little wolf."

A swirl of yellow sparks opened up nearby, cutting off our conversation. Phaidros was the first one through, his black, star-marked skin sharply contrasting the crisp white shirt he wore open to a deep vee. Unlike my sweatpants, his legs were clad in shiny black leather trousers.

In my mind, I painted them with blood. First his mother, and then he would follow.

But the figure who stepped through behind him was not the icy, inhuman goddess I'd seen in the heavens. No, they were distinctly masculine, towering nearly seven feet tall, with shoulders far broader than Cole's or Phaidros's lithe builds.

But that was not what made the creature stand out. It was the fact that he wasn't solid, not the way the rest of us were. His body was transparent. His outline was clear, but the space inside his form was a pale blue, with little sparks of light trapped inside.

One of the many souls the Moon Goddess had stolen

for her army. A shifter, who had spent untold years trapped among her stars. A ghost of a soul.

"Where is she?" I demanded.

Phaidros simply shrugged. "She sent a proxy."

I snarled, my animal side rising to the surface.

The shifter ghost turned at the sound. He appeared intrigued for a moment. His eyes were intelligent, if obviously pained. Then, a second later, it was gone. His eyes went unseeing, trained ahead. Even across realms, the Moon Goddess could control him.

"You can't truly expect her to be stupid enough to go into your realm, where the two of you have absolute control," Phaidros chided.

I *had* expected that. Because I would never be the kind of leader who sent others to do my dirty work because I was scared. "We have a deal not to harm each other while the trials are in play."

Phaidros arched a brow. "What can I say? My mother is a paranoid psychopath and doesn't care."

"Whatever. Let's get this over with."

Cole stepped forward. "Now that we're all here, I'll explain the trial of this realm. Underneath the ground, there is a labyrinth. It stretches miles in all directions. At the center, there is an imp. Imps are scentless, making the challenge *fair* since the Moon Goddess lacks a shifter's sense of smell. You will be required to capture it—and imps are wily by nature and do not enjoy being caught. Once you have the imp, you must walk from the center and find your way back to the exit." He spoke his next words, looking directly at me. "Do not be deceived: the second half of the trial is just as challenging as the first."

CHAPTER XXV

W E WAITED A BEAT, all eyes on Phaidros. As the arbitrator of the challenge, it was up to him to meet his Styx-bound vow and agree this was an acceptable contest.

"This is acceptable. Even if both contestants wound up having a shifter's senses," the demon said, a bright grin on his face.

There was no time for me to respond. The ground opened up beneath me and the shifter ghost. For a moment, my heart slipped into my throat and I choked, recalling the way the ground had split to take Cole to Tartarus.

Instead of the pits, we fell just a short distance.

The labyrinth was massive, as Cole had warned. Smooth stone walls stretched out in front, an opening. The ghost shifter moved into wolf form, its see-through body contorting painfully until it stretched out on all four paws. It stared me down, as if debating if it shouldn't just take me out.

My lips curled back, my inner alpha snarling, *Try it.*

A high-pitched laugh sang out. The wolf's ears twitched, following the sound. It took off in a blur.

I resisted the urge to give chase. Cole had warned getting back out would be the real test. I wasn't going to fail *any* part of this. I called on my magic and a thin vine sprouted from beneath my feet. It grew taller and taller until it reached my waist. I knotted it around my wrist, giving an experimental tug. Sturdy. The vine might be thin, but it would continue to grow and hopefully ensure that once I got the imp, I got back out.

The underground maze was well-lit, at least for what I needed. Torches hung against the stone in even intervals. The ground was unblemished concrete; my feet left no trace and the whole system was oddly scentless. Back when I had first died and wandered into Cole's castle, my so-called shifter senses had been nearly useless. I'd been effectively blind, and that castle had been as winding as the maze now was. For a wolf who counted on those senses, they would be stressed and anxious, even from beyond the grave. Me, I refused to panic. I had dealt with this before, after all.

I set off in the opposite direction of the wolf. It may have decided to chase the imp, but I didn't trust it not to come for me if given a chance. There was no way the ghost wolf could beat me. But defeating it... I didn't want to imagine what agony that might inflict on its already tormented, enslaved soul. If I could spare the creature that, I would.

Cole hadn't been joking about the labyrinth running for miles. Every ten steps I came to another fork. At first, I tried to reason it out. But there was no rhyme or reason to the maze. It would be a game of speed, and critical to not lose time weighing my options like they weren't luck-based. At least my ever-growing vine ensured I had a way back.

I listened for any sign of the ghost wolf, but there was none. Part of me was inclined to panic. What if he got there first? But fear was a useless emotion in a situation like this. I was here. I had to stay focused. If I gave into despair, it would all be lost.

I hadn't surrendered to despair in the godsdamned pits of Tartarus. I certainly wouldn't do so within my own realm.

Hours passed. The air was stagnant, stifling. Sweat beaded on my neck, dripping down my spine. There was no chance of a cooling breeze down here.

The shadows seemed to move around me. The light from the torches cast the entire space with an eerie glow. Any sudden flicker of the light could have been the ghost shifter. I still wanted to avoid that confrontation, especially once I had the imp. I hadn't dealt much with imps, even in my previous incarnation. They were solitary things and distrusted others by nature. Catching one wouldn't be easy, not when they were built to flee. They stayed at the edges of society, darting in and out to take what they needed. Other creatures scorned them for it, seeing them as leeches. The creatures didn't even have souls; I couldn't see them on my mental map of the realm. They were simply the realm's physical manifestation of *want*. Me, I just thought of all the times I had to sneak into the mess hall after hours or risk going hungry because my pack wouldn't let me eat around them.

I frowned as I came to one intersection, considering. It seemed just like the other hundred I'd gone through, but an awareness pricked at my senses.

Left or right? The same choice I'd had to make over and over again.

Why does this feel different? There was no obvious reason. Both paths were identical, lined with twin flames at equal intervals. The ground was the same; the same scentless air floated from them.

I took a step towards the left, then paused, reconsidering, and pivoted to the right.

The first torch on the right went out.

This... this hadn't happened before.

I took another cautious step, and a second torched went out, then as I took one more, a third, shrouding the passage in shadows.

Weird. I retreated and the third torch lit once more. Two more steps and they both came back. Grimacing, I angled back to the left and stepped forward. No torches went out.

A trick, or was the maze guiding me? Was this Cole's doing?

Cole wasn't above cheating—not if my survival was on the line. Still, I doubted it was his doing. Phaidros had exacted a large number of vows, including ones of noninterference. Cole was powerful, nearly omnipotent, while he held the mantle of the realm. But even he couldn't break a vow to the Styx.

I went through the left passageway.

The ever-parallel walls widened for the first time in all of the maze. A sign I was on the right path came when the walls widened to a circular room.

The heart of the labyrinth.

And there, in the center of the room, crunching on a piece of stale bread, was the child I had rescued in the bazaar. He was as tiny as I remembered, nearly emaciated. His little legs swung up and down under the table he was perched on. The rest of the room was empty.

"Dario?" I whispered, keeping my voice low so as not to startle him, nor to alert the ghost shifter I'd found the imp.

He looked up at me, his large eyes wide as he looked at me.

"I'm Avery. Do you remember me?"

He nodded, looking conflicted. "I'm supposed to run from strangers who want to catch me."

He still had the same lisp from those months ago. Despite it all, it made me smile.

"I'm not a stranger," I countered softly. "I just need you to come with me for a little bit so we can get out of the maze. Then you can go anywhere you like."

If he ran, I suspected I could catch him relatively easily.

If he decided to simply *poof* away, I was fucked. Cole's rules had stipulated I needed to walk out with the imp; I couldn't simply teleport us back to the starting line.

To my relief, after weighing his options, Dario gave me a toothy smile, hopped off the table, and held out his hand to me.

Thus began the not-at-all-quick process of retracing my steps to get us out of the underground maze. At least the vine would guide us back. We walked in silence. I kept glancing around. A bad feeling fell over me like a dark cloud. When Dario complained his legs were tired—why walk when you can poof away all the time?—I lifted him into my arms and picked up the pace. I went from a fast walk to a jog to nearly a sprint, never losing sight of the vine.

But my bad feeling was confirmed when I turned a corner and the vine simply... ended.

It hadn't snapped. A sickening pit opened in my stomach. If it had snapped, then the rest of it would be right behind, easy enough to follow. No, it had been pulled apart and redirected.

"Very good, life-giver. You found the imp." The Moon Goddess's voice echoed off the walls.

The ghost wolf rounded the corner, his jaw contorted into an unnatural canine smile.

I set Dario down and moved in front of him. The ghost's grin grew wider.

"I never cared for imps. So fragile, so... worthless. Not like your—pardon, *my*—shifters."

"Step aside," I warned, trying to get through to the ghost shifter. "I've won." Let his instincts tell him I was the stronger wolf and he should back down. But her grip on his psyche was absolute.

"You do have the imp," the Moon Goddess agreed conversationally. The wolf took a shuddering step forward, his paws halting with each movement. "I never stood a chance at winning a challenge in your realm. However, you have not *won*. The conditions say the imp must leave with you. As I said, they are so fragile... and if I kill it, then we have a stalemate."

The wolf lunged. Any halting movement from before was gone. I could've dodged, but that would expose Dario. I summoned my magic, thorny vines ripping from the ground, but they passed straight through his glimmering body.

We collided. I hadn't had a chance to shift. I kicked and punched, tried to focus enough to sprout a vine that would guide Dario away from the violence. The ghost wolf tore into my chest. I cried out as fiery pain erupted. He ripped out a piece of my flesh; I healed it in an instant. I shifted, turning into a wolf in a flash, and tackled the ghost wolf.

I ripped out his throat. It was bloody, but it was quick.

Part of me wanted to mourn as the wolf shimmered, disintegrating before me. Would it go back to its astral prison, or down to the pits? It deserved neither. It deserved peace, not to be used as a pawn in the games of a greedy goddess.

I shifted back, wiping a tear from my eye. I was used to violence. I would spill a lot of blood to keep my kingdom safe. But the wolf had been innocent.

"Dario?" I called.

I found him a moment later, cowered behind a corner with my vine wrapped around him like a security blanket. A few moments of reassurances and I had him back in my arms, trying to find my way out. Without the vines to guide me, it would be several more hours. He'd had a long, frightful day, and I wanted to get him out of the maze.

The light dimmed, torches going out all around me. The only ones lit were the ones directly in front of me and down a path to the right. This time, I didn't hesitate to follow. The trend continued; there was only one lit passage at every intersection. Eventually, I found the remains of my vine, but continued to follow the torches instead—I'd taken a rather circuitous route by the way the thread of greenery wove in and out of my path.

I led Dario all the way back to the hole, where I grew a fruit tree from the ground to carry us up, plucking a fresh peach for him to eat.

Phaidros and Cole were there, watching.

"We won," I told Cole.

I wished I would have felt more celebratory. But if this was the easiest of the challenges, we were in trouble.

CHAPTER XXVI

T HE NEXT CHALLENGE WOULD take place in the land of the living. Phaidros organized it to begin the very next day.

We met at Moon Rock the next morning.

Daphne had managed to unite two packs to our cause, the Wind-Bloods and the Fangs. She stood by Xander, and when Cole and I stepped through the portal, she rushed over to hug me. I breathed in her scent, as familiar as my own, and let myself hope.

On the other side, the Moon-Ghosts appeared. They looked on with hateful eyes, Sabine at the center. Jett was nowhere to be seen. The pack had seen better days. Losing their Alpha to his fanaticism had cost them. While Jett was still alive—for now—they lacked the leadership needed to survive.

I hated them. Gods, I hated them. But in that moment, I pitied them too.

I had been with the packs from the beginning. Had created the shifters from nothing. Seeing what they'd fallen to was an insult to everything I had worked towards. I wanted a better world for them. I'd told the mantle as much during my trials, and I would see it through.

The last to arrive was Phaidros, once again followed by the Moon Goddess's chosen representative.

Jett.

The Moon-Ghost Alpha had seen better days. After I'd crushed his wrist, the Moon Goddess had patched him up with a star-made splint that seemed borderline useless. Whatever magic it was, he was in pain, but able to hold the silver broadsword. His eyes were hollow, dark circles under them, but he had enough life to contort his face into a taunting grin when he spotted me. His eyes flashed over with stars and then back to his normal shade in quick succession, over and over.

Violent energy rolled off Cole. I squeezed his hand. This was the closest he'd ever been to the mate who'd forsaken me, the male who'd made my life miserable for years and years. He wanted to kill Jett. I could feel it, like a warm blanket draped over me. He wanted to tear him limb from limb, and the only thing stopping him was the fact it would get him sent to the pits.

But Cole would find a way. One day, when we didn't have all of this restoring-balance-to-the-realms nonsense to worry about, he would get his vengeance on my behalf.

"Today's game is simple," Phaidros announced. "It's called 'capture the flag.' You will form two teams of ten. The objective is to capture the other team's flag and bring it back to your own base. Violence is, of course, encouraged. Using magic to heal, teleport, or fight, however, is strictly prohibited and will result in an immediate forfeit. You have one hour to prepare from the time you both reach your bases. I will tell you when."

He held up two simple pieces of fabric, one white, one black. We got the black one.

Our team was made up of myself, Cole, Daphne, Xander, two other Wind-Bloods, and four Fang wolves. One was the Alpha, a shifter who appeared to be in his thirties, while the other was his beta. We agreed to use the Fang's territory as our base rather than the Wind-Blood. I knew from Daphne that the Moon-Ghost attack a few weeks ago had been devastating. The pack still hadn't recovered, not from the loss of their Alpha, nor the destruction the Moon-Ghosts had caused.

Phaidros finished explaining a few other details of the rules, mainly about what counted as winning—placing the enemy flag on a clearly marked resting spot of our own flag. We portaled over to the Fang's base. The Alpha, Ian, led us into what looked like a bar. Several motorcycles were parked outside, though in order to keep the situation fair, shifters who were not on either team would remain by Moon Rock.

"We split into two teams," Cole said, quickly taking command. "Avery, you, Daphne, Xander, and two of the Fangs will get the flag, since you two know the territory the best and the rest join you on the bikes."

The Fang Beta grumbled at the idea of sharing their motorcycles with the rest of us.

Cole gave him one *look*, and the grumbling stopped with an audible click of the male's jaw.

"Ian, Lewis, the two Wind-Bloods, and I will defend. The plan is simple—get it, get out. Try to avoid confrontation. We will hold out here for as long as we have to."

It made sense to split us up. Cole and I could defend ourselves, but we couldn't actually kill anyone. Something the living shifters were all able to do without repercussions. I didn't want to split up from Cole, though. This was dangerous, and without magic...

"Trust me, little wolf," he murmured, bending low to kiss my hair. His words were soft enough even the other shifters would struggle to hear, and they were already engrossed in their own discussion of tactics. "I can survive just fine without my magic. As can you."

I sighed. In the short time since I'd discovered it, my magic had become another limb. By ruling out healing, hurting, or teleporting, they'd basically handcuffed us. The only magic that could be used was the Moon Goddess's creepy mind control she had over the wolves, it seemed. I couldn't risk accidentally unleashing and costing us the challenge. We would have to be careful, and as Cole said, avoid coming into contact with the other team.

"I think you should go with Daphne and Xander."

He frowned. "Why? You know the territory better than I do."

"Because..." I couldn't find the words to explain.

Yet Cole knew me better than myself. "Is it because of last time? What happened to Hector?"

I nodded. I knew it was irrational, but the last time I'd been with them, not only had Hector gotten killed, but Xander had lost his father. *No, his father had been murdered,* I corrected myself. Because of me. Because I had brought them into a conflict and hadn't been able to protect them.

"I will go with them," Cole assured me, "if that is what you wish. But you cannot blame yourself for what happened to those under you."

"I do, though."

Cole curled a finger under my chin and tilted my head up. "This is a selfishness we cannot afford as rulers. Guilt, self-blame... these luxuries cost us the ability to protect those who have entrusted their lives to us."

Something uncurled in my chest. His words weren't gentle. If there was only one thing I would love about Cole, it's that he would tell me the hard truths. That was what I needed. "You're right."

One side of his mouth lifted. "You do hate to say those words."

"Only because it usually means I'm wrong," I teased.

His expression turned serious again. "If you still wish for

me to go with them, I will."

I considered. "I think I would. It's not just the guilt. I told myself I would look after all the shifters, and this is my chance to learn more about the Fangs. Daphne will show you both the way since Xander will need a guide, so it won't change the plan too much."

"Then I will go with them."

Cole kissed me then. He tugged me closer, and I fell into his embrace, tasting him, savoring him. The kiss was gentle, reassuring. Promising me he would return to me, as he always did.

"Cozy," Phaidros said dryly.

I turned and glared. He had opened up two portals on either side of him so he could communicate with both teams at once. Past him, a crowd of familiar Moon-Ghost faces looked out at me. Even Jett and Sabine stood around, though I couldn't tell exactly where. Daphne's father, the pack's old Beta, was there too. I wanted to growl at the sight.

"Can we start?" I snapped.

"Yes." The demon looked back and forth between our groups. "The second trial begins now."

Cole and the others took off. They'd agreed to borrow the motorcycles from the Fangs, something the Alpha had agreed to with no small amount of reluctance. Getting to the other camp as soon as possible was critical.

As I watched them go, I realized in my decision to trade

places, I had failed to consider how I'd feel sending all the people I cared about off while I stayed back with strangers.

"I always wanted to ride one of those," I mused.

Ian snorted. "The men or the bikes?"

My urge to smile was stifled by my worry. "The bikes. I was a shitty shifter, but I figured if I could ride, it wouldn't matter so much."

"I could take you for a spin," Lewis offered, an easy grin on his face.

The Fang Alpha glared. "I don't think her mate would like that. And I wouldn't get on the wrong side of him if I were you."

I blinked. For a moment, my mind conjured an image of Jett. But of course, they'd seen the markings Cole and I had left on each other. We were mates. In the eyes of all the shifters around us, we belonged to each other.

It soothed me.

"Come on. I'm not letting the flag out of our sight." I went back into the bar and sat at the round table we'd chosen for our base. Per Phaidros's many rules, the flag could not be hidden or held by a member of the team unless it had been taken by the opposing team and snatched back. Otherwise, we could just bury the flag and no one would ever find it. We'd settled for barring the door. It wasn't much, but at least it would give us some warning if they came in.

"You play?" Lewis asked, producing a deck of cards from

seemingly nowhere.

"Depends on the game," I hedged. If it could be played by two people, Daphne and I had done it. If it needed more, then no, I hadn't. "I think the one game we're playing is enough."

Ian shrugged. "May as well pass the time. It'll take them a couple hours to get to the base on the bikes, and twice that long for those prissy Moon-Ghosts to get here. They'll likely drive at least part way, of course, and finish the rest on foot, but in any case, we have some time."

Moon-Ghost territory and Fang territory were next to each other, while Moon Rock and Wind-Blood territory were both south. I'd have to take his word on the distances, but we shouldn't be facing them anytime soon.

Ian had a point, so I relented. Lewis dealt each of us a hand, and they taught me one of their pack's preferred games. The two were easier to talk to than expected, and the Wind-Bloods relaxed, joining us as well. The Fangs had a reputation for toughness that was thoroughly belayed by the easy laughs around the table. They told me more about their pack, which seemed to operate differently from both others, and I filled in the gaps that had been left from Daphne's sparse but highly effective recruitment pitch.

Lewis had just slammed his losing hand down with a good-natured moan when I froze in my seat.

I closed my eyes, trying to get a better listen, then stood.

"They're here."

No sooner did I give my warning than eight massive wolves hurled themselves through the bar's windows.

CHAPTER XXVII

A RAIN OF GLASS fell around us. The sound pierced the quiet of the night, our peaceful game destroyed as the world descended into chaos.

Nine on five. Bad odds.

Jett hopped over the wreckage, unshifted, the silver sword glowing in his hands. Sabine joined him, wielding silver daggers with gloves.

Make that ten on five.

Had they really not left anyone to defend their base?

Lewis and Ian tossed aside their leather jackets and began to shift. The Wind-Bloods stood behind, readying themselves.

Sabine didn't hesitate, hurling her two silver daggers straight at the Fang Alpha and Beta in their vulnerable state. I managed to knock aside the one headed for Ian. Lewis landed straight in his throat. A fountain of red erupted as he choked.

I might have been able to heal him. For a split second, I hesitated. That would cost us the trial. That moment cost us. By the time I could've considered otherwise, he was gone.

Furious, I launched myself at the nearest wolf, Ian doing

the same, an angry howl on his lips. They rushed us, and we dissolved into a mass of blood and fangs. A coppery scent filled the air. The room would be painted red in a matter of minutes.

I nearly killed the first shifter I reached on instinct. Doing that would've guaranteed me a spot back in the pits, so I had to settle for dismembering my opponent enough that her shifter healing would keep her alive, but she wouldn't be a threat. It wasn't quick. My back was to the table. Ian and the Wind-Blood wolves circled it, trying to keep them from getting our flag. We were sorely outnumbered, and unlike the Moon-Ghost, we weren't a cohesive pack. We might be strong individually, but wolves work best when they know their allies.

Still, I was happier to have the four of them at my side than any of my old packmates.

Someone went for the flag and I tackled them. Another shifter piled on. His scent was familiar, even as he clawed my flank. *Daphne's father.*

I didn't want to maim her blood relatives, however worthless. I managed to fling him aside, buying me time to claw at the underbelly of the other shifter.

Ian was still facing off two others, drawing them away from the table. The other Wind-Bloods were matched one-on-one and barely holding their own. That awful starry glow came over the Moon-Ghost wolf's eyes, turning their attacks nearly feral.

All that left was Jett, twirling the silver sword in his grip, his gaze trained firmly on me.

I'd been wounded several times over. I could heal myself with magic, but that was as good as forfeiting. If I didn't, however, I might pass out soon.

I bared my teeth at the Moon-Ghost Alpha and growled.

"So brave for someone so weak," Jett crooned.

I charged.

He slashed me with silver. The wound burned. I bit his leg, but that just gave him the opportunity to fight at my back. There was no way I would let this male ruin our chance at victory. I had people to fight for. Kingdoms to fight for. No matter how he cut me, how he attacked, I would not give up. Even if it cost my life, I would stop him.

An engine roared outside the bar.

What now?

The second of distraction cost me. Jett didn't lose focus, continuing to attack. I had to keep him away from the flag. Had to. But without my magic, with the silver sword reaching between us, I was on the retreat. My back hit the table leg. Jett's grin was nearly feral, his eyes promising a world of pain. If he killed me, he would not make it quick. But I wouldn't let him. I would never let him harm me like that again. I snarled, even as it hurt to breathe, my body shaky from the blood loss.

"Get away from my wife!"

Cole flew through the broken windows, shifting into a massive black wolf that towered over the others. He slammed into Jett from behind, his claws digging deep. Jett stumbled, and I got out of his way before he fell on me. Jett turned as he fell, waving the silver blade wildly. Cole easily dodged it as a wolf, knocking his sword to the ground and crushing Jett's wrist once more with his massive paw.

"You kill me and you go to Tartarus," Jett snarled.

Cole shifted back, towering over the other male.

"It's true, I can't kill you," Cole mused. "But I can make you wish you were dead."

He lifted the silver blade and cut Jett's right arm clean off. Then the left.

Jett screamed. I'd never heard a sound like that before. Pure wounded animal. No... I had heard those sounds. I had *made* those sounds. They had been brutal to me, and I had cried. Sobbed, begged, humiliated myself asking for a shred of kindness. *That* was what Jett sounded like.

Good, the wolfish part of me thought. *He deserves it.*

A cold gleam came over Cole's face. It was no mercy to spare Jett's life.

"You used those hands to hurt my wife. You don't deserve them." His voice was ice.

He lifted the blade, his fingers blistering under the silver, but Cole didn't care. With another brutal stroke, he removed Jett's left leg.

"You used these legs to chase her." Another slash. Jett was little more than a stump oozing blood.

Jett kept screaming and screaming.

Then his screams turned to laughter.

The Moon Goddess's voice came out of his mouth.

"He'll die from this, Lord of the Dead." She laughed. "Even if you try to stop the bleeding, he will die, and you will go to the pits."

"No, he won't," a new voice cut in.

Daphne had returned, Xander no doubt nearby.

Could we win? I wondered. *Two for two?*

"Because even if Cole can't kill him, I can."

With one savage jerk, a move I didn't even know she was capable of, she ripped Jett's head clear off.

"That's for forsaking my best friend," she snarled.

It was the nicest thing anybody had ever done for me. But there was no time to savor it. I ran to help the others. Cole followed my lead, getting there first.

It was bloody, but we'd won. I turned back to howl in triumph.

And saw Sabine with a silver knife at Daphne's neck.

CHAPTER XXVIII

"**S**HIFT BACK, OR SHE dies," Sabine purred.

Somehow, she had slipped away from the fray and sneaked up on Daphne. I growled, but did as she commanded. Cole followed immediately, flanking me.

"Do as she says," I told Ian and the remaining Wind-Blood. We'd been too late to help the other. "Let her go, Sabine. You've lost."

"Have I?" Sabine simply smiled.

"Your Alpha is dead. And Xander has the flag."

As if on cue, the Wind-Blood Alpha came into the room, the white banner dangling from his arms. He took in the sight before him and snarled.

"Yes, all that is true, I suppose. But see, I know something about you, Avery. You're a weak little wolf, and you would do anything to save the one person who had been kind to you. Including damn everyone else. Am I wrong?"

I said nothing. Daphne's eyes were pleading, begging me not to give in. But if I let Sabine kill her, she'd be sent to the starry prison the Moon Goddess had created. Her soul would join the painful cries I'd heard in my short time there.

"That's what I thought." Sabine's lips curled up in satis-faction. "So here's how this is going to go. To start, you're going to drop the banner on the floor and give it to Beta Rourke for safekeeping."

Daphne's eyes found Xander. "Don't do it—"

Her words ended in a gasp as Sabine pressed the knife hard enough to draw blood.

"None of that now."

Xander ground his teeth, but I knew no matter what I said, he would trade the flag for Daphne's life. I couldn't blame him.

"Do it," I commanded.

He kicked the banner over. Beta Rourke stood from where he'd been buried by the other bodies and took the scrap of fabric. Her father. The one I'd resisted killing.

"Now, the Beta will also take your flag and take it back over to our base. You're going to stay here with me, and vow to the Styx or whatever it is that you will not attempt to stop him."

"Avery," Cole warned.

"I don't have a choice."

He sighed in defeat, but he knew me. He knew what Daphne meant to me. He would never ask me to trade her life.

We made the vow, and the Beta snapped up the flag. He was injured, but he would make it with his shifter healing.

"Isn't this nice?" Sabine said conversationally. "In just a little while, you'll have lost, and will see the superiority of the Moon Goddess."

"I wouldn't be so sure."

Sabine raised a brow at me. "Oh? Why's that? You've vowed not to interfere with Rourke, and I have your pretty little friend here to make sure you don't misbehave."

"Because you've guaranteed we lose this round. And if we've already lost, there's nothing to stop me from doing *this*."

I reached my open palm out towards Sabine and crushed my fingers into a fist. At the same time, the wood beneath Sabine sprouted and a solid wooden spear impaled Sabine clean through, less than an inch from her heart. Her silver knife clattered to the ground, harmless.

WE HAD LOST THE second round. And worse, I couldn't help but feel like we had lost it for nothing. Good wolves had died to help us, and what did we have to show for it?

Dead wolves. Those I'd disabled, including Sabine, were finished off by the Wind-Bloods. Those who'd fought with us, I'd been able to do nothing for. The Moon-Ghosts hadn't pulled any punches.

The entire place stank of copper.

"They knew the risk we were taking," Cole assured me.

As he had said, guilt was a luxury I couldn't afford. I desperately wished I could, though. The best I could do was heal our wounded while I waited for Phaidros to show up. Cole had insisted I start with myself. Actually, he had threatened to portal me back to Hell and hold me there until I healed unless I prioritized myself. I'd agreed, since I didn't want to waste time arguing and I knew he wasn't joking. Now we were waiting.

"You should have won," Daphne snapped.

"She didn't have a choice," Xander argued. His whole body sagged with exhaustion. "Your life was on the line."

"And I was willing to die for it," Daphne snarled. "Everyone who came here knew what was at stake. *You* should have kept the flag and put it on the base."

Her words were directed at Xander. Something flashed between them, a silent argument that was ready to explode. Their scents were separate, but I knew there was something between them. It was cruel of Daphne to ask him to do that. Sabine would've killed her. Even now, with my healing magic running low, there was still a faint scar from where the knife had pressed against her neck.

But just as Hector's loss affected me, it hurt her even more. For the first time, she had let someone in, and he had given his life for me. She had been denied the same right. Maybe I was wrong to take that choice from her. Maybe I should've let her. Bile rose in my throat at the thought of Daphne joining the piles of bodies littered on the floor.

"You don't get to challenge my wife's decisions," Cole snarled.

I blinked, not expecting him to jump in. His amber eyes flashed in anger.

"She is the Queen of Hell. She does not answer to any of you. If you wish to serve her in this war, you have our thanks. If you don't, there's the door."

Ian very wisely ignored pointing out it was *his* door that Cole gestured towards.

"There have been, and there are, a lot of damn tough choices that will have to be made. You want to die a hero? Earn it. Don't let some asshole shifter use you as bait. Because that was what put my wife in the situation where she had to choose between your life—not just your life, but your soul—and letting that evil goddess win a round. If you want to blame someone, blame yourself, and don't waste our time. And if you really believed in Avery, you wouldn't be doubting that we'd win the next round. Then your death would have been for nothing. Do you really think so little of your closest friend?"

"Hey," Xander snapped. "That's over the line."

Cole rounded on Xander, ready to attack.

"No, he's right." Daphne's voice was quiet. "I do believe in you, Avery. If it's anyone's fault, it's mine, and I accept that."

I moved to hug my best friend. "It's not your fault. The truth is, it was a hard decision. Yes, we could've won. But something else could've gone wrong. Tough calls will happen, but I won't ever let myself believe the right option is sacrificing you." I turned to look at all the wolves around us, but especially Cole. "*Any* of you."

"Spoken like a queen," Phaidros said, finally arriving from his portal. "A sentimental, inexperienced queen who managed to somehow fuck up this extremely easy challenge I put together for you."

"Gee, thanks," I snapped.

"You're welcome."

"Say your piece, demon, and then let us leave." Cole took a step towards Phaidros.

The demon was unfazed. "The Moon Goddess has officially won this round, tying the score. The final challenge will take place three weeks and three days from now."

"Oddly specific," Daphne grumbled.

But predictable. "It's the full moon. She'll be at the height of her power."

Phaidros nodded in confirmation. "Yes. But there's a problem."

CHAPTER XXIX

"**W**HAT DO YOU MEAN, she's not letting us into the realm?"

The problem was that, though the Moon Goddess had set a date for the challenge, she wasn't actually allowing us up to compete.

"You're a Libra demon," I continued. "You should be able to portal anywhere." Even I couldn't fully block Phaidros from coming and going into my realm. I could make it difficult, but not impossible.

"It's a matter of my birth." Phaidros's admission came through gritted teeth. He loathed admitting the weakness. He glanced back to where Daphne and Xander were standing shoulder to shoulder, their argument forgotten as they united against a common enemy. "I suggest we go elsewhere to speak."

"No. You'll explain now." I wasn't wasting time to protect the demon's ego.

"Because my magic is not strictly my own, but rather a seed of hers, she has unique control over me. Hence the reason we entered this alliance at all. The goal was for you to win the first two contests, not be drawn into a third. Especially not one you can't win *because she will not let you into the realm*. If neither you nor a representative shows up, it's an automatic forfeit."

Cole was furious. "You expect us to consider this a fair contest? We said all your vows, demon. You were to exact the same ones from your mother."

"I did. But there are always loopholes, and she took advantage of this one. You have safe harbor within the realm, outside of the challenge, but only if you are in the realm. The vows did not stipulate that the ruler of the realm had to allow passage because she had never restricted my access to my home before."

"So what you're saying is you were betrayed. Guess the apple doesn't fall far from the tree," Daphne said dryly. "Or actually, that you were too stupid to anticipate it."

Phaidros turned on Daphne. "Your mouth is much prettier when it's *shut*, love."

Xander growled. "Don't talk to her that way."

Phaidros simply arched a brow. "You need this oaf to fight your battles now? Moved on so quickly from your knight in shining armor?"

Daphne snarled, showing all the teeth her "pretty mouth" had. "If you can't hold up your end of the bargain, then there's no reason for me not to avenge Hector."

She took a step towards the demon.

Phaidros took one in turn, yellow sparks dancing around him. "Love, if you think you are a match for me in anything but bed sport, I'm more than happy to give a lesson."

"I think I'm more than a match for you, momma's boy." Fur rippled over her skin, the shift imminent.

"Enough!" I cried. "Quit bickering and let's focus on solving this issue."

Hurt and shame flashed in Daphne's eyes. I knew what it was, to be lost in your grief. Phaidros had caused so much pain, but arguing with him when he was our only chance at fixing this was a bad idea.

"Let's take a day," Cole said. "We're all exhausted and covered in blood. Take a day to bury our dead, to mourn, and then we will find a way to solve this. We have three weeks. If the Moon Goddess truly believed there was no way for us to get in, she would have set the challenge for this very night. It's merely a matter of solving this puzzle." He took my hand, lifting my blood-covered fingers to his lips. "And we will."

W E RETURNED TO HELL and filled Hecate in on what happened.

"We need to figure something out. Maybe if I go to the library I can find something," I said, looking between the two.

"I meant what I said," Cole said, his voice low and commanding. He was all Alpha, and my wolf side appreciated that fully. "You are *exhausted*, little queen. Don't think I'm above tying you to our bed to see that you rest." His voice tipped lower. "You know I'll enjoy it."

Hecate, who had an impressive poker face, simply nodded in agreement. "I will look into it. In the meantime, *both* of you would benefit from taking time to recuperate."

So, Cole succeeded in getting me into bed.

What he didn't manage to do was make me rest.

I was on my stomach, my arms tucked under the pillow. Cole was rubbing my sore back. The wolf in me was loving the physical touch.

"You're too tense," Cole chastised.

I snorted. "I can't imagine why that would be. Between getting several shifters slaughtered and handing a victory to the Moon Goddess, I should be on cloud nine."

I didn't have to see Cole to know he'd frowned. His hands stilled, resting on my shoulder blades. "It wasn't your fault, little wolf."

But wasn't it? "I'm the one who insisted we change places. If I'd gone with Daphne and Xander, you'd have been there to protect Lewis and Adam." The other Wind-Blood had been a cousin of Xander's. The second family member of his I was responsible for killing. "I'm the one who brought Hector to the realm of the living. I'm the one who made a deal with

Phaidros to begin with and got us into this whole mess. I'm a failure as queen. No one should listen to me—I just keep making terrible decisions that get people killed."

Face-down on the pillow, I fought the pinpricks of tears. Even if Cole couldn't see them, he'd be able to scent the salty aroma.

But he wouldn't let me have the refuge of the pillow. In a single movement, he flipped me over, his legs still straddling me.

"You are *not* a failure as a queen. Hector would have chosen to give his life for you a thousand times over, and he only got hurt because you were rescuing me. You walked into the under-realm and walked out with another soul. I think you forget how incredible that is. As for today, yes, we lost good people. It will never not hurt. Had I stayed, would the results have been different? Maybe. It's impossible to say. The rest of it... little wolf, that deal only hastened the inevitable. We've been on a collision course with this destiny for far longer than you or I can remember."

He wiped away my tears. I leaned into the touch, but he tilted my head back to face him with his palm.

"You doubt me."

"I doubt myself," I admitted. "I can remember the years of ruling at your side, confident in my decisions. The years before, guiding the realm of the living. But it still feels like a different person at times. It may be my soul, and I may have finally pieced it all together, but I'm still me. Avery Ward, shifter reject, the one no one wanted."

"The one *I* wanted," Cole countered. "My queen. My mate."

I glanced at his exposed mark. "Yours," I agreed.

He saw where my gaze landed, and a smirk came to his lips. He was so proud of that mark. It was the best decision I had ever made. Then again, there wasn't exactly stiff competition around that title.

"You do make good choices, little wolf. And I know how I'm going to show you."

He knelt back on his knees, still straddling me, so his hips lined up halfway down my thighs. We were both naked, so I felt every inch of his skin against me.

"You're going to command me."

I blinked at him. "Do you think your wolf will like that?"

"My wolf *is* me," Cole reminded me. "And yes, I think we both will enjoy being bossed around by our mate."

I frowned. "Are you calling me bossy?"

Cole couldn't have pulled off an innocent look if he tried. "I think you've forgotten how much you like trying to boss me around. The difference is, this time, I'll listen."

Something in me lit with interest. It was a game... but it was also a test.

"Is that so?"

"Try me."

I eyed him up and down. Dark hair, falling in short waves just above his eyes. The winding dragon tattoo curved from his shoulder to his hips. He was hungry for me, that much was obvious. But he sat back on his heels, waiting for me. Even on his knees, Cole couldn't look anything less than utterly dominant. I liked that. It was no fun if he'd suddenly changed.

I slid my legs out from under him and lifted myself up so I was standing on my knees facing him. My fingers traced over that tattoo, barely more than a brush. Involuntarily, my husband gave a shudder.

"Stay still," I told him.

He obeyed without protest.

My touches went further. I stroked his length. Feeling him grow harder under my touch was an aphrodisiac. Before now, every time I touched Cole, he had touched me back. Now, there was an asymmetry. It should've created distance, but instead I felt more connected to Cole than ever. Like I finally had all my thoughts about me and could tease him as much as I pleased. That he trusted me with his body, with his soul.

"Any other commands?" Cole said through gritted teeth when my stroking had gone on for several minutes. I'd kept the same slow, torturous pace, almost lazy even though I was anything but.

I withdrew my hand, tapping a finger to my chin. "Hmm. My next one should be to tell you not to speak. Lucky for you, I like your grumbly voice."

"Lucky, indeed." His voice had dropped lower than usual for those words. "Then what is your next one?"

I considered. "Touch me."

I expected Cole to jump at the chance, but he stayed put. "Where should I touch you, mate?"

The word made me want to say "right between the legs would be great," but there was something about the slow, drawn-out game that appealed to me. "My breasts."

Obediently—a word I never would have expected to apply to Cole—his hands rose to my chest and slowly massaged. His touch was gentle.

Too gentle. "Harder."

His touches turned to kneading, and satisfaction raced through me. Still, I wanted more. His fingers were careful to avoid my sensitive peaks. Clearly, he wasn't going to take any of his usual liberties. He wanted me to tell him everything. "Touch my nipples," I demanded.

"My pleasure." His voice was a low rumble.

Once more, Cole obliged. Soon, my commands came in quick succession. My breasts. My stomach. My hips. My thighs. My *clit*.

"I want you inside me," I hissed as his thumb went in slow, taunting circles.

"Then order me to be," Cole growled. His erection was straining. The slow, controlled touches he'd done to assure me he was following the letter of my commands and nothing further had tormented him as much as it had me. "It's my favorite command to obey."

I drew in for a kiss and nipped his lip hard enough to draw blood. "Then fuck me. Fuck me like you can't stop yourself."

With that, the gentle petting ending.

And Cole *unleashed*.

He positioned me flat on my stomach, taking me from behind. He slid inside without resistance. I was wet and desperate for him. The fullness felt right. *Perfection*. I gripped the covers for support as he held my hips, slamming into me over and over.

"Is this what you wanted?" He bent over me, never ceasing his relentless pace. "Do you like feeling me like this?"

I nodded, even though he couldn't see it.

"You own me, little wolf. Any demand you make, forever. I will do it. If you tell me to fuck you, I will. If you tell me to carve out my damn heart and hand it to you on a platter, I'll do it without hesitation."

His words were dark, violent. There must've been something wrong with me, because they just amplified the pressure in my core.

"You're mine, and no one, not some bitch goddess, not the pits of Tartarus themselves, will ever take you from me again. Don't doubt yourself. Because I will never doubt you."

Tears pricked at my eyes. Different from before. Because there was such confidence, such truth in Cole's words. He meant everything he said.

"Now, little goddess, there's one more command for you to give me."

I knew exactly the three words he was waiting for. And this time, I didn't tease us.

"Make me come, Cole." It was a plea as much as it was an order.

Cole obeyed all the same.

When my release crashed over me, something warm and precious settled in my chest. Because he hadn't just given me pleasure. He'd given me something far more dear—his heart, and his trust.

And even if I lacked that faith in myself, I would honor his, and borrow it.

I would find a way to save us.

No matter what.

CHAPTER XXX

COLE HAD AN IDEA for how to get to the Moon Goddess's realm.

More specifically, he had a plan for how I could get to the realm.

Even Hecate was bewildered at his declaration. "How?" she demanded.

Cole's gaze never left my face. "Libra demons are thought to be the only creatures that can go between realms. They're born as slivers of the realm itself, Phaidros being an exception. They're part of the balance. Neutral, relatively weak entities that provide holes between the realms so the universe can breathe."

"If Phaidros can't get in, I doubt another Libra demon will solve our problem," I pointed out.

Cole shook his head. "I said they're thought to be the only creatures that can go between realms. But there is one other being powerful enough." He tugged aside his shirt collar. At first, I thought he was going to flash his mate mark again, but he pulled the other side, exposing the head of his dragon tattoo. He'd had that design for as long as I'd known him—both lifetimes included.

"I've never heard of dragons having this power," Hecate argued.

He arched a brow at the enchantress. "As rare as it is, sometimes your king knows something you don't."

"If dragons can go between realms, why didn't we try this before?" I asked.

"Because we weren't that desperate," Cole said plainly. "And it's not that simple. There are three issues. First, you need to draw out the dragon. Even I don't know how to do that."

"How come?" I frowned. "Didn't you do it before?"

"My circumstances were different. It's a long story, and it's not one we have time for now. You can't go and simply hunt the dragon down either," he added, ready for my next question. "Dragons come to you. They're too powerful to be caught against their will. That leads to the second problem, which is you need to offer the dragon something worthwhile."

I bit back a sigh. "Another deal?"

"No." Cole's refusal was sharp. "Dragons don't make deals. You must offer something freely and forever given. If they consider it a worthy offering, they'll accept. If not, they take it anyway."

"What's the third issue?"

"You're the only one who can call the dragon. There are two in every realm, in some form or another. The King's Dragon, and the Queen's Dragon. The King's is gone, which leaves yours."

"Okay. So to recap, I just need to figure out how to summon an ancient powerful dragon which none of you remember how to do, offer something immensely valuable in hopes the dragon decides to help us get into the heavens, and then we can finally decide if we are going to Tartarus for eternity in a tie-breaker match that is decided by the Moon Hag herself."

"It's a better plan than we had before," Cole said simply.

The worst part is he was right.

"Where do we start then?"

"The library would be a likely place to begin, Soteria." Hecate nodded down to the right, in the direction of the palace's massive library.

We teleported over. It was even larger than the one in the one in the castle I'd shared with Cole. In a prior life, that had been a pleasant escape for me. I'd loved reading then as much as I did now. The palace library was a hundred times larger. No one had ever read all the books in it—in fact, many of the books hadn't even been written. Not in the normal means. They simply appeared on their own whims. The tomes numbered not in the thousands, but in the millions. Even with the prior damage to the palace, the library had remained largely intact.

I winced. I knew the size of the library, of course, but being confronted with it visually again made our task seem impossible.

"I don't suppose you have a spell that can just find us the right book, or put all the knowledge in our brains?"

The enchantress shook her head. "Magic cannot help us here. There is such a spell to immediately memorize every word of text on a page, but applying it on such a scale would leave the recipient catatonic."

Great. So all we had to do was read a few million books in hopes of possibly finding some long-forgotten knowledge.

"We're going to need some help," I said, waving my hand to open a portal.

Help came in the form of Daphne, Xander, Ian, and a dozen shifters from both the Fangs and the Wind-Bloods. As many as could be spared without leaving the territories vulnerable to Moon-Ghost attack. Thirty shifters... and half the palace army.

Hecate had cautioned against bringing living shifters into the realm of the dead. Realistically, even if we had ten thousand people, we were running against the clock. But they were my pack. I needed them.

And, as I pointed out, if we failed to summon the dragon, we were all screwed anyway.

"Thank you for coming," I told Daphne as we went to a far corner of the library to pull some books. There were too many of us to fit into the massive library, so most people had scattered with their stacks of books to different corners of the palace to read.

"Of course. There's nowhere else I'd want to be, though I'm not sure how much help I'll be. I'm just one wolf."

I smiled. "I appreciate it all the same. You never know how much of a difference one person will make. Plus, I know it's not easy being here. You mentioned it feels like suffocating for shifters when they're here."

My best friend considered. "You know, it feels different this time. Last time, it felt like the entire realm was choking me. But this time it's not so bad. I still don't think I could shift. It's like there's a pane of glass between my wolf and me, when we should be one. But it's not so painful. I still know I don't belong here, but it doesn't feel like the entire realm is hostile towards me. Less Hell, more being-a-living-creature-in-the-underworld."

I tugged a gray book with a worn spine from a high shelf and handed it to her before picking another for myself, taking the time to turn her words over in my mind. Something had changed in the realm. I'd thought I just felt that because I'd taken the mantle, then because Cole and I were back in the capital. But maybe there was something to what she'd said. The realm had been the underworld when I'd ruled it, a neutral space. It had soured to Hell without any rulers caring for it, but there was no reason to believe it couldn't be restored.

Things I'd ponder later. For now, I had a dragon to catch.

I F I'D THOUGHT WE might get lucky and find the book on Day One, I was quickly disabused of that hope.

Same with every single day for the first week. Then the second. We were dancing dangerously close to the deadline.

If one of us didn't find a way to summon the dragon soon, Cole and I would be back in Tartarus. We spent hours and hours in the library, searching. Sometimes Daphne joined me, sometimes, when I got too irritable, she went off to Xander and Ian while Cole tried to reassure me.

But even he was growing anxious. Sleep was an extravagance we could seldom afford. The thought of each other in the pits kept us awake even when we tried to rest.

"We should talk to Phaidros. See if he found a way around it."

We were both loathe to ask the demon for anything, but we were out of options. It was past noon, and at midnight, it would be too late. Cole summoned Phaidros with his magic, but the demon simply sighed.

"Are you sure you've tried hard enough?" I prodded.

While I had dark circles under my eyes that would've qualified for their own realms and hadn't so much as bathed in—two, three, maybe more—days, the demon was in freshly pressed clothing, his star-studded skin nearly luminescent.

Now his expression narrowed. "I've tried to form portals until my magic threatened to swallow me whole and take me to realms that shouldn't even exist. Rest assured, dove, I haven't been sitting around reading." He cast a disdainful glance at the pile of books by my side.

We were in a corner of the library that was miraculously unoccupied. It wasn't a formal place to receive guests, but I didn't have the energy to care, and he wasn't a guest anyway.

If we did run out the clock, I'd simply kill the demon before the pits took us. At least I'd have that bit of justice to savor while the under-realm drove me mad.

"At least we're still looking for a solution," I snapped.

"Oh? And what do you expect to find?"

He was obviously fishing, but there was no point denying him. "We're looking for a way to summon a dragon."

Phaidros's mouth quirked, ready to scoff at us, before he paused the expression and considered. "That could work. My mother can block me, but even she can't stop one of the great sky beasts."

"Do you know a way?" Cole asked, contempt and fatigue bleeding into the words. "You've possessed a deal of knowledge you should not have, as though you've slunk into countless conversations where you didn't belong."

Phaidros grinned, like Cole had praised him, before turning serious. "I vow to the Styx I do not. If I did, I would tell you so you could kill my mother."

"But you *did* know a way," I argued, pieces clicking into place. "You summoned the undead dragon before."

"*You* summoned the Queen's Dragon in her decayed state," he corrected. "Sorry, darling, but planting-the-teeth-of-the-last-Queen's-dragon only works once while the dragon itself is sitting between the realms. Once you healed the dragon, that door closed."

I frowned. I'd been so caught up in everything that had happened immediately after I'd healed the dragon—Cole nearly dying, then getting dragged to the pits—I hadn't really thought about it.

Phaidros sat at an empty table and kicked his legs up. I glared. "You can go now."

To accentuate my point, I opened a portal right next to him.

He glanced at it, half amused. "If this is how my last hope dies, I may as well savor it."

"Optimistic, aren't you," I groused.

"I think I'll stay," he said cheerfully.

"I could force you to leave." Cole's voice was low, threatening.

"Not without breaking your vows, you can't," Phaidros chirped.

Cole's expression said that he didn't much care. He didn't like having the demon in his territory any more than I did, and his control was frayed after the past few weeks. Dark shadows gathered behind Phaidros, his death magic eager for a release.

"Fine. You can stay. But if you want all your internal organs to remain intact, keep away from Daphne. *She* hasn't made any unbreakable vows to not harm you."

"She can't still be mad about Harold," Phaidros huffed. "He was nothing, especially compared to *her*."

"I don't have time to spend guessing how your psychotic mind works. But rest assured, my best friend can hold grudges. I think you saw what she did to the last male who hurt someone she loved."

"Females." Phaidros sighed, clearly working up to some quip.

I cut him off by throwing a massive, dusty tome square at his chest. He caught it, but the dust scattered onto his freshly washed shirt. He glared, not appreciating my gift. I smirked.

"If you're staying, you can help look for a way out of this mess. And if you're too good for that, you can go find Daphne and see which of us knows her better."

Chapter XXXI

WE HAD HOURS LEFT.

I was barely reading anymore. I pulled a book, flipped through the pages, and discarded it. I was tempted to go to Hecate and tell her we should try the knowledge potion even if it left the user catatonic in hopes it found us something.

The latest book was useless. A recipe book for how to cook Scorpio demons without poisoning yourself. I hurled it away in frustration, knocking several more books from the shelf down.

Cole was immediately by my side, trying to soothe me.

"We'll figure it out," he promised, wrapping his arms around my waist.

I leaned back against him, finding comfort in his scent even though everything was a disaster.

"I want to believe that," I whispered. "But we're running out of time—wait."

I broke out of his arms and he followed me over to the pile of books I'd knocked down. It was a section of the library I'd gone through before. I'd moved on from it and onto the side that had Cookbooks From Literal Hell, which had been an improvement over the section that had extremely detailed tax law, which, given my state of sleep deprivation, was particularly dangerous.

But there, among the pile of legal books, was a title I recognized.

Portals.

The one-word title had been my lifeline when I'd first died and searched for a way out. I'd read the book cover to cover. It didn't mention dragons once. Yet I kept looking at it, trying to make the puzzle pieces fit.

Cole frowned. "I didn't see that book there before."

"It wasn't here. I'm positive. When the pocket-realm was destroyed, it should've been destroyed too."

"The realm has its own mind. Perhaps it's a gift, to help us keep the balance."

I plucked the book from the pile. It even had the piece of cloth I'd used as a marker. It was the same book.

"When I was in the first trial, I was lost. It should've taken me days to get out, if I could even get Dario to stay with me long enough. But instead of wandering for ages, the lights shifted, guiding me down the right path. Was that you?" I asked, already knowing the answer.

Cole shook his head. "If I could have helped you, I would have. But any interference would've cost us the round." A pause. "It must have been the realm."

I flipped open the cover of the book, tracing my fingers down the aged parchment. "Then maybe it's helping us again."

I didn't have time to reread every book word-by-word, but I didn't have to. One quick visit with Hecate, and she enchanted the book so that the next person who opened it would absorb all of its words, as promised.

It would be exhausting. But it was survivable, and that was all I needed.

I opened the book.

Words upon words assailed me. I fell to my knees, crying out as they all tried to fit into my head. There was no me, no library, no realm, just the words fighting for space. I tried to study them, to put them into coherent thoughts, but they fell apart at every attempt.

My head felt like it had a vise around it, tightening and tightening until I thought I would burst.

And then... clarity. The words slowed, coming together as I matched the endless stream with what I remembered from the book.

Between all the chapters I'd read before, there was something new. Words that hadn't been there before, but were exactly what we needed.

"I know how to draw out the dragon."

N EVER LET IT BE said dragons weren't specific.

If we hadn't found the book—if the realm hadn't sent the book to me—we would have failed. The list of ingredients went a mile long and required a cauldron to fit them all. Herbal ingredients I knew, both common and rare. A full deer carcass. Pounds and pounds of charcoal. An assortment of animal eggs that were half-rotted, which Hecate was miraculously in possession of. Flesh of a living demon, which Phaidros reluctantly provided.

Well, which Daphne took from him, with a little too much glee in her knife work.

Now, at least, we could manage the first part of the challenge.

It remained to be seen if the dragon would come in time.

We were on the palace roof. The living shifters had been evacuated back to their own realm. The cauldron sat squarely in the center, and four of us gathered around.

I set the cauldron on fire with my magic.

It was the smoke from a pyre my magic ignited that would find the dragon. In the wind that would reach every corner of the realm and draw the dragon out. By now, it was late. We were less than two hours from the deadline.

"Do you know what you will offer the dragon, Soteria?"

I appreciated Hecate's confidence the dragon would come.

"Not a clue. Any advice would definitely be appreciated."

"Something only you can give," Hecate said with confidence that I don't think any of us felt.

How could she know when neither of us had handled a dragon before? I pressed my lips together and watched the horizon.

Like imps, dragons didn't have souls exactly, so I couldn't see it in my mind's eye. But that didn't mean I wouldn't be aware of its arrival.

Something shifted in the air. An awareness. Cole felt it too. He adjusted his stance, drawing closer to me.

The last time he had faced this dragon, he had nearly died to keep me safe. He was more than willing to do it again.

I shut my eyes and felt the creature's presence wash over me. It was miles away, but the air shifted, as if in anticipation. It was almost an echo of my own magic, but something entirely different. Like when I'd stepped foot in the mantle.

The thunderous sound of beating wings burst through the skies. The rhythmic pulse was a warning. To me, it sounded like hope.

The giant green beast crested over the cliffs and came into view.

It was magnificent.

Where once there had been decaying flesh, covering the skeleton in an uneven patchwork, there were now only glistening emerald scales. The dragon roared its arrival and even

Cole leaned back at the sound.

I took a step forward. *Come to me*, I thought towards the creature.

"It didn't feel like this before," I whispered to Cole. There was a pull to the dragon I'd never felt in all my years of existence. How had I never found this creature before? "It feels almost like a part of me."

"In a way, the dragon is a part of you," Cole explained. "Both your magic and the dragon's is tied to the mantle, and thus, the two of you are bonded. What happens to one affects the other."

The dragon roared again. The ground shook.

"When I went to the pits with the mantle... it decayed because of me. It suffered because of me." How could I ask this creature for anything, when I had been the source of its pain?

The dragon came to the edge of the city and then landed.

"You suffered too," Cole said, tilting my head up. "You suffered to keep the rest of us safe. There is no shame in that."

I nodded.

"Then let's go get your dragon." He grinned at me and teleported us over.

Up close, the creature was even more breathtaking. I hadn't been able to process it as anything more than a threat, and a means for survival, when it had attacked the capital. But now, even with a new threat looming over us, its majesty was undeniable.

The dragon didn't roar again. It stood on all fours, staring down at us as if we were nothing more than mice. Its wings were spread wide, the membranous material letting through the barest hint of light. Its talons were smooth and nearly as tall as I was. Past the rest of its body, its tail lashed from side to side in anticipation.

Waiting for its offering.

I swallowed.

What could I offer a dragon?

Something only you can give, Hecate had said. But what special thing could I give it?

I stepped forward. Being this close to the creature should have been terrifying, but instead, it felt like another piece of me.

"I don't know what dragons like exactly," I admitted. I could feel Cole's gaze at my back, silently promising support. I didn't break my gaze. Twin slitted pupils looked back at me, assessing. "I could offer you food or mountains of priceless jewels, but for a creature as wondrous as you, that's nothing special. You can feed yourself as you need, and no gemstone could compare to your own scales."

I drew closer.

"I would offer you my limbs, or organs, or even my soul, if I thought that might work. Those are things only I can give you, after all. My magic. My very essence. They're special, in their own way, but I would give it all up to you to get what I want." I drew a shaky breath. "But you're not here for a deal. You're here for an offering. Something given without demanding something in return. So this is what I can give you." My knees shook as I forced myself forward once more. I drew myself up to my full height, and when I looked up at the dragon, it wasn't as Queen of the Underworld. It was as Avery Ward, the shifter no one had wanted, the one who had been hurt over and over again by people who considered me less than nothing.

"I will give you two things. The first is an apology, for my actions a hundred years ago. I thought I was protecting the kingdom and the people I cared about, but you suffered too."

The dragon growled, a low rumble in its belly like it was debating opening its jaw and bathing me in fire. At this distance, even with all my healing magic, I would die.

But it deserved an apology all the same. Images flashed through my mind of the undead beast. I wasn't sure they were all my own—some seemed to come from the dragon's eyes. Its pain rolled through me as though it were my own. The agony, the loneliness. It would've been so easy to turn away from, to reject those feelings. I didn't do that. I let every emotion hit me, because this was pain that deserved to be felt. There were no words from the dragon, but there was a psychic link, and in it, I finally understood the dragon. It was a guardian of the realm. It watched, and it protected. But when my soul had been torn to shreds, it had been corrupted. The realm it protected turned into a hellscape. Those it cared for now feared it. It slumbered, the only thing it could do to avoid hurting others, and that exile had scarred it deeply.

"I am sorry," I murmured. "I can't undo the past. But I can offer you this—a home. A place where you are wanted. No matter what happens, you will always have a place in my kingdom. And if I lose this final challenge, before I go, I will return the mantle so that you do not suffer again because of my recklessness. You will have your home, here, where you are honored and cherished."

Giving up the mantle would hurt. I hadn't wanted it in this lifetime, but now it had become part of me. But it was the right thing to do. I would not put this creature through such torment again. Let a new ruler come, take the mantle, and keep the Queen's dragon safe.

The dragon stared, smoke billowing from its nostrils.

Maybe it hated my offering. Maybe I had just damned all of us. *Maybe I really should've just offered a kidney and been done with it.*

Then it lowered its head down, just a few inches from my face. I lifted my palm to meet it.

The tentative psychic link snapped into a solid connection. Words poured into my mind. *I accept your offering. And I will give you the gift you seek.*

The dragon lowered its left wing, offering its back to me.

I took a step forward, then turned back to Cole.

"You'll come with me?"

My husband looked back at me, his amber eyes unyielding.

"Always, my queen."

CHAPTER XXXII

THE DRAGON DIDN'T MAKE a portal once we were on its back.

No, the dragon stretched out, its hind legs launching upward. The wings beat loudly as we pushed higher and higher in the sky. I gripped Cole's shoulders, pressing my legs against the dragon's back, and held on for dear life. Wind ripped through my hair. We pierced clouds, nearly vertical as the dragon drove higher.

Then it ripped through the barrier that held the realm together.

The magic around me shifted—we were in the land of the living. The full moon glowed overhead, lighting the land in a silvery blanket. The dragon didn't slow as we pierced the skies again. I held on tighter, my heart pounding. Thousands and thousands of stars lit the night, not a single cloud obscuring them. They grew larger as the dragon pushed forward. The air turned thin.

I sensed the barrier between the heavens and the realm of the living. It crackled against my magic. We weren't wanted.

But that wasn't going to stop the dragon beneath us.

It pushed against the barrier, wings straining and straining without moving forward. I called on my magic too, trying to help. Cole's own power wrapped around mine, and the three of us pushed against the Moon Goddess.

With a great cry, the dragon pierced the veil between realms.

We landed in the great hall, the emerald dragon roaring at all who saw us. Cole dismounted and caught me as I jumped down.

Thank you, I thought to the dragon.

It gave a soft cry back, a sound I would hold in my heart forever. It said that it appreciated my gift and was glad it had fought for me.

Without warning, it burst into a mass of green sparks. The sparks swirled higher, coming together into a single column. Then they arched back down and slammed me square in the chest.

The dragon's magic pierced me. I was in my usual sweats and vine-made tank top. My exposed right arm was suddenly covered in a winding tattoo, the unmistakable shape of a dragon head landing right on my collar.

It had taken everything the creature had to get to where it was not wanted, to get us to the Moon Goddess's realm.

I slid a glance at Cole. His own tattoo, twin to the one on my skin, was hidden under his clothing. But he had to know.

"You didn't tell me this was a one-way ticket."

He shrugged, ever casual even as we were now in enemy territory, with our very souls at stake. "If we lose, it won't matter."

I rolled my eyes. "How practical."

His feral grin was answer enough.

"So good of you to join us," the frost-filled voice called from high above.

I turned from Cole and took in the room. The Moon Goddess was seated high above on her throne, but my gaze didn't land on her. No, all I could see were the thousands and thousands of ghost shifters lining the room. They had the same translucent outlines as the one she'd sent for the first trial, their bodies filled with stars. Some were in human form, others in wolf form. Every single one had a choking collar of stars around their neck. Their pain called out to me, begging to be heard. I bit down a snarl. Cole didn't, outwardly growling at the treatment of the Moon Goddess's enslaved army.

"Your plan failed. We're here," I called out.

Her head cocked once more in that stilted way of hers, a mockery of natural emotions. "Plan? I simply wanted to make certain you were suitably determined to continue on this path."

Yeah, and I had her a hunk of rock in the sky to sell her.

"Before we go any further, *Phoebe*, you need to allow your son to enter the realm. He's our referee and you have no right to block him."

The Moon Goddess seemed to twitch at the use of her given name. Well, she shouldn't have given it to me if she didn't want it used. It was that, or one of the more colorful nicknames I had saved up for her.

"Naturally, since you are here, I will do this," she assured us.

What a load of crap.

A portal opened high above in the sky. Unlike the smooth circles Phaidros and I conjured, hers was made of shifting rectangles, pure white sparks shrinking and enlarging. The edges seemed sharp as ice, like if they jerked at the wrong moment, they would cut whoever came through. Phaidros fell through the portal seconds later, the star-skinned demon nearly crashing to the ground before opening his own portal and landing on his feet like a proper cat shifter instead of a demon.

"Oh good, dove, your plan actually worked." Phaidros winked at me, though I saw the unease in his movements. He reached through another smaller portal and pulled out a flask.

When he pulled his hand back through the portal, though, his wrist was seized with a band of stars.

"Yet it is your plan I find myself more interested in." If possible, the Moon Goddess's voice got even less human. She was angry. "You thought to ally against me, *son*."

"Hardly." Phaidros managed to sound insulted, even

though that had been exactly true. "I simply—"

"Enough deception. I have indulged you too much. I did so because you were borne of a part of me, and I do not believe in treating any part of myself with less than reverence. Yet you have proved ungrateful, over and over. And like any good mother, I must teach you the consequences of such work. Again."

The white spots making up the constellations on Phaidros's black skin glowed brighter and brighter until they burned to look at. Phaidros cried out, a gasp cut off as he choked on blood. Hundreds of piercings went through Phaidros with no further notice. The stars pierced him clean through, as though each had been a tiny spear.

There were parts of him I could see straight through.

The demon fell to his knees, his pierced hands falling in front to catch him.

On instinct, I reached for my magic, wanting to heal such cruelty.

But just like the last time I was here, my magic was locked away. The Moon Goddess had absolute dominion over magic used in her realm.

He forced himself up on his own strength. It would have been nothing less than excruciating.

"If you can stand, perhaps I didn't do enough," the Moon Goddess purred in a distorted voice. "Why do you make me do this?"

"Enough!" I called. "He's neutral in this. We all swore a million vows to the Styx to keep the contest fair, and Phaidros swore to be impartial. He's done nothing to deserve such cruelty."

There was something like gratitude in Phaidros's eyes, there and gone before I could be certain.

I didn't like the demon by any stretch. But he didn't deserve this from his own mother. No wonder he wanted to kill her. I recalled the words of my own packmates, the ones who were supposed to help shelter me, who'd thrown similar condescending words out when I refused to yield. *Why do you make us teach you these lessons over and over, Avery? Why won't you just accept your place as the weak little Omega?* My mother might not have physically hurt me, but she had let the pack do whatever they pleased while she basically disowned me.

There was nothing I wanted less than to empathize with the demon.

"Cruelty? You insult me, life-giver. Phaidros is a piece of me, my property to do with as I see fit. Just as I make all those who belong to me do what I wish."

On silent command, every shifter dropped to their knees, head bowed.

She didn't deserve their submission.

"But," she continued, "if you think he is better off without me, then I shall oblige. Consider this a final gift before you return to the under-realm."

With a flex of her fingers, the stars piercing Phaidros's skin disappeared entirely. I could feel the change in the air, his magic gone. She had ripped out whatever shred of her soul had spawned him and taken it back. Phaidros roared, the angry, pained cry of someone who had something fundamental stolen from them.

If possible, the Moon Goddess glowed even brighter.

"That is better. Back where it belongs." She floated down the steps. "Now, I will give you what you came for. This is my trial: single combat between you and me. No interference from the death god." She cut a look to Cole. The hate in her eyes was the most human emotion she'd displayed yet.

My wolf wanted me to growl at the thought of her looking at our mate. But that part of me was once again locked away, unable to come out in the goddess's realm.

"I object to this," Cole snarled. "Let me take Avery's place fighting you. I'd like nothing more than to rip you apart."

"I'm sure that is true," the Moon Goddess said. "But I have chosen my opponent."

Cole turned to the lump on the ground that was Phaidros, lifting him up by his shirt lapels. "She was allowed to send a representative every other time. There's no way she can specify which of us can fight her."

"Just because you did not think to, does not mean I can't." The Moon Goddess's smile was hideous and perfect all at once.

"She's... right..." Phaidros groaned.

Cole dropped the demon to the floor in disgust, rounding on me. There was fury on his face, but behind it was concern. He would do anything for me, anything at all. But asking him to stand on the sidelines while his mate fought for her life?

"Single combat," I repeated. "No tricks."

"No tricks," she agreed. "To the death. First one to the pits loses."

CHAPTER XXXIII

I ROUNDED ON THE Moon Goddess. She was lovely, but she was scrawny. I had shifter strength, even if I couldn't access my wolf. I could beat her. She might not make it easy, but I could fight. I gripped the hilt of the sword at my side that I'd grabbed before we left. I wanted to bathe my sword in her blood and put an end to this war once and for all.

The space had cleared and elongated, leaving an arena for her and me to fight in. It was bigger than the gym rooftop I'd trained on with Cole. At the edges were her shifter ghosts, circling on all sides. At my back were Cole and Phaidros. I drew my mate's dark scent deep into my lungs. It wrapped around my insides, coating me with love. Support. He believed I could do this.

I would not fail him. I would not fail our kingdom. And most of all, I wouldn't fail *us*.

"Ready when you are, Phoebs."

Her entire face twitched at the nickname. I didn't hide my grin.

The smile faded when she lifted her hands above her head

as if in supplication.

A wash of white light fell over her, blinding us. When it faded, she was in a mass of silver armor, every inch of her body covered in the poisonous metal. A pure silver spear sat in her hand, pointed directly at me.

How was I going to defeat her if I couldn't touch her?

"Then we shall begin."

She launched the spear at me with unnatural strength. I dodged, but the next second she summoned another and threw it again.

Now, I bared my teeth at her. "How is it fair you can use your magic and I can't?"

Her initial answer was another spear. "My magic is *suppressing* your magic. You could use all the magic you liked—if you were stronger."

When she threw her next spear, I was ready. Instead of retreating, I charged, landing a high kick right to her helmet-covered head.

I collided with a *clang!*

The Moon Goddess didn't so much as flinch from inside her silver armor. This time, her newest spear slammed into me. Her movements were clunky and untested, but it didn't matter, because she packed loads of magic into every attack. What she lacked in skill, she made up for in raw power and an unending supply of silver. I tried to slash her with my blade, but the metal bounced off, not so much as scratching her armor.

This was not good.

Our dance began in earnest. I wove in and out, dodging her rainfall of silver spears while I tried to find some dent in her armor. There should've been something. But her armor wasn't normal. It wasn't made of overlapping plates of metal. Instead, it appeared solid, like it was molded to her body and constantly shifted shape to adjust as her body moved. Even her eyes were covered by bars of silver, allowing only the barest hint of her unsettling eyes to peek out.

Her attacks increased, joined by her astral magic, and it got harder to get close.

I was on the defensive. Exhaustion hit me, but worse than that was the chilling realization as she slowly amped up her attacks that this was just the beginning. *She was playing with me.*

"That is better, life-giver. Run while you can," she called across the field when I slipped past another of her spears.

"Is this all you can do?" I retorted, trying to catch my breath as I sank against the column. Hundreds of ghostly eyes met mine, their mouths open but silent. The star collars choked them, rendering them voiceless. "Throw shit at a distance, like it means something? Hiding like a coward behind your silver armor, how can you call yourself a goddess? Why don't you admit you're just scared to face me?"

I slipped behind a marble column in the nick of time as

three more spears stabbed where I'd just stood.

"Do you think this is all I can do?"

On silent command, the ghost shifters took a step forward.

"What is the meaning of this?" Cole shouted. "This is single combat. Restrain your slaves."

"I have violated no rule."

The shifters took another step forward. I kept my eyes trained on the largest one, brandishing my sword in front.

"Don't you see?" she continued. "They are part of me. They no longer are their own creatures, simply loyal subjects that I control."

The shifter at the center lunged in wolf form. I slashed into its ghostly shape. Unlike the last time, my sword made contact. The phantom disappeared, but as I swiped, its soul called out. The pained cry from my sword blow went straight through my skull.

I stumbled.

The wolves that had flanked it came forward.

I stepped back, hitting the column. Shit. I moved aside.

Oh no.

She hadn't just activated the shifters directly in front of me. She'd called on her magic to pull in every single one of her shifters. The worst part is she wasn't wrong—they were almost entirely made of her magic. Her cursed stars ran through them, giving them shape. Her collars controlled them. The only thing she didn't tamp down on was their pain. I fended off several with my sword. Each's suffering hit me squarely in the chest.

I had to hurt them to survive. They didn't deserve the pain I'd caused. But it was them or me.

The sea of creatures grew larger and larger. I tried to keep a circle of space around me, turning rapidly from side to side with my blade to keep the perimeter. I was a sitting duck. Cole couldn't reach me now, even if he could interfere. And if she wanted to hurl more of those spears, there was nowhere for me to go.

But no spears came. No, she wanted me to suffer.

"Give up," she called. "Even at your most powerful you could never beat me, and this is far from your most powerful."

On silent command, five wolves launched at me at once. I stabbed two and kicked one, but the other two landed on me, their translucent fangs drawing blood. I cried out from the pain of the ones I killed and the ones who I'd failed to defend against.

Over and over, I attacked them, but more took their place. I couldn't tell how long it went on. Even with my shifter stamina, I was flagging. There were too many. I was just one person.

The Moon Goddess laughed, the sound rising above the cacophony of wolf howls as magic amplified the sound. "These are the creatures you cherished. Look at how they turn on you. They know you're weak, and they can't resist."

I stabbed another straight through the chest. When it dissipated, I faltered, seeing the ones behind it.

"Look. These you know."

The ghost shifters around me flickered, replaced by ones I recognized. Jett. Maddox. Sabine. Other Moon-Ghost shifters we'd killed in the last trial.

"These ones knew from the start. You're weak. Unwanted. Unable to shift. And you thought you could challenge me?" She laughed again. "The most powerful creature in all the realms, and some pathetic upstart goddess thought she deserved a piece of the world."

They lunged at once. My sword clattered to the ground as Jett's fangs found my forearm. Maddox drew from my thighs.

The pain was so familiar. I hated it. I wanted to run from it. God, it was so familiar. Maybe this was how I ended. Destroyed by the same packmates who had killed me before. It hurt. It hurt so badly. I just wanted it to end, to go away. Hadn't I suffered it enough times? Should I just accept this death, alone, on my knees? If everyone wanted me dead, what choice did I have?

"Even now, I barely have to control them." Her voice echoed in my ears. "They hate you. Despise you. Aren't they right to? You abandoned them all those years ago. Came back weak and useless."

I fell to my knees, unable to stand. The worst part was, I didn't think she was lying. Always, they had hated me. All I'd ever wanted was to be free of them, to run away and never come back. But now, here I was, at their mercy again.

They had no mercy. Not in life, not in death.

Another shifter tore into my flesh.

"You are so much more than that."

There was no way Cole's words should have reached me without him yelling, but I heard my mate. My husband.

The male who believed in me. Who saw me, all of me, and thought I was enough. I didn't need a crown or magic or shifter strength in his eyes. Just being *me* was enough.

I fell on my hands and knees. With my left hand, I grabbed the blade and swung in a wild arc. I killed two of the Moon-Ghost shifters, but the rest persisted. I kicked several off, ignoring the bleeding in my legs, and regained my sword.

Somehow, on determination alone, I rebuilt my perimeter. It was only a matter of time before I was overwhelmed again. The marble beneath me was slippery with blood—and I was the only one bleeding.

But I wouldn't give up.

"Perhaps I'll offer you a final deal—submit now, while my wolves tear you to shreds, and I'll spare the other one. Oh, he'll have to give up the mantle and settle in some forgotten corner, but I can be generous. He likely will decide to join you, but at least he will have a few years to survive. Do you not want that for him?"

Half a dozen wolves hurled themselves at me, aiming for

my already weakened limbs.

I cried out. It hurt.

But I was made of hurt. I was made of hurt, and I was made of love. I wouldn't hide from the pain. I slashed them away with my blade, clarity coming with every strike.

I was made of hurt, and I wouldn't hide from the pain. Just like I hadn't with the dragon. I would feel it, because it was part of me. I couldn't outrun my past. I would always have Moon-Ghost roots. I would always be the weak Omega they'd bullied. That was who I was, but that was only part of the story.

I would embrace *every* part of myself. Mate, queen, goddess, Alpha, Omega. They couldn't be taken away from me. She had tried to cut up parts of me, to splinter my soul, but I still survived. And above all of them—I was a shifter.

I felt my wolf ripple under my skin. Not my wolf—just me. Because whether I was in my wolf form or my human form, I was still a single soul, just like Cole said. Our hearts beat together, one entity, perfectly in sync.

She thought she could control all shifters, including my own, suppressing it in her realm.

"Submit and perish with mercy, or perish for nothing."

I growled. The sound was pure wolf.

"Eloquent."

Her offer could've tempted me. It had, in another life. I'd taken the easy way out before. Made a deal, thinking it was possible I could trade my misery for everyone else's happiness.

But that wasn't how this worked. I'd never get the better end of a deal with one of these conniving creatures.

It was time I stopped making them.

My voice roughened. "What I'm saying is this—I'm not good with words." My forearms turned red as fur erupted over my skin. "I'm better with claws."

The change exploded out of me. As a wolf, I howled loudly and angrily. The wolves froze in their assault.

"How?" she sputtered. "No matter. You will go to the pits all the same."

She twisted her magic around, trying to push the wolves at me.

The wolves didn't move.

I still couldn't access my magic, but seeing me among them was its own magic. I howled again, telling them without words that I saw their pain. It was real. It was unfair.

And I would end it.

The wolves parted. The star collars tightened, trying to force them forward.

None of the shifters took a step towards me. Instead, they began to part, clearing a path to the Moon Goddess, still clad in her silver armor.

She stood there, stupidly, challenging. "You cannot harm me like that."

But I could. Because at last, I had found harmony with my

entire being. I moved slowly down the empty pathway, my teeth flashing with the urge to rip her apart. Slowly, so slowly, while the shifters continued to part, I went forward until they all finally left.

I went from stalking to running.

Running to leaping.

While the Moon Goddess stood there, overconfident in her silver armor, I landed, jaws first.

Then I ripped clean through her throat with my jaws, the silver armor shattering like glass.

CHAPTER XXXIV

T HE MOON GODDESS CRUMPLED to the floor. Blood spewed from her throat. The taste of copper filled my mouth. However she had styled herself, she still bled like the rest of us. Her face was frozen in disbelief—the most human expression she'd managed. With her death, the all-powerful control she'd had on the realm slipped away. Magic flowed back into my veins. I shifted back, summoning my vines to clothe myself and my healing powers to close the wounds I'd received from the shifter ghosts.

The ground beneath us began to shake. I leaped back, getting as far from the Moon Goddess's body as I could. The vibrations grew stronger and stronger. The marble columns that lined the arena fell, crashing down.

A pit opened right in the center of the arena. My throat constricted, memories of exactly what that pit had done in the past clogging my airway. I readied my magic, prepared to fight the under-realm itself.

But Tartarus did not claim me.

A crack opened beneath the Moon Goddess's

blood-soaked body and swallowed her whole, silver armor and all.

Once she disappeared beneath the surface, the ground smoothed itself over, as if this had never happened. But it had happened. We had succeeded—we had won the trials, and now the Moon Goddess was dead. We were free.

Two strong arms wrapped around me, embracing me from behind.

"I knew you could do it."

"How?" I tried to laugh, but the sound was too brittle. "I didn't."

Cole spun me in his arms, the certainty in his eyes capturing me entirely. "Because my wife can do anything she sets her mind to."

I grabbed the lapels of his shirt and tugged him down to kiss me. I'd feared I'd never taste my mate again, never feel him against my lips. So many times, we had failed. Had sacrificed for one another. But not today. Today, we had triumphed and had unlocked the rest of our future.

"Great work, love, but a little help wouldn't be amiss."

Reluctantly, I broke from Cole and went over to Phaidros. He had pulled himself to his knees, but his body was devastated by his mother's magic. Her death hadn't undone the damage.

I stared down at the demon. I'd felt pity for him, true. I understood his decisions had been complicated, driven by a need to wrest his freedom away from his evil mother. But that was no excuse.

"I don't see why I should."

The demon ground his pearly white teeth. "We had a deal to act as allies."

"We agreed to be allies until the trials were complete," I corrected. "I owe you nothing now."

The demon's gaze dropped. For once, he didn't argue, didn't try to twist the words. Maybe because there was no ambiguity there. No rule bound me to help him. He was too weak to make a portal. He would die here, likely within the hour from his injuries.

As much as I hated Phaidros, I was tired of the violence. It was necessary—death was essential, and I respected Cole's magic as much as my own. But my magic didn't crave death. It wanted to create life wherever it could be had.

I twisted my fingers in front of me, green sparks flying towards Phaidros and filling each puncture. The demon froze under the grips of my magic, as if unsure if I was truly going to heal him... or simply hasten his death.

I shut my eyes to concentrate, trusting Cole to keep watch. This wasn't an easy healing to do. I sensed the different magics in him, the hole from where the Moon Goddess had withdrawn her soul. My gut twisted. I could feel the brokenness of his being, not just physically, but in his very essence. When the stars on his skin had been ripped away and pierced him clean through, it had been more than a matter of skewering. It had been about desecrating his very being. For a moment, I wondered if it wouldn't be a mercy to end his suffering now and kill him. Not for spite, but just to end it.

But there was something new. Something in the demon I hadn't sensed before. I concentrated on that spark of magic. It was as though a piece of him had been locked away, stifled. My magic drew closer, circling it, then approached. I *pulled* that piece forward, filling in the gaps that had been left. Her magic was gone... but Phaidros had his own, a kind that had not been seen before.

A sharp intake of breath from Cole. My eyes snapped open.

I had healed Phaidros. His skin was mended. The stars had returned, but they weren't in the same shapes as before. Instead of the shackling, stagnant constellations, now they moved across his very skin. Judging by the night-dark wings on his back, I had done more than just heal his body. The stars on his skin moved over them as well. The wings flared wide, feathers grazing the ground. He forced himself off his knees, rolling his shoulders back as he stood.

"Thank you. I owe you a debt."

I shook my head. "No more debts, no more favors. Let's just have peace, Phaidros. The realms have longed for it."

His gaze drifted past me, to the ghost shifters who had been trapped by the Moon Goddess for ages. "Yes, they have."

I turned back to the shifters. Their star-ringed collars had fallen away when the Moon Goddess died. But they didn't move, didn't disappear. Just... looked at me, expecting some answer.

I called on my magic again, wanting to heal them. Yes, there were hundreds, if not thousands, but surely I could ease their pain. Green sparks flew through the air. I reached out to every single one with my magic, trying to heal them the way I had Phaidros.

Nothing happened.

A hand clapped down on my shoulder. I looked up at Cole. He shook his head.

"I have to save them," I protested.

"There is more than one way to do that. You saved the demon—for some reason—with your gifts of healing. You saved all of us with your claws and your bravery. But this is my domain."

The King of the Dead turned to face the army of ghost shifters.

"You have been wronged." His voice boomed across the open space. "You were led to believe your journey ended here, at the whims of a mad goddess. But it does not. You have felt agony that I can only imagine. But today, that ends. Today, you are free. Your souls are free to find rest."

Cole's magic exploded across the arena. But it wasn't his angry, hostile shadows that filled every inch of the space. Instead, it was a comforting darkness that complemented the night sky around us. It stretched forward, beckoning. The compassion for his fellow shifters, for the people whom I had loved.

One took a small step forward. It broke from the mass, walking, exploring, while the others hesitated. They had been deceived before.

But Cole's magic offered only exactly what he told them. Freedom. Rest.

Peace.

The lone shifter went farther and farther until it was nothing more than a speck of light. Then it winked out, fading away into the darkness. A few more stepped forward, then the whole group as one. As if they finally sensed the truth, the possibility they had been denied. The mass of shifters took off, running as if in slow motion and then fading in the distance, their blue glow dimming until there was nothing besides the darkness of space, pierced only by the glow of the moon.

The ground around us began to shake once more. *Tartarus, again?*

Instead of a pit opening up, it was the edges of the arena that began to fall away. Fragments fell apart, the marble floor cracking at a distance. When it reached the collapsed columns, those too fell into the ether. It was almost peaceful to watch.

Phaidros drew closer. "The realm is falling apart. An empty realm cannot exist. My moth—the Moon Goddess sustained this place for millennia. Then she siphoned the souls of the shifters to sustain it. That was why she wanted control of the other realms. She felt she deserved a throne in a true realm, not content with the kingdom of her own making. It was unnatural. The universe is setting things back in order."

I could feel it, as he said it. The magic of the realm was nearly gone, dwindling to nothing. Pieces slowly crumbled, falling away as though gravity just barely weighed on them.

I looked back out into the darkness. There were still stars in the distance. But they were normal stars, tiny things. Not giant bright masses made of the souls of imprisoned shifters. "Will they go to the underworld?"

Cole shook his head. "No. For them, their time in the cycle is done. They will go somewhere... beyond."

"I wonder where that is," I mused. I'd been raised my entire life to think that the stars were the ultimate destination.

"I pray we do not find out for a very long time." Cole dipped his head towards mine. "Now, we go home."

Chapter XXXV

I HADN'T KNOWN WHAT we would be walking back into, but the last thing I expected was for Hecate to inform us there was going to be a ball.

We had done the impossible—restored the balance of the realms, freed the souls of countless shifters, and kept ourselves from dying—again—and falling permanently into the pits of Tartarus.

And we weren't alone in our celebrating. Daphne and the others had gone back to the world of the living. She gave me a fierce hug before leaving.

"I'll still be able to see you, right?" she asked. "It won't throw the universe into life-threatening peril for you to visit your best friend?"

"Nothing could keep me from you," I promised. "Totally safe."

Hecate arched a brow, no doubt ready with a thousand reasons as to why it was a bad idea, but I meant what I said. Besides, as long as I didn't kill anyone while there—and maiming was totally fine—I'd be safe. Now that the Moon

Goddess was defeated, there wasn't a single being who could match my power.

My gaze slid to Cole, who was currently leaning against the wall, eyes firmly trained on me. *Well. Maybe one.*

Daphne hugged me again. "You are *so* transparent."

"Huh?"

She rolled her eyes. "I get that you want to jump your mate"—I opened my mouth to protest, but she didn't hesitate—"but if you can tear yourself away from whatever private party the two of you have planned, the packs are going to get together for a party."

"The packs?" I questioned.

She nodded. "Wind-Blood, the Fangs... and Moon-Ghost."

"Is that a good idea?"

She shrugged. "Probably not. Honestly, all three packs have been decimated by this war. Moon-Ghost lost all its Alphas, and most of those who had Alpha potential. The survivors have been mingling. We were kept separate for so long, and where did it lead? A party seems like a good way to let off some steam and start socializing."

"No way there won't be half a dozen matches breaking out and someone will have their intestines clawed out before the night is done."

My best friend grinned. "Like I said, letting off some steam. It's a shifter party after all."

Maybe she was right. Maybe this problem had gotten worse with the way our packs had become insular and distrusting of any others. Part of me didn't want the Moon-Ghosts to get adopted into other packs. They'd been so damn cruel to me. But those who had—Jett, Sabine, Maddox—were now dead. And they weren't all evil.

"Sounds like a blast."

"So you'll come?" she prodded.

"Wouldn't miss it."

She grinned. "Perfect. Just remember, us non-queenly shifters dress a bit more casual than the whole ball gown thing."

"I'll keep that in mind."

After Daphne and the others went through the portal, I made my way to Cole.

"We have a lot to do."

"Later," Cole huffed. "I believe a private party was mentioned."

My jaw dropped open. "You were eavesdropping!"

"I was," he said, shameless as ever. Then he pushed off the wall, closing the distance between us. "And I can scent that's exactly what you had in mind."

I wanted to deny it, but I was a shit liar. Apparently, near-death experiences got me going.

I expected Cole to teleport us back to the bedroom. He did nothing of the sort. Instead, the doors to the throne room slammed shut. He grabbed my wrists and spun me around, pressing me into the wall. With a swift jerk of his hand, my vine-made clothing was ripped off. He buried himself inside me without a moment's delay.

I gasped at the contact. The sudden fullness. But I didn't protest, because I wanted it. I rocked my hips up to meet him.

"Someone could come in," I warned.

"They wouldn't dare" was his answering growl.

He nipped at the mate mark on my neck and I arched.

Cole was fierce in his movements, relentless as he pounded into me. My first orgasm came quickly. I gasped under him, my moans echoing off the walls of the massive room.

"That's it. I want the whole palace to hear you."

I couldn't have contained the sounds of my pleasure if I'd tried. I expected him to continue, to go for his own release, but instead, his pace slowed. His magic wrapped around us, transporting us.

To our bedroom?

No, only across the room.

To his throne.

He moved our bodies deftly, so I was in his lap. His fingers pressed into my hips, holding me in place on his erection. The sensitivity between my legs was heightened in the wake of my orgasm, but Cole gave me only the briefest moment to recover. I went to move up and down on him, wanting to bring him to the edge of pleasure.

He growled. "At my pace."

His hands gripped me even more tightly. He controlled my pace, lifting me and lowering me with utter dominance. All too quickly, I was aching for more. I tried to speed up the process, but he was having none of that.

"Greedy for another, so soon?"

"I'm always greedy for you." The words were out before I could think.

"Good." He slammed me down with enough force to make me cry out. Pain twisted in the pleasure, making my eyes go wide. "Then you understand how I feel."

I nodded, arching in his lap.

"You understand that you are my heart. My soul. My goddess. My queen, looking so fucking perfect on my throne that it's taking everything in me not to come right now."

"I understand you're my mate, my king." It was a fight to get the words out. "You're more than my soul. You're my home when there's not a shred of me left."

"You're *mine.*"

That might have been my favorite title of all. "And you're *holding back.*"

The words snapped the last of Cole's control. He thrust up against me, pounding me as I met him with each thrust. Pleasure built in my body once more. A slower build than before, but even more potent.

Cole came with a roar, his gaze fixed on me. I tipped over

the edge, but I didn't let myself close my eyes or throw my head back. No, I wanted to see him as he finally let go. Here, he looked perfect on his throne. Instead of the imperial, inscrutable ruler, he was my mate, coming apart while inside me.

The forces of the universe could do their best to rip us apart. Could try to destroy us.

Let them try, I dared them. What was between us was powerful enough to defeat any enemy.

CHAPTER XXXVI

OUR APPEARANCE AT OUR own ball was rather brief. We wore our crowns, our finest clothes, and danced across the hall, opening the dance floor. Food from the kitchens piled high at the edges of the hall, which, after the first dance, was where Cole dragged me. With our weeks in the library leading up to the final trial, I hadn't had much of an appetite. A hungry mate, Cole informed me with a growl, was unacceptable.

Of course, once we left the dance floor, people were eager to approach us. I greeted each with a warm smile. These were the ones I had fought for. This was a celebration that had been earned with blood and death. Our people deserved to be part of our triumph, so we spoke to as many as we could in the span of two hours before disappearing without making excuses.

Perks of being the monarchs of a realm—no one calls you on your bad manners.

Because as much as I wanted to surround myself with my subjects, now that they were safe from danger, my longing to be with my friends overruled that. We changed before leaving.

"If you keep looking at me like that, we won't be going anywhere."

"Daphne would never forgive me," I grumbled, not tearing my eyes from Cole.

The King of Hell was in jeans.

And he looked damn good in them.

In the castle, when I'd first come to the realm, he'd worn fairly neutral, timeless outfits, while the castle had provided the more modern cuts I was familiar with. Since moving to the castle, he'd worn more formal clothes befitting his station.

But jeans suited him just fine. What's more, Cole didn't care half as much about upsetting Daphne by being late as I did.

I forced open a portal between us. We landed where Daphne had told us to—Moon Rock. Or at least, that was what it had once been called. With the Moon Goddess's tyranny revealed, the land had been recast as Pack Point, in honor of the fact it was where the three territories converged.

No one noticed our arrival right away, which gave me time to take in the sight. It wasn't something I had ever thought was possible in this lifetime. In my last reincarnation, it had been my dream.

The packs mingled freely among each other. I could taste the differences by scent—the familiar scents of Moon-Ghost, the earthy, breeze-coated scents from Wind-Blood, and the faint motor oil scent that clung to the Fangs. But looking at them, that was all. Some packmates clumped together, especially with Moon-Ghost having been the enemy just a day ago, but wolves craved acceptance. The shifters would follow the strongest wolf they trusted, and as long as they weren't betraying some loyalty to do it, the pack divide wasn't impossible to overcome.

My best friend had done all of this. Pride burned bright in my chest. While Cole and I had fought a war between Hell and the heavens, she had taken on countless challenges in the land of the living. Because while I had always wanted to leave, *her* dream had been to stay and make a better world for everyone. It wouldn't be easy. A successful party was one thing, but a lifetime was another. But if anyone was up for the challenge, Daphne Rourke was.

"Find her. I'll be here," Cole assured me.

I flashed a smile at him. "I thought you would want to keep an eye and make sure no one bothers me."

Cole raised a brow at me. "My mate can take care of herself. If anyone makes any untoward advances, despite you being painted with our blended scent and my mate mark, I have no doubt you'll put them in their place."

I grinned at the pride in his words.

"But," he continued, "if you'd like me to dismember anyone out of sentimentality, I'd be more than happy to oblige."

I patted his arm. "Let's try to make it through the night without maiming anybody."

A curious male shifter glanced over at us, and Cole growled at him. "No promises."

"I can handle myself, remember?" The male was a bit *friendly* in his appraising looks, but my mate mark was on full display, and no wolf would disrespect that.

"Yet I find myself rather sentimental."

I rolled my eyes and walked off, trusting Cole not to immediately hunt the shifter down. Despite his words, he was confident that I belonged to him—and him, me—just as I was confident he wouldn't actually gouge out the eyes of any male who looked at me.

A whimper came from behind me and I suppressed a wince. Okay, reasonably confident.

I found Daphne embroiled in a heated conversation with Ian, the Fang Alpha.

"Am I interrupting?" I asked.

She lit up, whatever argument forgotten as she embraced me. "You made it!"

"I did."

She released me, her gaze going up and down. "I can't get over how different you look."

A glance down at myself revealed I looked the most normal I ever had. "This is the exact same thing I wore all the time, before..."

I trailed off. Somehow it never got less awkward to say "before I died."

Daphne shook her head, long tresses of hair falling in front of her face before she brushed them back quickly. "That's just the thing. It's not the clothes you wear. It's how you carry yourself."

"You mean I'm not constantly cowering in fear of the Alpha Clique?" I laughed. It felt good and strange to be able to laugh at the figures that had once defined the bars of my prison.

"No, you were never half as afraid of them as you *should've* been. You gave as good as you got, even if you couldn't physically win a fight the way you can now. It's more than that. There's this sense of... peace around you. Like you've finally found your place. The pack where you belong."

She was right. I had found a place. It wasn't a conventional pack—Daphne would always be part of mine no matter where we were—but I had found people who cared for me. People I would do anything to protect.

"I guess I did. This dying thing worked out after all." Across the crowd, I found a pair of amber eyes watching me, and my heart fluttered.

Daphne twisted to follow my line of sight, a sad smile twisting on her face.

"Thinking of Hector?" I asked quietly.

"In the chaos, it was easy to put my grief aside. But now that everything is done, it keeps bubbling up. I wish it would stop," she confessed.

I wrapped her in my arms, squeezing her tight. "You have to let yourself feel that grief. You owe it to both of you."

"I guess." Her voice wavered. "Is he really in that awful place? When we were in the library, I came across a book that talked about the under-realm. It was awful, Avery. Awful."

I wished I could lie to her. "He is. That's what happens in the cycle."

Wetness touched my shirt. I gripped Daphne closer, wishing I could take away the pain.

"Will he ever be free? Like how you got free?" she asked.

"Maybe," was the most I could manage. "It's not the way of things. Tartarus doesn't like to part with the souls that fall to it."

Yet as I spoke, another thought came to me. The barest glimmer of possibility. I tried to push it aside and focus on comforting my friend, but she sensed the change in me. She might not have magic of her own, but she had known me since we were pups.

"What is it?"

I shook my head. "I can't talk about it now. Just... try to enjoy the party, Daphne. He wanted this for you, whatever happened. Hector wanted you to be happy."

Her gaze slid behind me, and she nodded slowly in acknowledgment. Instinct told me it was the Wind-Blood Alpha.

I let her go. There was someone I needed to find.

I left in search of the scent of cloves.

CHAPTER XXXVII

"WHAT ARE WE SEARCHING for, little wolf?"

The moment I'd left Daphne, Cole had come to my side, sensing my need.

"The Libra demon."

I didn't need to specify *which* Libra demon.

"He could be anywhere," Cole pointed out.

I shook my head. "He could. But he's nosy and he has nowhere to go. His home was destroyed. He's certainly not welcome in our realm. I think he'll be here." No doubt lingering in the shadows.

"Then let's find him."

My search took me deep into the woods. The same woods I'd fled to all that time ago. I braced for unpleasant memories to slam into me, as they often had before, but none came. Maybe because, even though I hadn't wanted to die, it had brought me back to Cole.

Or maybe because those who had wronged me were all dead now too.

I caught the scent of cloves a moment before Phaidros

emerged from the shadows.

His wings were bent stiffly behind his back, drawn in like he wished they'd go away. I reached for Cole with my magic to let him know I'd found our quarry.

"Looking for me, love?"

I nodded.

He sighed. "And here I thought you meant what you said about me not owing you a favor. What could you possibly need already?"

That favor thing really bugged him. "You don't owe me a favor for saving your life, though a thank you wouldn't be amiss."

"I thanked you before," he pointed out.

"Never hurts to hear it again." I waited a beat, but obviously, no such expression was coming. Phaidros obviously likened debts to being weak, and a thank you was an admission of the debt. He might have been willing when he'd been on the brink of death, but nothing less would compel him. I let it go. I didn't need thanks, though it was fun to needle the demon. I had done it because it was the right thing. "I wanted to talk to you because we didn't finish our game."

Cole appeared in my periphery. Phaidros's head tipped towards my husband and then back to me. "I believe we did. And even if not, the point is moot, darling. The Moon Goddess is rotting in the pits of Tartarus, where she belongs."

"We agreed to a trial for every realm," I reminded him.

"The under-realm is a realm as much as that of the living, the dead, and the heavens."

Phaidros drew a breath. "No."

"We had a deal, demon," Cole reminded him.

He didn't probe me for details on my plan. He trusted me.

"You've both been there. Can you honestly tell me you want to go back?" Phaidros hissed in disbelief.

"I don't," I admitted. "I'd like nothing more than to move on with my life and forget this whole thing ever happened. But it did. And I owe it to those who fought for us to fight for them now too."

Phaidros growled. "If you want to walk back into the shackles of eternal damnation, find another demon foolish enough to take you." He lifted his hand to make a portal.

The tree behind him sprang to life, branches wrapping around him. Phaidros strained against the bonds in outrage.

"It has to be you. I sensed it in your magic when I healed you. It's like you said—if the Moon Goddess was your mother, your father is Tartarus itself. You're the only one who can take us there." I hesitated for a moment, then added, "Please."

"And if you don't have the good sense to take my wife up on her request, I can make the alternative a lot less pleasant."

Dark magic swirled around the tree branches, echoing Cole's words.

Phaidros bared his teeth at me. "Fine If you want to return to that hellhole, be my guest."

"Hell, I rule," I corrected. "So the term doesn't really fit."

Phaidros hissed at me again but stopped fighting against the branches. I let him go. A massive, yellow portal sparked around us.

"Now's as good a time as any to lose our souls, I suppose."

TARTARUS WAS EVERY BIT as awful as I remembered. The same darkness I had walked through before engulfed us. It swallowed all the scents and smothered my magic. I tried to reach for Cole, but there was nothing. A cold sweat broke out across my brow. *This was a mistake.*

"Enough theatrics," Cole snapped, sounding less terrified out of his mind and more annoyed.

The darkness cleared away. In its wake, it revealed the same place Cole had been shackled, the silver manacles still hanging from twin towering rocks. I didn't hide my growl. Cole, who was only inches away, was rigid. Not a single muscle in his body moved. I wasn't sure he was even breathing.

That was what this place did. It dredged up your worst memories, the worst horrors it could inflict on you, and made you live them over and over again. Made you think that life could not get better and that the safer thing was to give up. That it was better to feel the same cruel torture a hundred times over than to hope it might be different *this* time—and be proven wrong.

I reached for my mate. "You're not there."

"Never again," he vowed.

I echoed the words, but he wasn't done.

"Never again will I let this place keep us apart."

A warm flicker of emotion sparked in my chest. There were some things the under-realm couldn't take away from us. Our promises echoed between us. Our bond was sewn across centuries; it spanned lifetimes. No one would ever take him from me again. I wouldn't allow it.

"I told you I would see both of you again before the end of time. How unwise of you to hasten your return."

My spine stiffened as the realm's voice echoed in my head.

"They come to make a *deal*," Phaidros spat. No doubt he would've disappeared in a moment given the opportunity, but he had vowed to the Styx he would be present at all trials to moderate.

"I am not beholden to bargains you make."

"He speaks for you. He is part of you," Cole countered.

"He is his own creature."

"He is," I agreed, earning an arched brow from Cole and a surprised look from Phaidros. I shrugged at my mate. This wasn't a winning argument. "But we need to carry out a trial for this realm just the same as we did the others. I want to bargain for the freedom of the souls in your domain."

The under-realm was silent. We waited several moments,

but no response came. The sweat on my palms slid against my fingers as I clenched them into fists. We couldn't let the realm refuse.

"You may not be beholden to your son's agreements, but you do have a penchant for deals. I will offer you an irresistible prize if you participate." Cole strode forward, nearing the same altar he'd been imprisoned at. "The same prize as before." He turned back to me. "Every instinct is screaming at me not to do this, but know this, mate. I trust you above everything." He turned away from me again, as if the words were too difficult to get out while looking at me. "I will offer the same prize of the other trials—the souls of Avery and I."

I swallowed. I hoped I was worthy of the honor of his trust.

No. Screw that. I would make sure I was worth it by winning the trial.

"Your kingdoms made sense to fight for. You are foolish to risk your souls. You think because I have allowed each of you to leave once before it is nothing for you to leave again. This greed for more will be your downfall, life-giver."

"It's not greed." My words were soft but strong. "It's about doing what's right. Eternal torture is about as far as you can get from right as it gets."

"How quick you are to denounce the natural order of things."

The cavern shook around us. The ground beneath me

split. I hurled myself across to get closer to Cole. He dove for me and we collided, rolling away from falling stalagmites. Phaidros floated over to us easily. Earthquakes were a lot less scary when you had freaking *wings*. The scene around us didn't change in an instant. Instead, it was as though the realm was carefully rearranging the set around us. The floor slid up on the cavern walls. The ceiling fell to the floor, walls bending wide and then coming dangerously close before receding again.

"Tell me again that you wish to free every soul. That you believe they do not deserve that which I give them by right."

The scene widened to reveal the Moon Goddess. She looked nothing like the last time I had seen her. Gone was her silver armor; gone were her gossamer sheer robes. She was nude, but it wasn't a seductive nude or even a natural one like after shifters changed shape. Her body was on display in ice. Arms spread in front of herself protectively. Her eyes were wide, stuck at unequal sizes.

Her pupils widened at our presence, eyes shifting to follow our movement while her mouth was frozen in a permanent scream.

I parted my lips to tell the pits it was cruel because it was. But could I say it wasn't what she deserved? The goddess who had played with the lives of countless shifters, tormenting them for years upon years?

I couldn't.

"I can feel your loathing, life-giver. Still so eager to fight for the souls of the fallen?"

I swallowed. Cole's jaw was ground shut. He didn't have an answer either. After how she'd tormented me, if anything, Cole likely felt she deserved worse.

But this was about more than grudges.

"She's not the only one I'm fighting for."

"Very well."

The scene shifted. Various figures appeared around us as the realm showed off its wares. Medusa, who did little more than hiss. The nixie. Demons who had challenged me. I braced for any of my old pack members, but they'd been set free to settle in the land beyond the stars. Was I glad they weren't in the realm? I hated them. Jett dying hadn't absolved him of a single sin in my book. But while I wanted him gone, I didn't need him to suffer for eternity. What would it accomplish? No doubt several creatures wanted me to rot in Tartarus, the Moon Goddess included. Was their hatred any less valid than mine?

Okay, yes, in a lot of cases, it was. But the point was, no one deserved eternal torture.

"I will give you a gift, life-giver."

I raised my head from the latest torments the under-realm displayed and looked to the emptiness above. "What's that?"

"Rescind your challenge, and I will allow you and

your death god to leave with your souls intact."

Phaidros shot me a look, clearly screaming internally at me to take the deal.

"No."

"If you do not want the souls of those who belong to me, what do you desire?"

"I want them to get to choose their destiny. I don't want more subjects. I want to break this cycle of life, then death, then eternal torture. Let them live, then when they die come to our realm to rest. When they wish to be reborn, set the souls free, the way mine was, to reincarnate. And when they are truly done, let them disappear to the nothingness beyond the stars. They deserve a chance to find where they belong."

"You ask a large price."

I shrugged. "I'm prepared to pay up. Here's what our challenge is. If I can convince the souls to leave, we win. If any stay behind, we lose." It was a big gamble. I was betting everything on it.

"The challenge is mine to declare, life-giver. You overstep."

Considering I was risking eternal torture for both Cole and myself, it was reasonable to say I was betting with chips I couldn't afford to lose. A little rudeness to the realm that would be torturing us for eternity if we lost? All the more incentive to *win*. "Since Cole and I are the ones laying our souls on the line, I think I should get to make the rules." I turned to Phaidros. "Do you agree this is a fair challenge to preside over?"

The demon nodded.

"Very well. I look forward to your return to my realm. For I recall, when you last intruded, you tried to force my subjects to leave and failed."

He was right. I had tried to make a bunch of the realm's victims escape with me, and I'd been summarily rejected.

The setting shifted around us. Gone was the empty space—now we were at the sight that had been burned into my mind when I'd last come. Miles and miles of torture.

"Did you truly try to rescue the souls trapped here?" Cole asked quietly, surveying the area around us.

"You were my priority, but yeah," I admitted. "It didn't seem right. But none would leave with me. In fact, they seemed to hate me for trying to take them away."

Cole tensed. "And now we need to convince all of them to do just that when not even one would before. Dare I hope there's a plan?"

I nodded. "There is. We're not going to convince them to leave." I drew in a sharp breath, taking a step towards the nearest pillar, where some long-forgotten creature was hung upside-down, his limbs at unnatural angles. "We're going to ask."

And so the process began. I slid down to my knees, coming eye level with the tormented soul.

When I came into view, his unfocused gaze slid around, trying to detect the change in his environment. I went for the chains, but as he hurled oath after oath at me, I gave up and simply asked—"Do you want to be free?"

The soul hesitated. This was the curse of Tartarus. There is no hope; there is no escape. They weren't just etched into the entrance of the realm, they were burned into the existences of every creature unfortunate enough to be here.

But they were lies. Because there was *always* hope. You could always pick another path, no matter how terrible the current one was.

My magic stirred under my skin. I nearly jolted from the sensation, like I was suddenly able to inhale when something had choked me. I braced for it to disappear again, but no. It stayed, as if it had never left.

"You can be free," I repeated. "You can choose what happens to you. If you want to escape back to the underworld. If you want a fresh shot at life. Or if you're done, and you just want it to be over—you can have that too." My magic flared, green light encasing us. The unfocused eyes looked at me with new awareness in them. "Or you can stay. It's all up to you."

I waited. I waited a thousand years in that moment.

And then, in a quiet, shaky voice, he replied, "I want rest. Eternal rest."

It was Cole's magic that I drew on. I wasn't sure exactly how. Maybe because it was twin to mine, maybe simply because we were blended in every way. But my green life magic turned to the black of death, and I gave the soul the true death. His chains broke.

He disappeared.

I turned back to face Cole. His expression was slack with awe. I offered a half-smile before turning to the next prisoner. "We have a lot of work to do."

Time was meaningless in Tartarus. Cole and I went from person to person for hours, days, weeks.

But each one chose to leave. Some wanted the final death, like the first. Others wanted to return to the underworld. Few were brave enough to venture back to the realm of the living and discard all their memories.

When I found Hector, I sobbed. He was without his always gleaming armor, his once bulky muscles atrophied into weak lumps. The realm had picked a particularly cruel torment for him—he was chained, watching others die, over and over. His sword was permanently out of reach from his bound hands. For a protector like him, there could be nothing worse. It was hard to ask him what his choice was, because the truth was, I wanted to beg his forgiveness for getting him killed. In equal measure, I wanted to demand he come with me to see Daphne, who still mourned him.

But I did none of that. Like the rest, I asked, not biasing him. It had to be *his* choice. He would have to choose to abandon the torment. He would have to decide he was willing to walk away from the destruction in front of him and take his own chance.

And he did. He chose to reincarnate in the realm of the living, rather than come back to the kingdom. My life-gift broke the ties and sent him away. I wondered if I would ever find him again.

On and on and on. Until we reached the very last soul.

The most recent to have come to the pits—the Moon Goddess.

The realm parted the ice around her just enough for her frozen lips to move. Before I could ask her, though, the realm spoke again.

"You have proved your point, life-giver. I will offer you another boon—you may leave this one with me. Just one final soul. You hate her. You do not need to show mercy. Leave her here, and you will still win and take the rest with you."

I hesitated. I could have everything I wanted and still leave the Moon Goddess to pay for her sins.

This time, I didn't look at Cole to silently ask his thoughts. His palm fell to my shoulder, reassuring me that whatever decision I made he would back me.

Her eyes were hateful. There was no pleading in them. She might decide to stay in the pits for spite. Would that force me to lose? It wasn't clear, and I was too terrified to ask.

But I didn't have the right to govern another soul so absolutely. Just as the Moon Goddess didn't. Just as Tartarus didn't.

"Thank you, but I decline." There was no kindness in my voice when I spoke to the goddess. "Choose, Phoebe. Do you want to stay here for eternity? Or do you want to free yourself from this miserable realm?"

The Moon Goddess stared at me for ages. Ice edged in and out of her face, as if wanting to resume its job torturing her.

My heart pounded so loudly that I was convinced even in the ice she could hear it.

I hated her. Truly, desperately.

Maybe I should've left her here. But who would I be then? The wolf who had her own choices taken away again and again, to turn around and do that to someone else?

At last she spoke.

"I could choose to trap you here with me." Her words were clearer than any of the others, likely because she hadn't been driven entirely mad yet by the realm.

"You could," Cole agreed. "You could continue to harm those who have done nothing to you, if that is all you wish to be. Despite the current setting, you hold all the power. Power you have abused time and time again. Or you could make a choice based on what you want, not what you wish for others to not have. You spent all those lifetimes trapped in a fake realm. You have your choice of any of them now, even ours. What will you pick?"

Silence reigned for a long moment.

"I will choose…" She trailed off, and I didn't so much as breathe until she spoke again. "I choose to find a new path. Into the nothingness, the land beyond the stars, whatever you wish to call it. I have had enough of the realms I have seen so far."

"Very well."

The death magic erupted around us. Darkness flooded the scene, blinding me. When it cleared a second later, the ice was empty.

We had won.

Chapter XXXVIII

TARTARUS LET US GO without a word.

We had truly won.

The return was a blur. Phaidros brought us out, and warned the doors to the pits were sealed even to him now. The cycle had broken. No more would souls face eternal torture at the end of their lives. Phaidros did not take us directly back to the underworld. Instead, he brought us back to the land of the living.

Though ages seemed to have passed in Tartarus, the night was just winding down, shifters lingering around Pack Point.

"My father granted you a final boon, for besting him three times." He gave me a reproachful look. "I'd advise against trying for a fourth."

"A boon?"

He pointed as a figure emerged in the crowd, popping into existence. At the sight of the familiar broad shoulders, my knees shook.

Hector.

"The other souls who chose to reincarnate will have to wait

and be reincarnated anew. But for this one… he is restored to the form he was in, except, of course, he is now alive."

The soldier didn't spot me. Instead, he marched purposefully to Daphne. My best friend, sensing the change, broke away from Xander and ran to him. Something lightened in my chest for the first time in ages. *We had really done it.*

Cole took a step forward to bring us over to them, but I grabbed his hand and shook my head. Later. The two split away from the party, no doubt with a lot to catch up on. I turned to thank Phaidros for what he had done—somehow I doubted the pits had decided to grant this specific gift all on their own—but true to form, the demon was already gone.

"Let's go home," Cole said softly.

Home. The place I had longed for all my life. "I'd like nothing better."

Though the party in the living realm was wrapping up, the ball in the underworld was still going strong. The room was filled to the brim, the mountain of food freshly replenished. Cole was more than ready to drag me away into an empty hallway and celebrate in our own right, but Hecate got to us first.

"Soteria."

The enchantress was in a deep blue dress, the same color as a starless sky. Her raven black hair was pinned back, loose waves falling through, her cheekbones prominent. Her violet eyes were narrowed in accusation.

"Hecate," I greeted.

"Is it at all *possible* you have something to do with the several hundred thousand souls that have just arrived in our kingdom?" The enchantress's eye was actually twitching.

How to put it delicately... "Um, yes."

"I expected as much. It was not enough for you to disrupt the balance of the universe to save *one* soul, is it, Soteria?"

I grinned. "This is the last time, I promise. But how come you didn't accuse Cole? He was with me."

She loosed a beleaguered sigh. "Because *he* would only go for you. You're the only one crazy enough to keep going back there."

"Very true," Cole agreed. "Let's go address our new subjects."

Cole brought us with his magic to the top of the massive gates that surrounded the city, or what had been left of them. From our position, we could see for miles. And every inch was filled with newly returned creatures. Some, I had no doubt, would cause trouble. Others were just unfortunate victims.

No matter. I would find a place for all of them.

But perhaps the most surprising part of the view wasn't the people on the ground, but instead, the sky. The sky that had been stained bloodred for as long as I'd remembered, even in my last lifetime. Now, it appeared just as it had in my dreams—the same soothing night sky as appeared in the land of the living. There was no moon or stars, but it filled the space all the same.

Cole and I exchanged a look, a thought passing between us in an instant. *We hadn't destroyed the natural order of the world. We had finally set it right.*

"Welcome back to the underworld." Cole's voice was loud, his magic projecting the words so all could hear. "You will find, for many of you, this is not the same place you remember. This is no longer Hell. Instead, you are in the underworld. Neither good nor bad. This place is what you make of it. No longer will the threat of eternal torture loom over you." He lifted a hand, gesturing to the sky. "These are new times."

He quieted, and I took that as my cue. "Thank you for coming with us." The same magic Cole used to amplify his voice took hold of mine. "I know it's scary to leave what you know, however terrible. I'm glad you did. Things are different now. If you've come here, it may take time to find your place. I will help you. If you decide you want to leave, to reincarnate and return to the world of the living for a fresh chance, I will help you with that as well."

My magic took hold of the crowd, the spark of life and possibility, touching each of them, the same way it had in Tartarus.

"Should you decide instead you are ready for eternal peace, then I will take that as my duty to guide you there as well." Cole's death magic replaced mine, following his words.

Wary, yet hopeful looks were exchanged throughout the

crowd.

My heart was full when I spoke next. "This place has been my home, and now, I hope you will find your own home here as well."

A *home*. I had wanted it for myself, and I wanted it for them. The wariness faded.

"If you have any questions this evening," Cole added, "seek out the witch, Hecate. Because though your queen would spend the entire night helping you, she has fought hard for you, and my wife has earned an evening of rest."

I spun to argue with Cole, but he flashed me an unabashed grin and teleported us back to our bedroom. Before I could get a word out, his lips were on me with bruising intensity.

"Hecate's not going to like that."

He snorted. "She'll handle it."

He dragged me into another kiss, lifting me onto the vanity where he wedged himself between my thighs.

"Rest, huh?"

"I thought that sounded more polite than 'I plan to fuck my wife until she's too tired to give me a godsdamn heart attack with her next plan.' But don't worry, little wolf, I'll make you scream loudly enough that no one in the city will have *any* questions."

I flushed at his words. "We have a lot of work to do."

His expression softened without losing any of the intensity that lit his amber eyes. "We'll figure it out. We always do." He adjusted his grip. "But right now... now is for *us*."

I wasn't arguing anymore.

This time, Cole didn't stop at kissing. Our clothes fell to the ground in tatters, shifted claws shredding them without restraint. This was the man I had fought for, killed for. I would love him no less fiercely than I would fight for him.

Across realms. Across lifetimes.

For eternity.

Cole buried himself in me, and I reveled at the closeness. It was more than a physical sensation. I wanted to feel him in every part of me. True to his word, I screamed. I moaned, I pleaded, and Cole forced out every emotion I'd locked away to get through our final fights.

He might be the king of the realm, and I might be its queen. But we belonged to each other first.

Dawn's light was trickling through the window by the time we finally collapsed in the bed. Even exhausted, our magics played with each other, green and black sparks filling the room. Two halves of a whole. Life and death. We had power over both, while we sat in the middle—not the final death, not alive. A place where we'd watch over the millions of souls that lived in that exact same space.

"We've made a big commitment," I mused, my head resting on Cole's chest. His fingers were laced in my hair, softly combing through the strands.

He chuckled. "Overseeing the cycle of souls? What could

be hard about that?"

I grinned, tucking myself into the crook of his arm. We had signed up for *forever*.

"Do you know what happens now to the souls?" I asked. "The ones who escaped the Moon Goddess's realms, and the ones that your magic led into darkness?"

He shook his head. "Even I do not know what lies beyond."

For a moment, there was no more sound than our soft inhales and exhales. My entire universe was the rise and fall of my mate's chest.

I swallowed, meeting his amber gaze. "Will you stay with me until we go into that darkness together?"

The King of the Underworld lifted my chin with a crooked finger, pressing his lips to mine. "I can think of no greater honor, little goddess."

EPILOGUE

"WHEN YOU SAID WE'D have a honeymoon, I didn't think it would take several years to happen."

Cole arched a brow at me. "Need I remind you, you were the one who insisted on seeing all the newly freed souls settled. Which given the nature of the pits, was not *quick*. I was ready to go the first day we got back from that harebrained trip to the pits."

"Hey, you *agreed* to that harebrained trip," I reminded him.

It didn't matter how much time passed, we still bickered with each other. I might have teased him about it having been several years, but the truth was, time had flown by. It seemed like only yesterday we'd returned from Tartarus and changed the order of the universe permanently. Taking care of all the souls—guiding them to where they wanted to go, whether in our kingdom to rest, to reincarnate in the land of the living, or to fade into the ether—on top of running an entire realm—which was no longer Hell, with all the bad

PR associated with it, but simply the underworld again—was several full-time jobs stacked together in a trench coat posing as something a person could reasonably accomplish.

I eyed the male next to me. Well, two people. Because though Cole might tease me now, he was every bit as committed. He took his duties as King and Alpha seriously. The same way I had found my home with him, we had helped countless others find a place where they belonged.

"Of course I agreed. Any male knows the first rule of a happy marriage is to back up his mate in all her *harebrained* schemes."

I huffed to cover the fact I still got butterflies when he called me his mate. Even now, his mate mark was on full display. Partly because I'd freshened it last night, right after he'd announced that he was done waiting, we were going on our honeymoon, and Hecate could rule in our absence or the realm could burn for all he cared.

"Really? Then why were we arguing over whether to install a second library or expand the main one last week?" I'd wanted to build a second, smaller library since ours was nearly busting at the seams. Cole had argued we could just bend physics with magic and expand it. There had been several heated arguments before Hecate reminded us we could simply do both.

"Because I'm happy to know my little wolf likes to argue." Cole smirked. "And she really likes making up after those arguments."

I raised a brow. "Are you implying you pick fights with me just to have make-up sex after?"

"Do you want me to admit that, or would you rather we leave it unsaid?"

I growled. Cole's smirk widened.

"If you'd like a spot for angry sex, that boulder over there is the perfect height for me to bend you over."

He pointed to an outcropping of rocks at the edge of the path. My cheeks warmed, his words conjuring an image immediately of me, exposed in the outdoors, while he pressed my chest into the cold stone. I fought a shiver.

His voice dropped to a low rumble. "I'm always more than happy to oblige my mate."

I forced myself to turn away from the stone and keep moving. "You're not getting off that easily." He grinned, and I flushed all over again. "You know what I mean. I was promised a secluded little cabin."

"And you'll have it," Cole assured me, rejoining my side.

We were in the realm of the living. Although we could've gone anywhere—could've portaled anywhere—Cole had insisted on walking, and I was glad of it. So much time was spent in the palace these days, and though it had every luxury, the nature of our creatures was to go outside and explore. I hadn't shifted and run in at least a week, and I was antsy to shed my human skin and hunt. Plus, it was nice just to have time with Cole, where we could flirt and tease without outside pressures. I loved our kingdom dearly and cared for every soul. But Cole was my mate, and after so much darkness, seeing him smirk at accidental entendres was a gift I didn't take for granted.

We could've created another pocket realm. In the last lifetime, that had been our oasis to get away. Even though Cole had wrecked it to rescue me, with the mantles residing squarely inside us, we had enough power. But the pocket realm had been a kind of stasis. I didn't want to stand apart from the realms I ruled.

And it *was* realms. Although we mainly resided in the underworld, we split our time between the two. I wouldn't repeat past mistakes of leaving the realm unguarded, even though I didn't directly rule or take a hand in the politics. These days, that fell to Daphne and the males who were besotted with her.

"It's just up ahead." Cole pointed down the path.

I admittedly had no clue where we were going. We were well past the edges of pack lands. We'd stopped to see Daphne and the others just briefly, enjoying a large meal with the recently reformed pack. It had somehow stopped feeling odd to eat a meal with a large group of shifters, no longer a vulnerable, dangerous time, but instead a relaxing visit. Something I'd never thought was possible as a pup. I'd thought my only way out would be to mate another wolf and escape to the bottom of a different pack—instead, we'd fixed the broken pack we'd been part of.

The trees cleared, and a cabin came into view, stealing my thoughts away. I hadn't known what to expect—actually, knowing Mr. Throw-a-Demon-at-Her-and-Call-It-Flirting, I expected either a lean-to or a simple clearing.

"How?"

"The usual way, I suppose. Found someone who had something I wanted, slaughtered them in front of their entire family as a message to vacate and took over."

I just looked at him, and he sighed.

"Fine. I had some help. Now, do you want to see the damn place or not?"

I grabbed his hand and darted forward. There were large stones leading up the path to the front door, which was unlocked. The setting inside was humble, but welcoming. A roaring fire blazed in the hearth at the edge of the room with two large chairs, perfect for reading in, set beside it. A love seat at one edge of the living room, with a basic kitchen on the other side.

"Xander helped design the cabin, since it's like the old Wind-Blood structures," Cole explained. "Daphne had strong opinions on the furniture. Ian helped haul materials up here, though I'll admit I wasn't fond of having another male's scent inside."

I inhaled. The entire place smelled like Cole, his scent layered over and over, like he'd been coming here for months and even as recently as the past day. Familiar spices hit my nose, and I walked in farther to the stove, which sat beneath a large window facing out the other side. I opened the oven, my stomach growling.

"And the pie?" I asked. Somehow it was still hot and steaming, reminding me of the enchanted kitchen at the castle in the pocket realm.

"That's my doing. Now don't ruin it by bur—"

I was already grabbing the piping hot plate from the oven, my fingers burning at the contact. Cole growled at my carelessness—or, more accurately, the sight of me being hurt. Even though I was able to heal myself with magic a blink later, he seemed irritated anytime I so much as scratched myself.

"I wouldn't have made them if I'd known you'd use them to hurt yourself like an eager pup," he groused.

"You're just mad because you want to be the only one leaving bruises on me." I rose to kiss his cheek before he could throw some retort. "I love it. Let's eat."

Two words that would end nearly any shifter argument. I dug out some cutlery and sliced us each a large piece. It definitely tasted... different from the perfect, magical pies in the castle, but I devoured it all the same. "I had no idea you baked."

"I didn't," Cole said. "But then I had a mate who was rather fond of them, so that changed."

A lot had changed. Even if the pie tasted weirdly salty instead of sweet, it didn't matter. Half of it was gone in a matter of minutes, and that time, I pressed my lips against Cole, licking a spare fleck of pumpkin off of him. Not content to be used so blatantly, he hoisted me onto the granite countertop and caged me in with his arms while deepening the kiss.

It was a slow, tender kiss. One that said he'd do anything to see me happy.

"Thank you," I said, half-breathless when we broke apart.

"You never have to thank me for that, little wolf. I promise I enjoyed it."

From the way we were lined up, I definitely felt the proof of his words, but I shook my head. "Not for the kiss. I mean, for doing all of this." No doubt magic had played a part, but there were too many homemade touches in the space for me to doubt Cole had spent a lot of time making the place perfect for us.

"I'm glad you like it, Avery. I wanted to make a home."

I frowned. "We already have one." A rather massive one.

"We have a palace," Cole agreed. "But I wanted you to have a home too. A place that was *just* yours, without a thousand servants floating in the hallways, or packmates looking over your shoulder."

Tears pricked at my eyes. How many times had I wished for that when I barricaded myself inside my tiny bedroom? "It's perfect. But you should know by now, my home is wherever you are. In any realm, in any life."

"And my heart is wherever you live. No matter where in the universe we are."

I gripped the lapels of his shirt and pulled him into me for another kiss. "Does this cabin come with a bedroom?"

"It does. But the floor is closer."

The floor it was. And then the couch and the chair and the wall, right against the reinforced glass window. Twilight played along the tree line by the time we finally collapsed in each other's arms, curled up on the floor with a blanket stolen from the love seat.

I eyed the window. With our supernatural stamina, we were never down for long, and the wilderness outside was calling to me.

Cole followed my gaze. "I think my little wolf wants to go for a run."

I flexed my fingers, eager to feel the dirt beneath my paws. "Maybe."

"If you run, I'll chase you," he warned. "And when I catch you, you'll regret it."

I couldn't stop the shiver of excitement. Running was fun, the wind in my fur urging me on. But running with a large, determined predator at my heels? Intoxicating. And Cole's version of regret tended to wind up with us both sweaty and exhausted, my body pushed to the brink but very sated.

Very, very intoxicating.

"I won't make it easy."

"You never do," he assured me. A playful glint lit his amber eyes. "But it's always worth it."

Thank you for reading Fatal Goddess! If you want to hear about future releases, be sure to sign up for my newsletter here, where you can get all the latest news plus exclusive content like the first time Cole and Avery *really* met + character art.

Acknowledgments

So... *the end*. It's one of those things that seems so simple when it's done. I started writing *Forsaken Mate* during late nights of 2021, and the story concluded with *Fatal Goddess* two and a half years later when I typed the last word in the manuscript. Wrapped up in a pretty bow, all done!

Ha. Not even close.

Writing isn't a solitary activity by any means. There are so many people who made this possible. Thank you to Magan for not only editing this entire series, but also for your comments which made me laugh out loud. Thank you to Christian for turning "It's book three, title is Fatal Goddess... maybe it could be blue?" into an absolutely amazing cover. To my ARC team for your kind messages and all you did to spread the word about this book. And to all of the friends I've made along the way, who chatted excitedly about covers in group chats or sent encouraging messages pleading for the next book, thank you as well.

Thank you to my day job for providing inspiration for the first part of this book and fueling my dreams of being a full-time author.

Thank you to my mother, whose wholehearted encouragement was so convincing it didn't occur to me until this year she was (probably) exaggerating to build my self-esteem. Thank you to my father, who will talk to me at any hour of the day about anything, and accepted me bastardizing his language throughout this series.

And thank you again to my parents who, in addition to supporting me absolutely in my writing, accepted the look of terror when they asked to read my books with enough grace that neither of us had to talk about the smut.

Last but certainly not least, thank you, dear reader. I cannot overstate my gratitude to you for picking up Forsaken Mate and following Avery's story to its conclusion. A book no one reads is just a pile of paper; without you, this story wouldn't be as alive as it is. Thank you for coming with me on this journey (cliffhangers and all). I hope to see you on the next one...

About the Author

Vasilisa Drake is based in New England and is constantly bouncing from city to city while she tries to find her home amidst overpriced rental apartments. *Forsaken Mate* was Vasilisa Drake's debut, though she's written contemporary romance under another name for several years. Fantasy romance is her first love, closely followed by pet dragons and men who are obsessed with their women. She can be found staying up way too late reading, organizing her bookshelf for the millionth time, and winning the imaginary arguments in her head at least 30% of the time.

She can be contacted via email at VasilisaDrakeBooks@gmail.com or on TikTok / Instagram @VasilisaDrakeBooks

FIND VASILISA

You can find Vasilisa on several platforms including:

Bookbub

Goodreads

Instagram

Romance.io

Storygraph

TikTok